to Sidney,
I hear you'r
Hope you en,
Robert Hutto

4-11-22
...
...des.

BITS AND PIECES

by

Robert Hutto, DDS

DORRANCE
PUBLISHING CO
EST. 1920
PITTSBURGH, PENNSYLVANIA 15238

Dorrance Publishing Co
585 Alpha Drive
Pittsburgh, PA 15238
Visit our website at *www.dorrancebookstore.com*

ISBN: 978-1-6366-1421-2
eISBN: 978-1-6366-1997-2

CHAPTER 1

June 8, 1980
San Diego, California

United Airlines flight 15, inbound from London to San Diego via Newark, NJ, was scheduled to arrive shortly at 10:45 P.M. June in San Diego is notorious for fog and late at night is particularly bad; the locals call it June gloom. Normally, flights are rerouted to LAX and passengers are transported by bus to San Diego. Tonight was anything but normal. The pilot had radioed that an indicator light flashed a fire warning in one engine and, a minute later, in the second engine too. He felt it would be safer to land in San Diego rather than to try to make it to Los Angeles even though he was flying strictly by radar.

The approach to Lindbergh Field is tricky even in ideal conditions. The terrain drops from an elevation of 266 feet to sea level in less than one nautical mile.

The first indication of any problem to the passengers on board was a shudder and flash from the right wing as it clipped a wire on a utility pole along Highway 5, which was adjacent to the runway. This was followed by another shudder and then . . . .

CHAPTER 2

DOC/BOB HUGHS

The phone rang. It was the San Diego Police. As the newly appointed coroner or medical examiner (ME), I was used to such interruptions. I had just spent five years completing my medical degree, more years obtaining a residency in anatomic pathology, then a fellowship in forensic pathology, and a year working in the coroner's office to earn this interruption. I guess you could say it fell into my lap . . . the former coroner died a couple of months ago with a pulmonary embolism. I was already here, I had the qualifications, and I got the title. My job was to investigate the cause and circumstances of death. San Diego was no different than any other place in the world: death was inevitable, often expected, sometimes not. I got the unexpected ones: violent, brutal, drug induced, and probable/suspicious suicides. Nice work if you can get it.

It was late, but I was still sitting at the desk in my office. It was cluttered with papers as usual. The room was nothing fancy; a single book shelf lined the back wall, filled with books on anatomy, forensics, pathology and even a few murder mysteries. It was spartan in decor. My diplomas and qualification certificates hung on the wall adjacent to the door. The only personal item was an 18 × 14-inch framed picture of me with my wife and daughter hanging over my desk. A happier time. The glass was cracked in the lower left corner. It had fallen off the wall a while back, courtesy of one of San Diego's not-so-minor earthquake tremors. It was the last picture I had of them. It was a spur of the moment thing we had done at a Kmart. I don't know why I kept it. It reminded me of them, but it also brought up the memory that they were no longer with me, having died in a particularly gruesome car crash a few years earlier. A tractor-trailer rig driving much too fast slammed into their car head on. Both were killed instantly. My daughter was not wearing a seat belt and was catapulted through the front windshield, crushing every bone in her face. I did not recognize her.

The phone rang again.

It was Detective Kelly, a Sergeant within the Special Investigative Division of the San Diego Police Department. We had a long history, but only recently with our current jobs. I had met him years earlier when we were in the Navy's Officer Candidate School or OCS, at Newport, Rhode Island. We both had just completed a four- year college degree and had been immediately anointed the title 1-A. That was now our military draft classification. In 1967, it stood for "enlist or get drafted."

The sixties were not the best years to lose one's 2-S school deferment status. The war in Vietnam was growing bigger and America needed more and more nineteen and twenty-year-old boys to defend the world against the spread of communism. I still remember politicians predicting "the domino effect." Somehow, I wasn't convinced and neither was my new friend, Joe Kelly, whom I met at the airport in Providence waiting to be picked up by Navy personnel. We sat together on the bus ride to the Navy base in Newport. In an attempt to avoid being a newly minted second lieutenant in the Army with a life expectancy of about twenty minutes in Vietnam, we chose to join the Navy as officers. It was that or flee to Canada. Don't think for a minute we didn't consider it! For four months we became best friends. We roomed together in Nimitz Hall, as members of Golf Company. I helped him with tactics, naval engineering and celestial navigation and he protected me from physical abuse. Joe was an athlete. A really good athlete. He said he was a gymnast in high school but grew too tall to really compete in college so he switched to swimming. He was good enough to nearly qualify for the Olympics. His best event was the 400-meter individual medley race: 100 meters of the backstroke, butterfly, breaststroke, and crawl. Ridiculously hard.

I wasn't an athlete. In fact, I was only five feet eight inches tall. I guess "tall" isn't quite accurate. I had always been short. When my dad was transferred to Kansas City in the middle of my ninth grade, I was four foot six inches, small. The picture they took for the year book that year showed all the new students standing together from the chest up. All you could see of me was from my nose up. I was four feet 11 and a half when I was graduated. I always included the half inch. Kind of like a four-year-old says they are four-and-*half* years old. Makes them feel more important. I did grow. My sophomore year in college I shot up to my present height. Still on the short side.

Initially, I think we bonded because we both just wanted out of there. But team work and an emphasis on taking care of each other made an impression. The fact was, we bonded because we learned to accept what the military preached: "Mission first; People always." That was the mantra of leadership, and it made sense. You may have a job to do, but it's your people that make it work. Take care of them. They'll take care of you. Even though I vowed never to remember OCS as anything but terrible, I will always remember those words and be grateful for the friendship and trust Joe Kelly and I developed.

After being harassed and ordered around for what seemed like an eternity, we were graduated as Ensigns in the United States Navy. I was, surprisingly, actually quite proud. My parents and brother even traveled across country to attend the graduation ceremony. My dad beamed.

We soon received orders from our Detailer, the Navy's assignment officer. I think it was the first time we were ever given a choice of what we wanted to do: "Pick a coast," he said. It was a given that everyone was going to a ship but you could choose the coast you wanted. There were two coasts. I chose the east coast . . . and I got my second choice! A ship out of San Diego, currently in Da Nang. Kelly applied for and got accepted into Buds, the Basic Underwater Demolition School; the SEAL training program in Coronado, California. His first choice. I was the smart one, he was even smarter. Someone is *always* smarter: A lesson I would be wise to remember . . .

CHAPTER 3

I don't like stalking around these neighborhoods; no telling who's out here, waiting to rob me . . . or worse. It isn't fun, believe me, but I've got my reason. This is the best place to hunt. I read somewhere there that there are over 20 million trafficking victims worldwide . . . and young girls make up 98% of those in sex trafficking. Innocent little girls, some as young as ten or twelve, forced to leave their families, live in squalor, and perform the most outrageous acts for despicable deviants. Few ever escape. Those that do and are caught, are beaten, tortured, often killed. Who cares? I certainly don't. They're a dime a dozen. That's why I'm here. Here's where I find them. Someone will soon care about a few of these girls though. The message will be clear, for I have a plan. It will definitely be clear to someone, one of these days . . .

What have we here? . . . A young girl hiding in the shadows over by that fence at the end of the alley. Crying. "Sweetheart. Are you hurt? Are you lost?" It's dark and I can barely make anything out. As I walk closer, I can see it's a pretty girl . . . maybe fifteen or sixteen years old. She looks cold, wearing a tattered brown cotton jacket over her dress. It was pink, like the color of the bow in her hair. She was wearing a pair of leather sandals. Her mother may be a whore, but she wanted her daughter to look pretty.

"Uh, Huh." She whispers. "Please help me."

"Sure, honey. Why are you out here all alone? How did you get here?"

"I came with my mom. She doesn't like me staying at home alone. She says there's too many men coming in and out of our house. She doesn't trust them. Usually I just come with her and wait behind this fence until she gets back. She meets a lot of men . . . and then we go home. But she hasn't come back tonight. I'm scared."

"Oh my, that's not good at all. Let's go see if we can find your mom, okay?" I put my arm around her shoulder and walked with her out of the alley. There was no one in sight. I bent down and suggested we go for help. "I think we should go the police."

"No. Please. My mom told me never to go to the police. They took her away once and put me in a house somewhere with an old lady. She was mean. My mom finally came to get me after a long time, but I don't want to do that again."

The girl didn't seem to understand her situation. Perhaps she was on drugs. It didn't matter. She was mine now.

"Okay. Let's go to my house. I'll bet you are hungry. I'll fix you some dinner."

We walked to my car, an old beater I found just for this purpose. Fake license plates and no other identification on it. There was no one around. We headed for my favorite spot.

My cutting room.

She was still cold and I offered her some apple juice and couple of Ambien tablets a doctor prescribed for me once when I had difficulty flying on long trips.

She was soon sleeping soundly.

A few hours later she was lying on her back on a table in the cutting room . . . she was not clothed, but had a towel draped over her. I'd washed her and fastened her legs securely. Her hands were at her side but bound by leather straps connected to each under her waist. She was also awake.

This was usually important. Not so much tonight. I always wanted the older girls to know what was coming next. Why I chose them. The runaways. They should be happy. No longer would they just be an unknown piece of human flesh to be used and used and used again only to be discarded in some trash heap like some piece of garbage. Unknown. Nobody. My . . . you'd think I was some kind of savior. Hardly . . . they just happen to fit my plan perfectly.

"I know you're scared, darling. But it's for the best. The future ahead of you is not worth the heartache and pain you'd have to endure. We'll take care of those problems tonight. Maybe we'll make you famous, even only for just a little while," *I whispered.*

Standing behind and in back of her head, I gently lifted it off the table by her hair. With my right hand I swiftly sliced the knife through her neck, severing her carotid arteries and jugular veins. The blood drained down the sides of the table into the trough at the end, collecting eventually into a container on the floor.

The vertebrae required more effort and I had to saw with my knife to completely sever the head from the body.

I wrapped it in plastic and placed it in the refrigerator.

This one was just right for my purpose . . .

CHAPTER 4

"What do you need, Joe?" I was the only one who ever called him Joe. He was Kelly to everyone else from the time he started grade school. It was a cool name, implying toughness and bravado. My name was Hughs, frequently pronounced Hugs. Not so cool.

"There's been a plane crash attempting to land at Lindbergh Field!" he yelled. "You need to get down here ASAP. Debris is scattered from Balboa to Point Loma. I'm telling you it's a mess. It's like the crash in '78; maybe worse."

"Okay. Let me get dressed and gather my forensic kit. I should be there in a half hour." The main job as the ME is to investigate the circumstances of the death scene: question everybody, collect evidence, photograph the scene, and prepare bodies for transport while preserving evidence tags. In the case of an aircraft crash it's not to determine the cause of the crash, but to identify the victims.

Joe's reference to 1978 brought back bad memories. I had just completed my anatomic pathology residency and was starting my year-long fellowship in forensic pathology when that crash happened. It was a PSA flight out of Sacramento via Los Angeles in-bound for San Diego. September 25. Unbelievably, it had collided in clear skies with a small Cessna on its approach to Lindbergh Field and crashed into several homes in the North Park area before exploding and catching fire. It completely destroyed everything in its path. I was invited to the scene with the San Diego coroner to investigate. Police had already cordoned off the area for several blocks. When we got there the only thing remotely resembling a plane was part of the tail section, some of the engine components, and the landing gear. Debris and rubble were scattered throughout the site. There were no intact bodies and their remains were burned to a crisp. Curiously, the severed head of a woman was found amidst a torn suitcase alongside one of the homes that was partially destroyed.

Just the head, no sign of the body. She appeared to be Hispanic.

I wasn't part of that investigation but I remembered the coroner saying they never did find out where the head came from and they never identified it. It was classified as a homicide, but after many months of search, it was placed in the cold case file. North Park was only about three miles from Lindbergh field. So close; so far, for the 135 people on board and the 7 who died on the ground.

A passing thought crossed my mind: my brother lived around North Park. I wonder if he witnessed the crash.

I was still not prepared for the scene at Lindbergh Field.

Aircraft debris and contents were scattered across Highway 5 and well over 100 yards down the runway. Police vehicles were blocking both north and south lanes of the highway. Motorists were not happy.

Fortunately, there was no explosion and little or no fire. I was thinking that would make identification easier. The plane was probably low on fuel as it slammed into the concrete tarmac. Still, at almost 200 miles per hour, the impact would be catastrophic. I was right. Suitcases and partial suitcases and tons of clothes littered the stretch of debris. I could see parts of the tail of the plane, engine parts, the wheels mangled with other pieces of the airframe. What I did not see . . . were bodies. I walked the length of the crash site. They had erected huge spotlights along the crash corridor and my vision was mesmerized by thousands of pieces of human flesh intermingled with the plane debris. No piece was larger than your hand. It was horrifying. It appeared that the bodies had been tumbled and ground along the runway like a cheese grater. I had been at many crash scenes of vehicles and brutal murders over the years, even the PSA crash, but nothing compared to this. As I walked along I spotted something sticking out of the rubble. It was the only piece that remained of a human body: the left eye and remnants of the associated cheek and nose. It was no bigger than a postcard . . .

And that was the largest piece we were to find after combing and collecting every human piece of flesh in the area. In the end we used dogs to complete the search. We then began collecting suitcases, noting the tags on the luggage for later identification. We would have to match the names on the passenger manifest to luggage tags, bracelets, rings, and the teeth and bones that were intact. I was hoping there could be some fingerprints.

Picking up a piece of luggage, I noted the location and the identifying tag and jotted it down in my notebook: Dean Meritt, with a hand-written address from somewhere in Chula Vista, California. But when I peered inside the damaged and partially open metal suitcase, my mouth dropped . . . inside was the severed head of a teenaged girl.

"Whoa!! What the hell? . . . What is this? Somebody get over here. I need to get a picture of this. Find Detective Kelly. He needs to see this."

Taking out my camera, I begin taking pictures of the suitcase. It was a grey metal case which appeared to have been locked but partially broken during the crash. Its identification was a paper United Airlines tag attached to the handle by a string. The kind one gets at the ticket counter when checking in. Inside was the head. It appeared to be that of a female no more than fifteen or sixteen years old. I would be better able to determine that back in my lab. There was no indication of trauma, other than the head had been separated from the body, and rigor mortis was not evident. After death, the muscles of the body partially contract, but they are unable to return to their relaxed state. They become fixed in place for 24 to 36 hours, sometimes even up to 72. Then they relax. It takes from ten minutes to several hours to set in. The face sets first, then the rest of the body.

I took several pictures of the head and face. Brunette, brown-eyed, a pink ribbon in her hair. I tagged the suitcase and the head and returned to photograph the rest of the crash site. This was now not only a terrible accident, but a murder scene.

CHAPTER 5

Kelly stood beside me looking at the head, a mercifully intact face alone amidst a sea of mangled bodies.

"Who is she? How did she get here? Who killed her? Where was she killed? Why was she killed? Why did they put her in a suitcase and transport her on a plane? Why this plane?" he wondered out loud.

Each question leading to another . . .

"Where does one begin?"

I was exhausted after spending the night at the crash scene. As I returned home, I was hoping to get a few hours of sleep before organizing the material I needed to identify the bodies. The phone rang.

"Bob . . . Doc. I need those pictures you took of the girl's head." It was Joe. "We need to get them out to all the police departments, hospitals, shelters, schools and news media as soon as possible. Both here and in Newark. Have you seen any identifying marks on the face or head that would help with the identification?

"Honestly, the only thing I looked at when I returned to the lab was her teeth. Her second molars and maxillary cuspids were fully erupted and the usual diastema between 8 and 9 had already closed."

"English, Bob . . . or, Doc. Significance?"

"Sorry. Her 12-year-old molars and her top eye teeth were in . . . which would indicate the normal space between her top two front teeth had closed. That usually occurs around eleven or twelve years old, when the cuspids erupt. No caries . . . or cavities. Her third molars have not erupted. That occurs around eighteen or nineteen years old. I'd say she between fifteen and seventeen years old. She was Hispanic. She has been dead for over 72 hours. There's little odor so she would have been killed or preserved in some way fairly soon before she was placed in the suitcase."

"Got it. Say, what do I call you now? It's been years since OCS and I 've only known you as Bob."

"I don't care, Joe. Whatever makes you comfortable. My first year in college I was called lunchbox. I never drank in high school so my experience at keg parties was laughable. Whenever I had one or two beers, up came my lunch."

"Okay, Bob it is," he laughed. "I can't quite equate that image with you being a doctor!

Change the subject. I've got a ton of things I have to investigate and I need to get started. I think I need to know how and where that bag got put on the plane. Maybe that's where the murder took place . . . and that's where we'll find the name of the victim."

"At least you know where to begin. All I've got are a bunch of bones, tissue samples and lots of broken jaws and teeth. Once I get the passenger manifest hopefully I can get their dental records and compare fillings and dental anomalies. If I can get some fingers or hands large enough to sample, I may get some fingerprints."*

"Otherwise, we can try to match luggage with names. I don't know where to begin: it's like trying to solve a 1000-piece puzzle with no border or corner pieces. I'm clueless . . ."

* Editor's note: Although DNA has been used to solve criminal cases since 1987, it wasn't used to routinely identify bodies until the early 1990's.

CHAPTER 6

DETECTIVE KELLY

"What have we got?" It was a rhetorical question, more to myself than anyone else. So far, the pictures we'd distributed had gotten us nowhere. The coroner had little to go on other than her age and race. Let's see. That narrows it down to about a million other girls in the United States. We went to missing persons. There were lots of them. "I've got two leads: the name on the suitcase and the origin and flight path of the plane." We started with the name . . .

We . . . as in Linda Meadows and I. My new partner in crime. She had just transferred over from being a patrol officer. She was about my age, maybe a little younger, but lots smarter. She was also a knockout. Five feet nine inches tall and curves where they should be. Long brown hair which she usually wore in a ponytail. Her teeth were perfect and matched her smile. Why was that the second thing I always noticed on a woman? Just so there's no confusion, her eyes were the third thing. She had worked her way up to detective similar to me in that she had to spend four years as a patrolman before she could take the detective exam. She passed it on her first try with the highest score. Graduating from San Francisco University, she also came from money. Her daddy had retired as a 3-Star Admiral in the Navy and followed that with membership on various corporate boards throughout the country. I heard they paid well.

She was single . . . divorced actually. Her marriage to a wealthy real estate developer soon turned sour after a couple of years when she discovered he was into more than real estate. Her name isn't important; neither is his . . .

She got into law enforcement when she realized how much fun she'd had snooping on her prick for a husband. And she got the house. A little 4000 square foot shack overlooking the Pacific Ocean in La Jolla. I guess "shack" doesn't adequately describe it.

We actually got along pretty well. We both had Navy backgrounds, had moved around a lot and were pretty familiar with the San Diego area. Only once did I make the mistake of referring to her as "Daddy's little seaman."

We started with Dean Meritt, Chula Vista, California. The phone book had no such person in Chula Vista. With no address, we started calling everyone with the last name, Meritt. Days later, we exhausted those leads in the San Diego area. We also traced the plane's flight path.

No one with an identification claiming to be Dean Meritt boarded United Airlines flight 15 departing London Heathrow Airport at 10:05 A.M. on the eighth of June. It landed at Newark, New Jersey (Liberty Air Field) at 1:05 P.M. Same day. It had a long layover of seven hours then departed at 8:00 P.M. carrying 125 passengers expecting to land at 10:45 P.M. Of course, it touched ground a bit earlier.

No one named Dean Meritt checked in at Newark either. But someone checked in their luggage and boarded on the plane, attaching a United paper identification tag on the suitcase with the name: Dean Meritt. It surely did not match their name, and the agents didn't check. No carry-on noted. We asked security at the Newark airport if checked bags were screened. They were, usually by dogs trained to sniff out drugs and weapons. Bags were not X-rayed unless they were viewed suspicious for various reasons. He didn't elaborate. I asked him if the dog could sniff out a human hand. As far as he knew the dogs were not trained to sniff out human remains. So, the head could have come from Newark, or New York City, just eight miles across the bay. Eight million people, a fake name, and no name.

Or they could have boarded in London . . .

A thought struck me. What if the fake Dean didn't know a head was in his bag? Maybe he was concealing his identity for something else and someone else put the head in the bag. Who would have access to the bags before they were placed in the cargo hold of the plane? A reach for sure, but a lead to investigate. Where do we start?

There she is. Showcased in the San Diego Union evening newspaper. She even made the local nightly news and was on national television! She's nearly a celebrity! Her pretty face was front and center for everyone to see. Perfect. I wonder if her mother will claim her . . .

16

CHAPTER 7

I got authorization for Linda and I to fly to Newark. It was as good a place to start as London . . . and much cheaper. We had to track down dozens of handlers, search the databases for past offenses, meet with their superiors, and observe their operation. We called NYCPD and the operational department at Newark Airport. By the time we arrived we had the names of every baggage handler that worked that night and their criminal record, if any. Most of them were long-time employees with minimal involvement with police authorities: parking violations, speeding tickets, you know the drill. There were a dozen or so that had worked there for only a year or less. This group contained some more ominous crimes: felonies, grand larceny, prison time.

They had served their probation in good fashion and had been given another opportunity by the airline to get on with their lives. Kudos . . .

It's not politically correct to pigeon-hole any group of people, but this latter group seemed like a good place to begin our investigation.

First, we petitioned the airlines to see if any customers had complained of missing anything in their luggage or having them indiscriminately opened like it was being searching for something. In fact, there were such complaints. More than just a few. In the past year alone exactly 337 complaints were registered . . . not all from United. Over 20 million passengers flew through Newark each year, roughly 60% on United. A few hundred complaints hardly registered. But what did these baggage complaints have to do with a severed head?

We elected to go undercover. We only had four days on our SDPD travel voucher. It was decided that Detective Meadows would pose as a wealthy young socialite from New York City heading to San Diego to meet her husband. She checked in two bags; free, as a courtesy to those flying first class.

"May I see your passport or driver's license?" The ticket agent was clearly not looking at her smile or eyes, either.

"Yes, it's right here in my purse, somewhere." The Gucci purse was large enough to hide a small dog. As she spilled out some of the contents it was obvious to all in the vicinity that there was some valuable jewelry inside. Who knew what she carried in her suitcases? Actually, we had planted a Rolex watch; fake, of course. The other bag was clean.

They made a bid deal about her luggage. The weight was too much. One bag weighed over fifty pounds. Sixty-two point eight, to be exact. The ticket agent was nice, though, and he helped her transfer some of the contents of the heavy bag into the lighter one. It was obvious there was some pretty expensive clothes in there for all to see, and the Rolex box. I was standing nearby taking pictures. Mostly of everyone standing within earshot of the ticket transaction. We didn't know who might be relaying information. We were told there were cameras stationed at various points in the process. Taking a suitcase off the belt and searching through it would be difficult without being seen. The best place might be when the bags were actually brought into the plane and stored. At any rate, we'd just have to wait to see if our Rolex had been stolen. We had about an hour to wait until the plane boarded so we made like every good cop and headed to the nearest Dunkin Donuts.

Women are funny. I wanted to talk about the case. She asked me if I'd ever been married. Where did that come from? When I said, "No," she wanted to know why. It started a short conversation about my past and present relationships.

"Okay," I began. "Graduation from San Diego State in 1967. Majored in Biology and Physical Education. Thought I might have been a trainer someday. Avoided the draft by going to the Navy's Officer Candidate School in New Port. I actually roomed with our new coroner, Bob Hughs. He's a good man. I qualified to try out for the Navy Seal Team in Coronado. Going through BUDS training was the toughest thing I've ever done. Two tours in Viet Nam. Nothing I care to brag about. Discharged late 1970. Joined the San Diego Police Department. Four years later I was promoted to detective in the Special Investigative Division. Also, not much to brag about."

"Come on," she smirked. "Surely you left out all the juicy details. You're six foot two and built like an Olympic gymnast. How come you never met a nice girl and settled down? Don't tell me you're gay. I've seen the way you 've checked out the front and rear ends of every pretty gal that walked by."

"There *was* a lady," I admitted. "I met her in the Philippines. She was a Navy nurse stationed at Subic Bay. We were both ensigns in the Navy but made Lieutenant Junior Grade about the same time shortly after I arrived. Back then it only took a year to be promoted to LTJG; I think it's two years now. The tours in Nam were usually thirteen months and about half way through we were granted thirty days liberty. They called it R and R: rest and recuperation. You couldn't go back to the mainland so most guys generally went to Bangkok or the Philippine Islands."

"Mainland?" she asked.

"The United States proper."

"Oh . . . of course, I knew that."

"Usually the married folks just met their wives in Hawaii. I always went to the P.I. Best liberty port in West Pac and maybe the world at that time. The beer was cheap and the women . . . friendly. Not only that, but Subic Bay was a great base to unwind: great facilities, good food, sailing, scuba diving, horseback riding, and a swimming pool. Cubi Point Naval Air Station was just up the hill. But I guess most men would say the best part was Olongapo. That was the little town right outside the gate. Just over the bridge crossing shit river. It really did stink like shit, hence the name. Small boys would sit in their Banca-boats yelling for the sailors to throw coins into the water. Then they would dive in to find them. I'm sure they all died of some nasty disease before they were thirty. The main drag was Magsaysay; night clubs on both sides of a muddy street a half-mile long all playing the sweetest sounds you've ever heard. I swear those Pilipino bands sounded just like the bands back home. I think the beer was fifteen cents a bottle. San Miguel . . . I had my wetting down when I made LTJG and rented an entire bar: food, drinks, music and entertainment for about $100.00 . . . total! At least thirty guys were invited."

Hesitating a little, I added, "Okay, the entertainment was extra."

She laughed, "Tell me about the nurse."

"Long story, but basically I was in the medical clinic there grinding through my daily routine of physical therapy. I had had a little injury a couple of months earlier and was still trying to get the kinks out. She, Mary, was stationed at the clinic. I was smitten, or at least horny. We just seemed to hit it off and we dated every night until I had to return to Da Nang." His voice cracked a little and he stared into his coffee cup for a second as he remembered those moments with her.

"What happened to the nurse?"

"That's the sad part, and the part I don't usually like to talk about. Mary put in for orders to Da Nang. We met there a couple of times between my assignments. It was just before the Tet Offensive in January, 1968. The Viet Cong staged a huge offensive over-running many installations before they were finally quashed. But it was the beginning of the end for us in 'Nam. I think everyone but the White House knew we couldn't keep this up. Our hands were tied. We were losing support from the South Vietnamese and we couldn't mount an offensive into North Vietnam. It was like being in a boxing match where you had one hand tied behind your back. All you could do is try to defend yourself and occasionally throw in a jab or two. You're going to lose."

He was quiet for a second. He took a sip of his coffee. Then he whispered, "Mary was captured and eventually killed. That's the part I usually leave out. When we were mopping up we uncovered miles and miles of underground tunnels around Na Trang. They'd been digging them before the French were there, and some of them were quite sophisticated. You wouldn't believe how large some of them were: thirty feet underground with rooms larger than most basements. They had hospitals down there! We found her in one of those rooms. Well, our tunnel rats did. That's what we called the smaller guys who risked their lives going down those holes looking for the enemy. They couldn't pay me enough to do that. Those guys had to have nerves of steel. Anyway, Mary was lying on a dirty cot . . . or what was left of her. After they had had their way with her they cut off her hands and feet and head . . . and jammed a bayonet into her . . . vagina. The tunnel rats took pictures of her body to try and identify her later."

"I don't know if I've ever completely gotten over those pictures. It's hard to love someone, vision a future together, and have it all taken away by a bunch of fucking butchers. And in the back of my mind, I can't help but feel it was my fault she was even in Viet Nam."

"My God, that's . . . that's terrible," she stammered, and reached out to touch my arm. "I'm so sorry. I should not have brought it up. I can't imagine how you feel. But I do understand your guilt. I've had to live with not understanding how someone I loved so dearly could just up and decide I'm not good enough anymore. Was I to blame? What was wrong with *me*? "

"Listen, I still feel guilty that I wasn't able to protect Mary. But there's nothing wrong with either of us. Shit happens. Unfortunately, those memories have taken their toll, hardened me, and the romance of dating has clearly taken a back seat in my life."

"You're right, of course. I *have* moved on as well . . . changed my name back to before I was married and vowed to shoot the SOB if I ever saw him again. Just kidding, of course . . . I think." She laughed.

Our sob stories over, we headed back to the gate. Passengers were starting to board. I watched as she got on the plane and then headed to security.

The bags were soon loaded and the plane was just about to leave the gate. I had base operations hold up the plane, telling the passengers that someone had to be removed at the last minute. Security personnel boarded and escorted Miss Linda off. They then off-loaded her luggage. We searched her bags. There was the Rolex.

"What did you expect?" boasted the security guard. He was obviously a little irked with us. "You California dicks think you're smarter than us? Our dogs are the best. We've got one dog named Peanut. She's a white beagle who somebody says is a lemon. Let me tell you, she's no lemon. She once sniffed out ten bricks of pure 'H' wrapped in plastic and covered with BenGay. We don't have a big problem with baggage theft or smuggling. Sure, occasionally someone puts in a claim, but I wouldn't put it past them to just be looking for insurance money on an item that didn't even exist. I'm not buying your story, either. You're obviously here for something else."

"I'll tell you, pal," I growled, getting irritated. "Did anyone see a picture of a missing girl several days ago? It probably wasn't shown on your TV, but we sent it to all the police precincts in your area."

"I think it was mentioned at the morning brief about a week ago, but I didn't pay that much attention to it. It's hard to keep up with the dozens of missing persons we get here every day. California doesn't always show up on our radar. Why are you guys looking through bags anyway?" he asked. "I don't think she's hiding in one them."

"Because we found her head in a suitcase. " Now, I *was* pissed. "Somebody killed her, chopped off her head and stuffed it in a suitcase which we found in a plane that crashed in San Diego en route from, you guessed it: Newark. You're right. We don't give a fuck about baggage theft. We didn't mention the girl because we didn't want to tip anyone off about our motive for the search. We're trying to figure out how that head got in a suitcase on your plane without anyone knowing about it. If we do, we might just figure out who killed her. We theorized it may have been possible that the same folks who were going through bags looking for valuables might have also slipped something into them. It obviously didn't pan out. In hindsight, maybe we should have let you guys in on it, but we didn't know if security personnel could have been involved as well. It was a bad idea."

Linda quickly changed the subject. "Listen, we apologize for the attitude, but we're kind of grasping at straws right now. We'd appreciate it if you would just keep an eye out for any suspicious behavior or items that might occur in checked baggage. We really do appreciate your help."

"Look, Detective, I understand. You've got a tough job. But you two came here like gang busters accusing us of sloppy security. We take pride in our job just like you take pride in yours. You'll excuse us for being a little sensitive to the way we conduct business. Now that we know what you're looking into, we'll be more than happy to assist. No hard feelings?"

"No hard feelings." We shook hands, forced smiles, and headed back to our hotel.

Unfortunately, we were right back where we started. No names, no motive, no idea where the suitcase came from or who or why it was placed on the plane. The baggage handlers in Newark seemed like a dead end . . . not dead, but on life support. One bag search is a pretty poor sample, but I thought it was in indicator. I didn't think the odds would change. We checked with the agents in London. Their baggage handling was even more restricted. It really didn't make sense to pursue that angle further.

CHAPTER 8

Seeing nothing else to go on, we decided to head back to San Diego. We'd leave tomorrow, a day early. We booked a plane leaving at 8:30 A.M. That's 5:30 back home. Checking in two hours earlier meant we wouldn't be getting much sleep, especially since I hadn't quite gotten over the jet lag. I told Linda I was going back to my room to write up our report. She should take the rest of the day to go shopping or something. Whatever floated her boat. She said she was tired and was headed back to her room as well. "How about dinner first?" she asked. Sounded reasonable . . .

There was a nice restaurant at the Marriott Airport Hotel. We decided since it was close we'd try that. We checked out of our earlier motel and got rooms at the Marriott. It was a little more than our expense account merited but since we were leaving a day early we decided to splurge. Besides, they had a free shuttle to the airport, so we turned our rental in today, eliminating that hassle in the morning.

Dinner was good, but it was mostly small talk about the case until Linda suggested wine. I ordered a bottle. Cheaper than by the glass. I'm not a drinker but wine with pasta seemed reasonable. Of course, one glass led to another and with the jet lag I was feeling a little bit tipsy. She might have been too.

"How long were you married?" I asked.

She looked up from her food and stared at me for a second. "What brought that up?"

"Just making conversation. You asked about my love life . . ."

"Two years. Actually, two years and three months. I thought I loved the guy. He was handsome, smart, and incredibly rich. He was also very good to me . . . at first. We honeymooned in Hawaii, on the island of Kauai. I couldn't have been happier."

"I take it that didn't last long."

"No . . . it didn't. Sean was obsessed with his job. As a real estate developer, in business with his brother who worked out of the East Coast. They were in competition everywhere they went . . . and they hated to lose. Sean had a temper I never saw when we were dating, and he would fly into a rage if someone got the better of him. Within a year of the marriage, he began to come home later and later from work. He always had an excuse. He claimed he was busy. Very busy. So busy that he had to fly all over the country meeting investors, putting together deals. At first, I went with him. It was like a honeymoon in a new city every week. As time passed, he went alone; he said he thought I'd be bored to tears alone in some hotel all day. He was probably right. The excitement of the honeymoon was definitely over. He wasn't all that romantic anymore either; 'exhausted from all that travel,' he said.

"I flew up to San Francisco to visit my mom one weekend while he was supposed to be in Minneapolis. I came home a day early and discovered he'd never left. He made some excuses for not going but I got suspicious when I found a strange brand of shampoo in our shower designed especially for 'Latinos.' The bra on the bathroom floor wasn't mine either; way too small. I guess that's why he was too tired for me. At first, I was hurt. Then I got mad, really mad, but I decided not to confront him . . . then."

She took another sip of wine and smiled, "I hired a private investigator to snoop. Sometimes I went with him. It took us a year to ferret out all of his activities. It was shocking. I documented so much evidence he didn't stand a chance when I sued him for divorce. That's why I got the house," she laughed. "Unfortunately, information regarding some of the women he had been screwing came out, and his business took a nasty turn. I haven't seen him since."

We finished the bottle. The severed head was the farthest thing on my mind.

With dinner over, we headed back to the elevator. Fourth floor; adjoining rooms.

Somehow, we adjourned to her room. Sitting on her bed. King size.

"This is not going to work," I said. "We're partners. We both know getting involved in a romantic relationship is asking for trouble." I got up and started to leave . . . really?

"Are you sure?" she smiled, removing her blouse, kicking off her shoes, and lying back on the bed. "We're both adults. We have needs. What's the harm?" She began taking off her bra and slid over onto the big pillows lined against the headboard. I was now looking at the *first* thing I looked at when meeting a woman . . . and I couldn't take my eyes off of them. "We don't have to have sex. Maybe we could just have some fun. I remember some politician who swore, 'I never had sex with that woman.' He was right: the cigar did!"[1] and she laughed.

"I've got an idea. Look into my purse and get that small plastic bottle labeled Massage Oil. She slipped off her panties and lay on her stomach.

"Just squirt some on my back and massage my shoulders and back muscles."

"You're kidding," I chuckled.

"Come on, it's just a massage."

Feeling a little silly, I took my shoes off and knelt down on the bed beside her and started rubbing. It did feel soothing. As I kneaded her muscles I actually began to enjoy it. I started on her shoulders and worked my way down her back. It was smooth and soft. I massaged that way for a couple of minutes. "Lower," she cooed. "Work the back of my legs too." I started at her toes, gently teasing each digit and then her calf muscles. "Kelly, you're really good at this. Knead a little harder, you won't hurt me." I started on her thighs. She spread her legs ever so slightly, and I could see she was completely shaven. I was sure I had heard a term for that before, but I couldn't think of it at that moment. I inched my efforts higher until I was kneading her buttocks.

"That feels so good," and she spread her legs just a little more. It felt good to me too.

I put more oil on her back and it ran down and over the crack of her ass and onto her vagina. She had a little catch in her voice as she implored me to please rub it in. By now I was getting into it. I caressed her crevices and ran my finger over her anus ever so gently, lingering just a moment, and then going lower over the slit between her lips. She was starting to move slowly, gyrating her hips to put more pressure on my finger. I never inserted it, rather just gently parting the lips and touching just the right spot, once, twice, and then moving back over her anus. She definitely didn't need any more oil. Up and down, rubbing and flicking my finger. "Please, don't stop," she begged. But I had no intention to. I slid my middle finger into her wetness. In and out . . . and then rubbed her clit. Slowly at first, then faster and faster. She moaned, she cried out, and I slid two fingers deep inside her. And then she screamed.

---

[1] Editor's note: This was long before a more recent headline. He wasn't the first politician to pursue a relationship with an aid.

Her body actually tensed, her butt cheeks clenched like she was having a cramp. She shuddered . . . and then she relaxed. Spent, her eyes closed, appearing to relive the moment. Then she turned and smiled at me.

I was hard as a rock.

She quickly helped me out of my pants and underwear. I think she was impressed because her eyes widened significantly as she took my member and licked the end of it. She stroked it and then put the head into her mouth. I closed my eyes.

It didn't take her long before she had results. Bringing my cock in and out of her mouth soon produced a copious spurt of semen. It ran down between her breasts. She laughed and continued sucking until I started to go soft. We lay down together . . . spent. I think I must have dozed off because when I opened my eyes she was no longer in bed and the shower was running. I called her name and she said she couldn't stay. Early plane tomorrow and we had work to do. Actually, she could stay. It was her room. I got up, dressed and left.

Well, "Slam bang, thank you Ma'am," was all I could think of.

Maybe that politician was right; maybe we didn't really have sex at all . . .

Very early the next morning we met outside for the shuttle. No words were spoken. It wasn't until after we had checked in and were having a cup of coffee awaiting boarding that she spoke: "Well, what do you think?"

"I'm thinking we shouldn't do that again. It's bad enough that I don't even carry condoms anymore but . . . damn it! We're partners . . ."

"I'm talking about the case. Grow up. That thing last night never happened."

Wow . . . she sounded just like most of the guys I knew at the precinct. "Chicks are everywhere in our line of work, and it doesn't pay to get involved. Look at our police department. Half the men are divorced and the other half wished they were." How many times had I heard that warning?

We both slept on the way back. That's not easy riding in the cattle car in the rear of the plane right next to the heads. I still called the lavatories "heads." Once in the Navy, always in the Navy, I guess. At least there were no little kids sitting behind me kicking the seat for hours.

CHAPTER 9

We still had work to do. We checked into the Lieutenant's office to get an update and to update him. He wasn't impressed. "I thought it was a wild goose chase before you left. Anyway, it's been way too long now. The news is growing old. You know how the press reacts . . . if it doesn't make the front pages anymore they move onto something else. Well, they have. We have just uncovered a major sex-trafficking ring operating south of Interstate Eight. The area has been serving as a kind of holding place. Somehow, they are bringing in girls through the border and dropping them off in National City to serve the sailors stationed at 32nd Street. As you know, the Navy's biggest base is right here in San Diego. Hell, 32nd Street is just the tip of their operations here. That's just their surface ships. I'll bet there are at least fifty ships stationed here. With at least eight piers, each over a quarter mile long they can dock a ton of ships. Then, you've got the marines at the Marine Corps Recruit Station near the airport, major recruit training at Naval Training Center at the north end of San Diego Bay, the submarines at Ballast Point on Point Loma, their largest Naval Hospital at Balboa Park, and the Naval Air Station in Miramar where they train the top gun pilots. Oh, I forgot, three aircraft carriers moored by the Naval Air Station on Coronado Island and the Seals at the Naval Amphibious Base. There is no shortage of young men looking for women, not to mention the deviants who prowl the streets."

I didn't think it was the time for me to mention the huge Marine Base in Camp Pendleton about 50 miles north of the city, home to over 35,000 marines of the First Division. There was also San Diego State College, the University of California at San Diego, the University of San Diego, National University, or the two-year Community College at Miramar. I was sure I was missing a few too. I let it rest.

"I'm putting you and Meadows back in sex-trafficking. They need all the help they can get and maybe you can find a connection with your unidentified head."

Our Lieutenant was Samuel Hill; like, "what in Sam Hill?" My dad used to say that. Don't ask me why. Never did know how that originated. Lt. Hill was a no-nonsense, seen-it-all black man who seemed to like me . . . or maybe it was Meadows. Anyway, He gave us a lot of rope in most crime cases.

We started looking at cases. Linda spit out, "This is disgusting."

The police had just arrested a thirty-two-year old male sexually molesting a six-year old girl. The only reason he was caught was the man's wife forgot to lock the door and their fifteen-year-old daughter walked in on all three of them. She was disgusted too . . . and called the cops.

There was the case of a seventeen-year-old runaway girl from L.A. who met a nice-looking man through a friend. Believing she might have a relationship with him and looking for a place to crash, she agreed to go with him down at his house in Chula Vista. Although she was probably under no illusions as to what he wanted, she actually brought her fourteen-year-old sister with her. After all, her situation at home was no better than hers. Her mother worked late, they had very little money, and her father liked little girls; especially his. Not much changed. When they got there, they discovered more girls and the nice-looking man pocketed several thousand bucks for the pair days later. We caught them too, but only because the nice-looking man tried the same tactic on one of our undercover girls working the downtown district. When we raided the flop house, the others were gone.

"Those girls were lucky. Most of the women come from broken homes or homes that are so poor that their parents actually sell them off to pay their rent or because they just can't afford another body to feed. Girls from Central American and Asian countries are the biggest victims. They are literally slaves. Often, they are promised their freedom once they pay off their passage to America and their room and board. That doesn't happen. And then they get hooked on drugs.

"That's another way for the gang to maintain control of their product. Drugs are easier to smuggle across the border than women. Obviously, many girls try to escape. But it's not so easy. San Diego is a big place. Where do you run? Where can you hide? They need money. Money to eat, money for a room, money to feed their habit. They *do* know how to get money: they turn back to taking tricks. And that's when they get caught again.

"A pimp does not take fancy into runaways. That costs him money . . . and it makes him look bad. The talk in his circle make it sound like he's not man enough to satisfy his harem; can't keep them happy. That's when the beatings start. Violent, contusive, but with rubber belts so as not to leave too many scars, kicks to the legs and buttocks, but never the face . . . that may cost him a trick or two. Usually they are chained or locked in a room. Sometimes for weeks. They might get enough to eat and drink if they are good, but they don't neglect to offer them drugs. Gradually, their confidence regained, their bruises healed, the addiction satisfied, promises made, they are released. Back to work.

"This may go on until the girl decides enough is enough and runs again, or they get too old or worn out to be useful. That's when we find them in the trash. This time they are beaten so badly that identification is really difficult. If the hands are still attached and located we can try to make a match with missing persons, but usually there is no one in the system with those characteristics. Same goes for teeth. You can't match someone unless you have something to match against.

"All we can do is try to catch the bad guys and put them out of business. We know that most of the women do not come from the United States proper. They are smuggled in. Some come from Canada . . . very few. Most cross our southern border somewhere along its 1,969 miles. It runs east from San Diego and Tijuana, Baja California; 15.6 miles known as the San Ysidro Port of Entry, to Nogales, Arizona; El Paso, Texas – Juarez Chihuahua; and Laredo, Texas – Nuevo Laredo Tamaulipas, Mexico. The whole thing is virtually wide-open. It's a nightmare for us. We can't cover all of it, and there are too many trying to cross. It's a losing battle . . .

"Years ago, our hands were really tied.

"In 1965 President Lyndon Johnson, in a major civil rights reform, changed the preference for immigration. Anyone who had family ties with someone currently residing in the United States could enter without restriction.

"In 1969, however, President Richard Nixon launched Operation Intercept which mandated surprise inspections of all border crossings between the United States and Mexico. Thousands of border patrol agents were dispatched along the border, virtually shutting down illegal immigration . . . by car . . . for the first time.

"Of course, crossings still continued by boat and all the territory that did not have roads. There were no barriers.

"Now, it appears that the laws have been amended . . . at least to the effect that there seems to be a lull in law enforcement. Pedestrians and cars are only stopped intermittently. We heard that an editor from some obscure newspaper actually smuggled someone's dog across the border covered in a blanket in the back seat of his car to prove how easy it was to smuggle someone across the border. No one looked. I wonder what was in the trunk. I'm not a politician, but I think someday we're going to have a real problem with illegal immigration. The United States is just too rich a country to not attract a whole lot of people, destitute with their lives, not to want a piece of the pie."

CHAPTER 10

DOC HUGHS

One would think that it would be easy getting antecedent dental records. I mean, I have the names and addresses of the victims on the plane manifest. Searching relatives, I can usually narrow down the names of their dentists. One would be amazed at how many people have not been to the dentist, or it has been many, many years. Even when I find one with fairly new radiographs, trying to match a filling in a fragment of a jaw or tooth is time-consuming, to say the least. They don't all look the same, you know. The size and shape and location of a filling is determined by the extent of decay and the ability of the dentist to remove it while adhering to the patient's occlusion. They must also insure it will not fall out and it must match the original shape of the tooth. Matching a restoration from a postmortem X-ray to an antecedent X-ray *is* just as reliable as a fingerprint. But not everyone has a full set of teeth. Periodontal disease for the elderly is particularly evil. When there is no bone or tissue to hold the tooth in place, it eventually just falls out. It stinks too. Third molars, or wisdom teeth, erupt at around seventeen or eighteen and are sometimes extracted, usually when they are partially obstructed and cause pain. For the life of me, I do not know why they are called wisdom teeth. It's an obvious misnomer. Eighteen-year-olds rarely show much wisdom.

Every tooth is different and decay patterns are different. The shape and size of the tooth's roots are different too. Dentists are like miniature architects; building foundations for their restorations so the filling material will not leak and stay in place. Most of the restorations are in amalgam, a mixture of mercury, tin, and silver. Copper is starting to be used as well. I know, mercury is toxic, but when it is bound up in the tin and silver, hence the term amalgam, it is rendered harmless. The best restorations are usually in gold. Dentists are starting to use composite fillings too because they're more tooth-colored. Unfortunately, they usually leak and hide underlying caries. I imagine future generations of composites will improve. There are also dentures and removable partial dentures to contend with as well. Fortunately, I don't have to do this by myself. I've enlisted ten Navy dentists over at the 32nd Street dental clinic going through their Advanced Education in General Dentistry program to help. They've been great. I expect in a year or two we will be finished . . . just kidding. I expect with the luggage match, seating chart matched with a passenger sitting in that seat (not necessarily the right seat) and family members missing a loved one who was supposed to be on board, we'll match everyone. Even a Dean Meritt will be found, although it probably isn't his correct name.

I still don't know who the detached head of the young girl belongs to. Detective Kelly's trip back to Newark was in vain. I've still got a lot of work to do.

---

* Editor's note: Although DNA has been used to solve criminal cases since 1987, it wasn't used to routinely to identify bodies until the early 1990's.

Chapter 11

It's time for action. *I need to create more awareness . . .*

Tonight, I'm prowling the streets in National City. It's a Navy hangout. There are street girls and massage parlors galore. I've found them very helpful in finding unwanted women. I know they are victims of sex trafficking. They're usually from China, Korea, or Latin America. Look at their faces: flush with make-up to make them look more attractive . . . some want to be a bit older; most want to be younger. It doesn't hide the despair I see in their eyes: "How many more tricks? I'm tired; I need a fix." They carry huge debts or are under extreme financial pressure, speak little English, no education, and are usually in their thirties or forties.

I ask for a massage. I want one of the younger girls. The room is little more than an eight by ten-foot stall. Inside is a six-foot-long table with a sheet covering it and a pillow with a hole in it to place your head. I guess so you can breathe. There are no chairs. The masseuse is "younger," probably close to thirty. She's wearing short-shorts and a bra. She said for an extra ten spot she'll take off her bra. I ask her how much would it take for me to take you out of here. She laughs, "You can't afford that, cowboy. How about I just give you a special right here and we'll both be happy? Only twenty bucks more and I'll drop my shorts just for you."

"How about I talk to your boss instead? I'll bet he'll agree."

I have to pay her "manager" a "traveling fee," but I can afford it. He'll never recognize me. Long hair, false teeth with one front tooth missing. I had a dentist make that up for me to go with a Halloween costume I wore one year. I smile for the full effect. And the Texas twang! I've even worn a short scraggly beard, bow tie and black cowboy hat. Where do I think up these guises? I'll bet he looked to see if my horse was tied up out front!

I offer to take the girl to a motel down the street. She's been there before.

"Get in the car, sweetie, I'm too old to be walking the four blocks up the street. Your boy can watch us. He's got the license plate."

We never checked in. She asked me where we were going. I told her I was taking her out of there. I've paid off your debt and now you're free. I have a place we can stay and I'll help you get off the drugs. You can have a life now. It's not too late." I think she believed me . . . or at least she wanted to. She didn't object.

She started talking as I headed to my house.

"You just don't know what my life has been like," she volunteered. "I lived in Nicaragua. A one-bedroom house with my mother and two sisters. My dad, actually I don't know who my dad was, never was around. He could have been anybody who frequented the house.

A different man came and went every night. They never spoke to us, just spent the night with my mother. We had no money to speak of. My mom worked doing laundry by day and spent the night with men. I think they may have given her a little money. Yeah, I know she was prostituting herself, but I don't like to think of her that way. She did what she had to do to survive. Three kids didn't help. That's why I left, because my mother finally *did* ask for my help. I was fourteen at the time. It was the first time she ever invited me into her room at night. We kids always slept on cots in the main room. She told me she was scared, and wanted me to watch out for her. I was confused but I sat on the chair by her bed and waited. Soon, a man entered the room. He smiled at my mother and then looked at me and said, "What have we here? A present for my birthday?" He laughed loudly. As my mom started to undress, she looked at me and said, "Just watch, honey, it's okay." I watched this man drop his pants, climb on top of my mom and proceed to fuck her. He was rough and demanding and when he was about to cum he pulled out of her and stuck his dick in her mouth. "Swallow it, bitch," he cried.

He then looked at me. "Don't worry sweetheart, I'm through. I'm not going to hurt you. But my buddy standing at the door has other plans." With that he backed off the bed, put on his clothes and threw some money on the dresser.

As he walked out the door, his "buddy" came in. He was already naked. My mother whispered, "don't hurt her, please, it's her first time," as she left the room. He grabbed me by my hair, pulled me over to the bed and forced me to take his dick in my mouth. After a few strokes he got hard and told me take off all my clothes and lay on my stomach. He made me get up on my knees and then he started to fuck me in the ass. Jesus! I was still a virgin. I screamed and screamed, but he wouldn't stop . . . until he was finished. "You're *still* a virgin," he laughed. "Tomorrow I will make you a real woman."

"Tomorrow . . . I left. I had heard some people say they were getting out of Nicaragua. They were heading north, into Mexico and then to the United States. It would be a long trip, possibly dangerous, but no worse than here. There was money to be made there and laws to protect you, not take advantage of you. That was the hook.

"Couldn't you call the police and have that guy arrested?" I asked.

"Are you kidding me?" she cried. "The guy who raped me in the ass actually *was* a policeman!"

"That won't happen here, I promise. You don't have to worry about that any longer. You're safe with me," I lied.

"My mom gave me some money. She cried as I left. But I think she was happy for me. The journey was hard, like they promised. It took us over a month and in that time, I had sex with many men to pay for the trip. At fourteen, I was attractive and had lots of customers. Soon, I didn't even care. I was just a product, like a piece of toilet paper, to be used once and thrown away. No one knew my name, no one cared where I came from, no one knew of my family."

"Come here, kid. Spread your legs, I'll get you to the border."

"That was a lifetime ago. Since then I've worked the streets. I started on my own but it's too dangerous. The competition is brutal and you have to have protection. The regulars have the best corners. You need a pimp. They all know each other and as long as you stay in your own territory you won't be hassled. Of course, pimps are a pain because you do all the work and they take the money! The pay is food, a lousy flop house to stay in, and enough drugs to keep you going. I don't think I could do this without the drugs. A couple of years ago, I got lucky. My pimp got shot in a drug deal that went sour. I got hooked up with some lady who hired me to work in that massage parlor. I still have to fuck for a living, but the environment is better"

She was tired and hungry and thirsty by the time we got to my place. I fed her, gave her some tea and a couple of my trusty Ambien pills and waited for her to fall asleep.

She woke up in the cutting room.

Same story as before but she fought me a little. It's easier if they just hold still and allow me to slice. She turned her head back and forth, screaming for me to let her go. Way too much noise. I plunged the knife into her heart and she stopped struggling.

A gurgle or two more and I held her head high in triumph. Such a touching story she told. Nobody missed her before. Nobody paid attention to her before. But somebody would. I'll take care of that. I just had to find the right moment and place. Man, I just love their stories . . . like I give a shit.

CHAPTER 12

Trouble. I got a phone call from a mortician in San Carlos. That's not too far from Jack Murphy Stadium. The San Diego Padres and Chargers play there. They play like old people fuck. They know all the moves, but just aren't very good at it.

The mortician's name was Anderson; George Anderson. He said he had been looking for me for a while but just couldn't bring himself to talk to me. He said he was embarrassed.

"What can I do for you, Mr. Anderson?" I queried. "I'm a coroner. You can't embarrass me."

"You know your brother, Jim, works for me, don't you?"

"Well, I knew he worked for a funeral home, but didn't really know where. We haven't spoken for some time. James was a little envious of my position, being a doctor and now Medical Examiner for San Diego County. We don't hang with the same crowds. He doesn't have any formal education. Never went into the service; asthma, I think. Last I heard, he was doing well, had a job, and was renting a house somewhere near North Park."

"Yeah, that's him. And don't get me wrong. He's a good employee. After I have received the death certificate from an attending medical doctor, he handles the transportation of the deceased from the assisted-living and memory care units around the county. Once I have read the will and know how the deceased is going to be interred, he will either bring them to our funeral home for embalming if it's to be an open casket for viewing, or to the crematory. James has always been very respectful and careful with the bodies. I have never had a problem with him."

"I sense a *but* coming, sir. Has he done something wrong?"

"Yesterday after he took the body from the funeral home to the crematory I went looking for him. He'd already left. There was another death call. Your brother was needed to retrieve the deceased. That's when I noticed a disturbing thing. A female body was laid out nude on the table as usual preparing to be wrapped in plastic and taped before entering the crematory. But the body had been mutilated. I was shocked and didn't look further. I confronted him with what I saw when he returned and he was visibly shaken. He didn't deny it. He said he was sorry. He said it was the first time he had done it and he didn't know why. He said the deceased, a young woman, looked so peaceful and beautiful. It was almost romantic in a way. He was overwhelmed and he got carried away."

"But I knew it was wrong. In fact, I was going to call the police but then thought this would just cause him and me all kinds of trouble. The person was dead, they were going to be cremated. Really, what lasting harm was done; who would know?"

"So, I called you. I'm putting this in your hands. You work for the police. You know your brother. You know his history; I don't. He seems like a good young man and I don't want to see him hurt. He is my most dependable employee and he doesn't deserve to go to jail or even have a police record. I am at a loss over what to do. Will you help me?"

Yeah, I knew his history. I could write a book about it. I told George I'd handle it. Don't look for it in the papers. I was starting to worry about my brother . . .

CHAPTER 13

James was four years younger than me. I actually raised him when we lived on the farm. It was a chicken farm. When my Dad retired from the Navy we lived in Newport, Rhode Island. He had been raised on a farm in Kansas and decided it was a good life and a good way to raise a family. He bought a six-acre farm near Fall River, Massachusetts. It had three barns on it and a big old farm house. My dad grew up learning how to fix anything. He went through the depression in the thirties at a time when they had no money. He told me he moved a lot. "Every time the rent was due, we moved," he would laugh.

So, he began fixing up the farm. He remodeled the barns to accommodate chickens. We eventually ended up with over 3500 of them. We didn't kill the chickens for food; rather, we sold their eggs. Lots of them. A chicken will lay an egg almost every day as long as it doesn't reach its clutch. That's four eggs for a chicken. Every bird has a clutch. So as long as you never let a bird reach its clutch, they will continue to lay. Three thousand chickens produce a lot of eggs every day. And we weren't automated, which meant someone had to gather all those eggs. It didn't stop there. They had to be washed, candled to look for impurities, sized, and packed for sale. That was my mom's job. She even had a wholesaler she sold to in Boston once a week. We moved into the old farmhouse and even rented the upstairs because it was so big. I don't know when it was built, but there were no nails it in, just small spikes. It really was old. It had three fireplaces and no other heat. Anyway, we settled in and with all the work being done by my mom and dad, I was left to watch my brother. And watch him I did. He was curious. Curious in the way he acted. I don't mean that he was retarded, but he was sure a little bit screwed up mentally. He liked to cut up things. Not just things, but living things. He had this dark side. He, we, went down to a small pond across the street almost daily in the summer. We would catch frogs, snakes, and turtles. I never could figure out how fish got in that pond, but there were bluegills and perch to catch as well. I built a little terrarium and put it in the garage. When I'd catch a big bull frog I'd keep it there. When my brother caught a frog, he would try to figure out what was inside it. It was like he was fascinated with its internal organs! But it was more than that. He would cut off their legs, throw them in the water, and watch them die. Once he dismembered a frog, eviscerated it, and placed it on top of an anthill. He laughed as the ants ate it alive. One fourth of July, he caught a big old bull frog and stuck a firecracker up its ass. It hopped about three jumps and its whole ass end blew off. Sick.

We had about thirteen cats on our farm. He once caught several of the new baby kittens and tried to drown them. He told my mom he was giving them a bath. He was covered with scratches and cat hair and he and my mom both laughed. She stopped him before they were killed. I knew if she hadn't seen him, they would have been drowned and dissected as well. He seemed obsessed with death. I had a baby map turtle I caught at the pond. I named him Toby. One day James saw me playing with little Toby on the driveway. He walked over and stomped on it. He laughed. When I shoved him to the ground, he laughed again. I called him a little asshole even though he was still only five years old.

I don't know why I protected him and never disclosed his dark side. He liked to kill things. He was fascinated with death. Did that brand him as evil? He was just a kid. Maybe he would grow out or it. We moved to San Diego in 1963. My mom told my dad, "It's me or the farm. I've had it." After more than a little thought, my dad sold the farm and took a job in Civil Service, eventually working his way to the Social Security office here in San Diego. She divorced him anyway.

I started college. James soon went to high school. He was smart but made only average to poor grades. He went out of his way to irritate our mother. She pushed him way too hard. It wasn't enough to just do his assigned homework from school. She demanded more. She tutored him in math, made him read book after book and make reports for each of them. Like a father trying to make his son into an elite athlete, she was going to make him into a child genius. I don't think that James ever realized she did the same thing to me. She just wanted us to succeed. Like it or not, two kids raised in the same environment, by the same parents, with the same moral values, do not always turn out the same. We're all different.

James *was* a good athlete and he was always good at art. He could draw or render anything. Halloween was his favorite holiday. He'd dream up the neatest costumes, mostly monsters, and scare everyone. He hardly dated, not only because mom was always hounding him to study more but because he just didn't seem interested in girls. But that wasn't entirely true . . . I came home from college during a spring break and caught my brother in his bedroom with a blow-up doll. He may have seen me but I quickly left the room. We never talked about it . . . then.

I decided to call him. To have a chat and see what was going on. But I had a good idea what he was doing . . .

The phone rang. I was just coming through the door holding a cup of coffee in my hand when I heard it.

"Bob, I've been trying to reach you for the last ten minutes. There's been another incident. Looks like it was intentional. You need to come and evaluate the scene, collect the bodies. There are several of them."

It was Joe, again. "Sorry, I went out for coffee. Where am I going? Send me the directions." I gathered my kit.

CHAPTER 14

It was in Chula Vista. An older home that someone had set afire. The fire department had doused the flames but were not entering any more than they had to in order to preserve any evidence there might be. That was my job. The police made sure the scene was safe and secured from onlookers, while separating them from any potential witnesses. They found several occupants huddled in the back room. Their bodies were almost completely charred. Much more than they should have been considering the small amount of damage to the other interior rooms or the outside of the house. The smell of gasoline was still in the air. I asked a group of cops standing nearby if they knew who had been the first officer on the scene. One of them pointed to my left: "Peters, he's over there talking to a witness."

I walked over and he confirmed that they had not touched or moved anything, this was just as they found the bodies. There were three of them. It was obvious a whole lot of gas had been poured on them and set afire. They were in what some folks called the fighter's stance. A tell-tale posture, fingers clenched, arms up. It's what bodies do as they burn and the muscles and tissues tighten.

I had brought with me a portable X-ray machine. It was occasionally handy in cases like this. Burned, charred bodies were difficult to examine, and difficult to move. Taking an X-ray of their heads, more specifically their jaws and teeth, at the scene sometimes is more practical than lugging them back to the lab. Sometimes. Teeth outlast all body tissue. But I needed more room. There was a closet located right beside the bodies. It looked like it hadn't been damaged badly. I opened the door and stepped inside a little to better position the X-ray machine. It was a difficult task. First, I had to find their heads. Then, where

I thought their mouths might be. It was like looking at a charred lump of meat. It took me awhile. Meadows tried to help me. I would still have to resect their jaws back at my lab to get better pictures. That was not always easy. I had to cut both the maxilla and mandible separately from the head. Access to the teeth is very difficult as the tissue is very rigid, but it allows me to take X-rays at an angle more consistent with the radiographs taken in a dental office. Postmortem X-rays are only useful when compared to the antecedent matches though. Again, I didn't think we'd find any.

When I was done, I walked outside to talk to Joe, who had just returned. He said they had found a witness who saw a man walk to the door wearing a white cowboy hat and a false mask that looked like Richard Nixon. He had two bags with him and what looked like a five-gallon container of gasoline. A few minutes later a different man ran out of there like he was shot. Looked Hispanic. He took off in a '57 Chevy Impala up the street. He remembered that because it was a classic. The witness said he then went back into his house. Several minutes later he heard shooting. Not uncommon in this neighborhood. His wife finally convinced him to call 9-1-1 but by the time anyone came to the house the masked guy had taken off in a newer model Ford. He didn't get the license plate. 9-1-1 notified the police but because the witness neglected to mention the house fire, it took longer for the fire department to arrive. That's probably why the bodies were so badly burned.

"Well, I'll need to look for gunshot wounds, but if it was a shotgun there won't be any bullets to compare with other weapons. I didn't see any shell casings I can match either."

Just then detective Meadows came running out. "Kelly, Doc, you both need to see this!" she yelled. We went back in the back room and there in the closet was another suitcase. I hadn't noticed it when I was there, but I wasn't focused on the contents of the closet. It had been opened by Meadows. Inside was another severed head!

Okay. This was clearly different. Another suitcase, another head. But this one hadn't been on an airplane, and there was no address on the suitcase. It was a different kind of case, too. Looked more like a bowling ball bag. Maybe the shooter was carrying the can of gas and the other bags held the gun and the head. It dawned on me that maybe Meritt didn't bring that suitcase with him from Newark. It was planted right here in San Diego. Was there a connection?

"We need to get an ambulance in here to carry out the bodies. I've photographed the entire scene and have initiated a chain of custody to record the description of each body and object in the room and the exact location where it was found as well as who is in possession of the evidence."

"Somehow I don't think it will help, Doc," Joe volunteered. "This whole area has been marked by us for some time as a place for moving girls. They hold them up in one of these "safe houses" for a while and then transport them to cities across the country."

"The girls are nameless, homeless, and unwanted. There's no one looking for them. You're looking at a whole lot of work that's probably going nowhere."

CHAPTER 15

Days later, after doing a more thorough look at the bodies, I was able to determine that one of the dead bodies was still alive when it caught fire. The trachea showed signs of smoke and soot . . . and indicator she was still breathing amidst the flames. It was also determined by looking at the bones of the pelvic region that they were all women. No evidence of pregnancy. And fairly young: no missing teeth, recently erupted third molars, no dentures, minimal abrasion of the enamel and very few, if any, caries. There was also evidence of fluorosis. That's a brownish stain in the enamel that can be caused by excessive fluoride in the water. It significantly reduces caries and occurs naturally in the Southwest; Texas/Mexico areas. Maybe that could pinpoint where they came from.

I also got some fingerprints off of a couple of the victims. Sometimes when the fingers curl up they protect the tips from the fire. Perhaps we could match their prints to something or someone. The only thing different about the severed head was the age of the victim, clearly older than the plane victim, probably in her late twenties, early thirties, judging by the wear patterns in her teeth, teeth eruption, and caries pattern. I also noted she wasn't decapitated cleanly. There must have been a struggle; instead of a single knife stroke, she had several deep lacerations above the final cut as well.

I had forgotten about my brother in all the excitement of this investigation. I still was undecided about what to do. I decided to confront him. See what he says. A phone call wouldn't cut it, I needed a face-to-face meet. I called to set it up . . .

"James, this is your brother, can you talk now, it's important?"

"No, Bob, I can't. And don't call me James. You know I hate that name. It reminds me of Mom and gives me nightmares," he shouted.

"Okay. How about we meet for lunch or dinner tomorrow whenever you are free. I'll come by to pick you up. Where will you be?"

"Don't bother, I'll meet you at 11:30 at that little cafe in the Barrio. You know where it is, on Main Street down by the Coronado Bridge near Chicano Park. You used to take me there after you got your driver's license. We both liked their Mexican food."

"Got it, and Jam . . . or Jim, this is important. Don't stand me up."

I got there a little after 11:30. We were lucky. There was only one car in front of the diner. It was a 1967 Chevy Corvair. His first car. Dad bought it for him for his eighteenth birthday.

The place was just as I remembered it. A little hole in the wall. The neighborhood was a little shaky . . . especially after dark. Graffiti everywhere. The café was small. There weren't a lot of tables. Most folks ordered to go. We were lucky. He was already there and had gotten a place to sit. I sat down and watched a cockroach dance across the table. James had already ordered a big chicken burrito. It looked pretty good so I ordered one too, with extra guac.

We didn't speak for a while and then he asked, "So, what do you want? What have I done now?"

'It's what you've been doing for some time now, Jim. Only this time someone besides me has caught you. Your boss, Mr. Anderson, called me last week concerned with what he found at the crematory. You know, the mutilated, naked body of that deceased young girl you picked up. How long has this been going on?

I thought you'd quit when I saw you years ago. The blowup doll was one thing, but doing it with that dead girl *was* a little sick, don't you think? There's even a term for it: 'necrophilia.' I protected you back then. You were only in high school when we found the body while hiking in the hills past Escondido. I told you to stay with her while I notified the authorities. When I got back you were going at it. What's wrong with you? That's disgusting!"

"Who are *you* to talk? What do you know about my life? You left me to go to college, join the Navy, and spend a million years getting a doctor's degree, and now a coroner, no less. Mr. Bigshot. Too important to even call me anymore. I don't have any friends. Never did. Mom died in '65, thank God. Who knows where Dad is. You were the only one who ever cared about me. Mom was too embarrassed to be with me. Dad was too busy. Girls never looked at me twice. The only ones who never left, never turned me down, always satisfied me, were the ones who couldn't. They never said no. Making love to them was so gentle, so peaceful; romantic really . . . and I had an irresistible urge to connect with them. So, I did. I found a place that made it easy to find the bodies. I was all alone, could take my time. It was really all I could ask for; all I needed. Shit, now I even get paid for it.

"Did you know there is no law in California against necrophilia? I know the word, smart ass. I looked it up."

"Well, you need to be careful, Jim. I think you are one sick puppy and now that your boss is on to you, he's going to be checking your behavior more carefully. Next time, he won't call me. And I won't be around to cover your ass when they find you with another body in the hills."

"Don't worry," he smiled. "I have the perfect place to take them. And they'll never be able identify the girls. I'm smarter than you, he whispered. You just never knew it."

Louder, he threatened, "Who knows, someday I might take you there too."

We didn't have much to say after that, so I finished my burrito. I was struck by so much that had changed in our relationship over the years. Sure, I wasn't around much. Christ, I was going to school. I enlisted in the Navy. I have a career. But we were always close when he was younger. I was his mother and his father. I taught him how to swim. I taught him how to play all kinds of sports. When he was eleven he won our town's "Punt, Pass and Kick" contest for ages twelve and under. He got his name in the paper. That was a big deal. We had practiced for months. I was so proud of him. In high school he played soccer. He was good enough to play on a traveling team that included the best players from other schools in the area. Soccer was just beginning to be popular in the States. Most of the really good players were Hispanic. I took him to the movies with me when I was in high school. Some guys had dates; I had my little brother. What happened to us?

He didn't even acknowledge me when I said goodbye. As I got into my car, another thought struck me: Could this ever be connected to the severed heads we were finding? I was starting to worry.

CHAPTER 16

KELLY

The police forensic team was having a field-day collecting evidence from the crime scene. Fingerprints were everywhere. Clothes, drugs, and empty beer bottles were found. It appeared this house had been used for some time. I guess the neighbors were either afraid to notify the police or figured it was none of their business. They didn't know those women . . . and no one was asking for help.

It didn't take long to match a print to a guy who was in the system. Petty crimes. Booked and released several times. Paid a fine; did some community service. Looked like he was a mover now. Police quickly found him a day later up in Miramar. He ran a light and was pulled over driving an old Chevy, registered to someone named Reynolds. He said it was a friend of his. It hadn't been reported stolen. The registered owner verified he had loaned it to Manny. Last name Rodriguez. Manny, or Miguel, was in possession of a current California driver's license. Not sure how he got that.

Joe found Manny down at the station.

"Man, am I under arrest?"

"Nope, we just want to talk to you. Do you *want* us to arrest you? Do you have any reason to not want to cooperate with us?"

Quickly, he asked, "What's your name?"

"Manny."

"That your real name? It says here it's Miguel; Miguel Rodriguez."

"Okay, man, but everyone calls me Manny."

Manny was Mexican. His driver's license indicated he was born in Ensenada, south of Tijuana. His place of residence now was Hillcrest, CA. His file said he was twenty-seven. The picture made him look like he was about forty. But he looked a lot younger in person. He was on the short side. He was wearing hand-me-downs. He needed a haircut and a shave. Obviously, he had not lived a charmed life. I was not inclined to believe he was anything but a keeper. Give that guy a hundred bucks and he was set for a month; no questions asked. He said he came to the U.S. when he was around eight with his brother. He still lived with him in Hillcrest. We noted he was also here in the United States illegally. His temporary residency permit had expired long ago. That wasn't our concern. He was going to jail.

"What were you doing in that house in Chula Vista? You don't need to lie. We have your prints. They're all over the house."

"I just watched over the place. Man, nobody told me nothing. They just said watch the girls and don't let them leave."

"Who's they?"

"I don't know, man. They never mentioned names. I was told never to leave the house. One or both of the men would fuck a girl before they left. They told me I could fuck them any time I wished; just don't hurt them or make any marks on them."

I was thinking, a dream come true, for handsome Manny.

"So, the men stayed awhile with you? What did you talk about?"

"Nothing. I swear. They just fucked the girls and left."

"Did you ever talk to the girls?"

"Sometimes, man. When we ate. Or after we fucked. Once we had a threesome. Me and two girls, not me and the two boys. Them girls were all from south of the border. They cried a lot; didn't understand what was happening to them. I think they were all hooked on something. One of the girls was sick. They all slept a lot. One of them, a young girl, told me she had hiked by foot from Honduras half way through Mexico before a group of men rounded her up with some other women. They eventually took them to a little shack which had a false door behind a closet that led down into a tunnel. The got into a cart of some sort mounted on a track. They rode in that until they got to another ladder which took them up into another house. They stayed there a couple of days and then came to my house."

"Now you're making sense, Manny. Where was the tunnel located?"

"How the fuck would I know? I just watch the girls! When them gals arrived, like I said, they were muddy and wet. I was told to wash their clothes and make them look good."

"What did the men look like?"

"They were young guys . . . maybe early twenties. One was white, the other was more Latino, maybe black, maybe mixed. They wore nice clothes. Nothing I could afford. Tennis shoes: they always wore tennis shoes. Don't white people wear regular shoes anymore? That's all I know, man."

"That's too bad Manny. Did you know withholding information in a murder, or murders in your case, will cost you a lot of prison time? As a matter of fact, we're not sure you didn't start the fire to cover up the murder of those girls before you ran away. That would make you an accessory, and that's life."

"Wait a minute. I didn't start no fire. And I sure as hell didn't kill nobody. He killed them girls? Man, I ran out as soon as the masked dude came in. He told me to get the fuck out . . . and I left."

"Why did he let you go? Did he know you?"

"I don't know . . . maybe he was afraid of me. Jesus, you ask a lot of questions . . . "

"You do look ferocious, Manny. That's probably it; he was afraid of you."

"Did you get a look at him?"

"Yeah, he had a mask on that looked like some president and he was wearing a white cowboy hat and tennis shoes."

"Okay. Did any of the men who dropped off the women or picked them up say where they were going or where they had come from?"

"Yeah, one of the guys mentioned heading to L.A. He was the white dude. He was concerned about going through some customs stop halfway to Ocean City. They planned to stop before they got there. He would herd the girls up over a hill and beyond the roadblock and meet the truck on the other side."

"How often did they come?"

"Once a week, man, like clockwork. Always the same night. Always the same guys. They always had two girls. Those guys would drop them off and when they had eight or ten girls stashed, they'd come back a few hours later to pick them all up."

"Why would they do that? Why not just keep going?"

"They said they had to get gas and get something to eat. They would bring food and water back for me and the women."

"When was the last time they made a delivery?"

"The day before that crazy guy showed up."

"Was that Tuesday? Or Wednesday?"

"I think it was Tuesday . . . no Wednesday. The cowboy showed up yesterday. Today's Friday, ain't it?"

"Yes, so to be clear, the cowboy showed up on Thursday. Right? And the pizza van showed up on Wednesday."

"Shit, man, you are confusing the hell out of me!"

Meadows laughed, "Did you get a look at the delivery vehicle?"

"They used the same one every time. It was white, but covered with dust and mud. There was writing on the side but it was hard to make out. I think it said something about pizza delivery. There was a big picture of a pizza on both sides."

"Anything else you can remember?"

"Nah. Wait . . . I was told to turn the light on by the front porch. If the light was off, it meant there was a problem and they'd know not to stop. I kept it off all the time otherwise."

"Okay, Manny. You did good. Now you are under arrest. Sex trafficking is a serious crime and you were in the middle of it. But don't worry, I'll be sure to tell the DA how you were so cooperative."

"I hope you catch the asshole who killed them girls. They were real nice. Man, I never had that much pussy my whole life . . ."

I read him his rights. We'd gotten all we were going to get out of him, but I had a nagging feeling he was not telling us everything, and what he did tell was probably bogus. Maybe a couple of days in a cell would provide some additional information. That is, if some court-appointed lawyer didn't shut him up for good.

We both had a good laugh after we left when Meadows cracked: "It's not hard to figure out why they call him Manny."

This guy was just a soldier, a throwaway, in the operation. He saw the guy come in, take out the shotgun, and he took off. The health and safety of the girls was the farthest thing on his mind.

CHAPTER 17

Detective Meadows and I had desks across from each other at headquarters. I brought in a couple cups of coffee and sat down to chat. We started with what we now knew. One: we had an idea how the girls were being smuggled across the border. We didn't know where or when. We only knew when they were transported to the safe house. Two: they went to the same "safe" house every time, the same day, at night.

Three: since the house had caught fire, they would have to find a new location. Four: they might not know their house was compromised yet.

And five: we now had another unexplained severed head.

First things first.

Their next delivery of girls was not expected until next Wednesday. It was now Friday. Maybe we'd get lucky.

"How do you want to work this, Kelly?" she asked. "I don't think the exterior of the house was so badly burned as to be that noticeable from the street in the dark. If we stationed a few undercover guys in houses across the street and a couple inside the house we should be able to stop them. Let's not forget about the light either."

"True. And we should probably have some unmarked cars parked at either end of the street in case that get skittish and try to bail. I also think we should start our surveillance at least a day or two early. Just in case they fill their quota quickly . . . and Manny was lying through his teeth."

"Agreed. Let's go tell the LT. I don't think we should investigate the tunnel until we know more. Our best bet is to catch the delivery guys. They could lead us to both ends of the shuttle."

That was too risky . . . . I'm going to have to be more careful. I'm not in a huge hurry; there's a time to be bold and a time for patience. Perhaps I'll just wait a few months or so and see what develops. Let's see what kind of attention this girl will get . . . My plan is perfect right now. No one could ever suspect me . . .

CHAPTER 18

So now we wait. The LT okayed the plan, we had the agents we needed briefed, the lookout houses selected with permission from their owners, and personnel ready to rescue the women and tend to their injuries or health as the case may be.

Detective Meadows and I had completed our reports of the Newark sting and were headed home when she offered an invitation.

"Want to see something special?" she asked. "You remember I told you that in the divorce of my ex I got the house? Well, it really is something. It's in La Jolla with a grand view of the Pacific. With the glass doors open to the veranda you can hear the waves breaking over the rocks. In the evening, the sunsets are to die for. It's also very lonely. I've got this humongous kitchen stocked to the gills with food and no one to share."

"And I love to cook. Got the gift from my mother. Why don't you let me cook a nice dinner? My treat. You can watch TV or just have a drink and watch the sun set. What do you say?"

"I say it sounds like a trap. After our little tryst back in Newark I'm not sure we should go back there again. Don't get me wrong, I'm not complaining. That was definitely special. I just don't want to compromise our official positions within the police department with any unofficial positions."

"Come on Kelly. You need to live a little. It's just dinner. That's all it is; you can leave any time you want. I won't even ask you to help me clean up."

"Okay, it's a deal. But I better not see any massage oil on the table."

She was right. Her house was spectacular. She took hold of my hand and offered to show me around. It was a single-level home situated directly above the sand at one of La Jolla's best beaches. And La Jolla was the premier real estate in Southern California. It was on an acre lot! She told me it had been built in 1970 but they had had it remodeled. I wasn't an expert on architecture but it appeared to be a Spanish or Mediterranean style house built around a large courtyard. It had a four-car garage. We entered through large oak double doors into an open concept space. Most of the homes I had lived in started with a staircase, a hallway with a room on the left, room on the right, maybe two bedrooms upstairs. One bathroom. Six or seven rooms at the most. This was obviously different. I could see across the entire house from the front door! Weight-bearing columns served to separate and delineate the rooms.

I commented on the beautiful tile floors.

She corrected me, "They're marble. The rugs are Persian, what's-his-name had them flown over from Iran." They were strategically arranged in various areas. Each area of the house had its own ceiling fan. You know, the kind where each blade looks like a giant palm leaf. At least twelve-foot ceilings.

"His mother bought the crystal chandelier over the dining room table for us. A little bit over the top for my taste. Fortunately, the divorce also included the Mother-in-law . . . I let him have her just to be fair. She was nasty."

"This is my favorite room." We were in the kitchen. It was ridiculous. A huge room with at least a ten-foot island down the middle. Marble counter tops, several sinks, a gigantic gas stove and hood and a refrigerator that was large enough to hold a whole cow. "I love to cook, got the bug from my mother. She once told me to pick out any recipe I liked in a big Betty Crocker cook book, and start cooking. She'd buy the ingredients and if I needed any help, give her a call. I never looked back."

The living room, or den, or whatever you called it, had a stone fireplace and a large television set against another wall. It looked more like a movie screen. "I spend too much time here, alone," she said. There were comfortable sofas with pillows piled atop and chairs everywhere. Off to one side was a small enclave with a baby grand piano.

"Do you play? I asked.

"No, the Ex did. He was pretty talented. It's just for show now. I would sell it, but I don't know what I would put in its place."

I recognized one of the big pictures above the mantle of the fireplace: A Peter Max. It looked like the head of the Statue of Liberty in New York. "What's the story behind that? It looks like an original," I asked.

"Again, my Ex's. But I kind of like it. Guess I'm a little patriotic myself. Besides, he told me that it was going to worth a fortune someday. I just love to piss him off!"

All the walls facing the ocean were glass. At one end of the house was a wrought-iron staircase and a short hallway leading to a bedroom with a bath and walk-in closet. That seemed strange to me; only one bedroom . . . and why the stairs? She read my mind and led me down the stairs: there *was* more. I had been wrong; there was another level. The way the house was built one actually entered the upper level. Downstairs were three more bedrooms. Each one had an extra-large rectangular picture window looking out into the Pacific; eye level while lying on a bed. They also had their own bathroom and walk-in closet. There was a door leading down some steps directly out onto the beach from what I assumed might be the master bedroom. That was her room, I guessed. The shower connected to her room was big enough for three people and had a water spigot on both sides and a rain shower overhead.

I said it could handle three persons.

We went back upstairs and she took me outside onto her veranda. It stretched the length of the house. You could see the sand below and hear the sounds of the waves crashing against the rocks. She was right. On one side was an outdoor kitchen set-up and a hot tub on the other. There was even a thirty-foot lap pool. Finally, there was the stairway to the beach. Only thirty polished granite steps away. Not exactly my style of home, but I could get used to it.

"Make yourself comfortable," she said, as she gave me a swat on the butt and headed to the kitchen. She gestured for me to follow.

"There's a bottle of red wine over by the fridge and a corkscrew in the top drawer by the sink. Pop the cork. I'm thirsty. Let me get dinner started."

I poured us each a glass and then went out on the veranda and watched the waves. So, this is how rich people live, I thought.

She came out a little later. "Everything's done, it just has to cook. We're having lasagna tonight. It's my mother's favorite recipe and now mine as well." She sat down beside me and snuggled up against my side.

"Isn't this beautiful?" she purred. The sun was just beginning to set. They say you can see a green flash of light when the sun sets over the ocean's horizon. Personally, I'd never seen it, but we both looked for it just in case. Must have been a bad night.

We watched a high-flying plane scratch across the sky. It brought back memories . . . "When I was a kid, I used to watch planes flying overhead and wish I was on one. I didn't care where it was going . . . I just wanted to be on it. It wasn't that I wanted to leave home . . . I just wanted to be somewhere else. Sounds silly, doesn't it?"

She thought for a second. "I don't know. I was a Navy junior . . . the Army called us brats . . . and I traveled a lot. I just longed to stay in one place. I guess it's just human nature; no matter what we've got, we want something more."

We had another glass of wine and she got up and began setting the table. The food smelled delicious and tasted even better. I began to think this girl had a lot of hidden talents. Too bad she couldn't play the piano.

By the time dinner was over and I had helped her clean everything up she declared, "It's ten o'clock; I'm going to take a shower and go to bed. We've got to get up early tomorrow. I've got a date with Doc Hughs to go over his forensic findings. Come on, you can stay the night if you want. I'll show you the guest room. It has its own bathroom."

She went into her bedroom and closed the door, so I went into my room. Undressing, I crawled into bed and thought, "What the hell just happened?" I know I made it sound like I wasn't interested in romance, but really . . . didn't I expect it?

Women. I'd never understand them.

I was awakened by the sound of my door slowly opening. As she tiptoed into my room, I saw she was naked and felt her slip into my bed beside me. "You really didn't think I was going to leave you alone tonight, did you?" she giggled.

Sadly, I really had . . .

The sex was different this time. It was intense, not gentle. No more caresses; no more teasing. I was hard as soon as she touched me and couldn't wait to mount her. She was ready. She spread her legs and pulled her knees up to her chest with both of her hands as I entered. We didn't need any massage oil. My thrusts were hard and got faster as I went deeper and deeper into her body. She screamed. We both came, and I moved slower, milking the last drop into her wetness . . . and then we slept.

She stayed with me all night. In the morning we enjoyed each other again. Slower, more intimate. I don't know which time I enjoyed more.

I enjoyed it even more when I found out she had started taking the pill.

CHAPTER 19

Fast forward to Monday. We were setting up our sting. It was decided that I would stay in the safe house, Meadows would be right across the street in one of our lookout homes. We would be in radio contact with each other at all times and with the two unmarked cars at either end of the block. We started our surveillance around 7:30, before it started to get dark. In the summer, nightfall usually didn't set in until after 8 – 8:30. Manny had indicated it was later at night so we shouldn't miss them. Besides, we were starting a couple of days earlier than they usually arrived. I didn't trust Manny.

In fact, I left the porch light *off* . . .

By one in the morning I was giving up hope. Then the radio buzzed. Our car at the west end of the block just had an off-white delivery truck pass. It had the picture of a large slice of pizza on the side: Pepperoni. Manny had lied. The truck came on Monday, not Wednesday. I hoped he lied about the porch light too.

"Okay, folks. Get ready. I don't want to make any moves until one, and preferably both of the men are out of the truck and go into the house."

We watched as the passenger, the white guy, got out of the truck and headed for the house. As he opened the door, he shouted "Manny, everything okay?"

I was in the back room and grunted, "Hang on man, I'm almost done."

"Jesus, Manny, all you ever do is fuck!" He laughed and signaled the driver to come on in. He turned around to enter the living room when he smelled the gasoline. He turned on a light and noticed the burn evidence. "Dave: It's a trap!"

Too late. Meadows and the other officer were onto Dave before he could make any kind of escape. I came out of the bedroom holding my gun. The party was over. They did not try to resist. Turned out Dave was a white guy too.

Manny, Manny, Manny . . .

Meadows ran over to the back of the van and opened the doors. There were two of them, huddled in the rear corner. They were scared, but a little relieved to see a woman standing there instead of their two drivers.

I went outside to look at the vehicle. It was bigger than a regular van. It looked more like a box truck or city delivery van. It looked large enough to hold eight to ten women comfortably and at least fifteen jammed in tightly. Both sides were painted with a picture of a slice of pizza and "Pizza Delivery" printed below. There was no address or phone number. I looked at the tires: brand new. I got the feeling they didn't want a breakdown between here and wherever they were headed. Inside the glove box was the registration: Whitmore Corporation in Pasadena, California. The gas tank was almost empty. I found a knife under the driver's seat.

We took everyone downtown, calling an ambulance to take the women to a hospital to check them for injuries or disease. I suppose they'd end up in a shelter somewhere.

The boys were booked. I say boys, because that's what they were. College boys. One white dude was Phil Lighty, son of a minister in Coronado. Life never fails to amuse me. He was a junior at San Diego State. He said he got hooked up with his partner by answering an ad in the San Diego Union offering good wages for local drivers. His partner, the other white dude, was Dave Eustace, a fraternity brother. Together they had been driving for a company called "Collegiate Movers" for two years. They were told the girls were of legal age and were hired to work in massage parlors in Los Angeles. They said they didn't know they were coming across the border illegally. The pay was good and the benefits better. When I asked about 'benefits,' they indicated sexual favors. I knew they were lying, not about the sexual favors, but about their stories. I placed them under arrest.

I talked to each of them individually. Meadows was in the room as well. You know the room: four bare walls with a table in the middle. A chair on each side. The perp's hands were handcuffed to a set of iron bars attached to the table. One door. Behind me was a window. Actually, a one-way window. It allowed watching from the other side without being seen.

"Phil, you're in a shit-load of trouble. You must know that. I'd like to ask you some questions. Your answers might just make things go easier on you. Okay? Before I do, I need to read you your rights. You have the right to remain silent. You have the right to an attorney. If you can't afford one, one will be provided to you at no cost to you. Anything you say to me can be used against you in a court of law. Do you understand these rights?"

"Yes sir."

"Good, there are still some facts we need to clear up."

He never asked for a lawyer. That happens more than you'd think. Especially with first-time offenders.

"Let's start with where you picked up the girls."

"There's a little building, more like a construction shack, in an industrial park just northeast of Tijuana. Over in Otay Mesa, on the U.S. side. When we get there the girls are sitting on a wooden bench, usually with one or two Mexican guys in the room. I have to give them a thousand dollars for each girl and then they are loaded up into the back of our van."

"Where'd you get the money?"

"That comes from the other end, when we drop off the women in L.A. That's the hard part. Dave goes to school at USC. He knows the area really well . . . and it is a war zone around the school. I know it's a beautiful campus and all, but the neighborhood surrounding it is scary. I try to get in and get out as fast as I can. Anyway, we drop our cargo off at a big ugly dude's crib, that's what he calls it. He's a black guy; must be six eight at least and over three hundred pounds. He's got one gold front tooth. We don't make the drop until we've got eight to ten women. That's when we get paid. Fifteen hundred bucks for each of them and five hundred for Dave and me."

"Sounds like you boys are making a nice profit. Five hundred extra per girl more than you paid for them and a nice retainer of five hundred apiece for gas. Drop off ten women and you've got a tidy six-grand to split and ten-grand to pay for more."

"Do you see a problem here? Are you guys so stupid that you don't understand the magnitude of your crime? First of all, several of the girls are underage. They're not here under their own free will. You're selling them for a profit. That's called slavery."

"Second, you're assisting them crossing the border between the United States and Mexico illegally. And don't tell me you didn't know that. You're a college junior. Why do you think you had to pay to pick them up?"

"Third, you have admitted, and we have a witness, that you have been fucking these underage girls. That's called rape, with or without their consent.

Unless you want to go to jail for a very long time, we're going to need your help."

I got up and left him with Meadows.

As I was getting ready to interview Dave, I was struck with a thought. How ironic: desperation had replaced the iron chains and slave ships of the past; now they were coming to us, making slaves of themselves. They didn't have papers, they didn't know their rights, and they were desperate for money. Easy pickings for smugglers who would profit by augmenting their truckloads of weapons, drugs and other contraband with human cargo.

Dave proved to be a little less talkative.

I began as I had with Phil. After I told him he was under arrest for sex trafficking, read him his rights and asked if he understood, he said, "I want a lawyer."

"No problem," I replied. "Your pal, Phil, has already given us everything we need to put you away for at least twenty years. He'll probably get a lot less because he cooperated."

I got up and started to leave when he blurted "Okay, Okay, forget the lawyer. Can we make a deal? I know a lot more than Phil does about the business. All he did is help me drive the truck. I know where the girls go. I know where they're kept. Deal?"

"I don't make deals. All I can do is recommend to the District Attorney. Your cooperation goes a long way towards that recommendation. It also depends upon how valuable your information is. Like I said, Phillip was real cooperative."

"Why don't we begin from the beginning? Just so you know, this whole conversation is being taped. If at any time you want to stop, just say the word."

"We know about your run down by Tijuana. Where did you get the truck?"

"We own the truck, that is, the frat owns it. Theta Eta Zeta. We own three."

"Three? Where does a college fraternity get the money to own three trucks?"

He hesitated. "What do you mean?"

It was a classic give-away. He needed some time to think. He was lying.

I repeated my question: "Where did you get the money for three trucks? Why do you need three?"

"I told you. We're in business."

"Hauling women around from San Diego to Los Angeles? At two or three a time it takes you a month to round up eight or ten before you make your delivery. According to Phil you each make two or three grand a month. That's not bad, but it hardly pays for three trucks. Why do you need three? Do you switch them out to avoid suspicion?"

"No, San Diego to L.A. is my run. Another truck goes to San Francisco and the larger truck heads to Phoenix. That's where the real dough is made. They can pack in as many as 20 girls in that truck. They only go a couple of times a month but they make over twenty-five hundred a head each time. Of course, it's not all profit. Lots of overhead. Gas, repairs, safe house rentals, sitters like Manny, kick-backs to guys like Phil and of course the payment at the initial pick-up. It's a sweet deal, man. We pick up the women, feed them, keep them safe, and deliver them to their place of business. They work in massage parlors."

"You're scaring me, son. You mean to tell me you have no idea what 'business' those girls are in?"

"Okay, sure, some of them are hookers. But what they do in L.A. is not my problem. All I am is a delivery man. It's like the sign says on the side of our truck: Pizza Delivery. Besides the girls don't object. In fact, they're even excited. They're eager to get out of Mexico. Is there a law against trying to make money in America?"

"No, but there's a law against murder . . ."

"Murder? Who said anything about murder?"

"I guess you didn't know about that. It appears that someone took out your 'product' last week. Those girls you left with Manny were killed. Someone shot the three of them and set them on fire. That ups the stakes on your little business venture."

"Holy shit! I got nothing to do with that. Man, you need to talk to Jake."

"Jake?"

"Yeah, Dr. Whitmore. He's our business professor at USC. He told us we could call him Jake."

"What's he got to do with this?"

"He teaches a class called entrepreneurship. We get three credits for it. It's amazing how much money there is to be made if you can come up with the right business model. He's been teaching the class for a couple of years."

"Any idea why someone would want to put you out of business? Whoever shot those girls and set them on fire seemed to know a lot about what was going on."

"That's why you need to talk to Jake. He warned us to be careful. He told us that when business gets too good, other folks start to compete. In our business, competition might be dangerous."

"Okay. Sit tight. I'll be back in a little while." I'd heard enough . . . for now.

I headed over to see Meadows. She was still talking to Phil.

"Anything new to share? I asked.

"Not much. He said the info about the ad in the paper looking for drivers wasn't true. He found out about the job from a party at his frat house. They had invited frat guys from the University of Southern California to join them. That's where he met Dave. He got him off to the side and proposed an opportunity that seemed just too good to be true. All he had to do was help him drive a truck with its cargo from San Diego to L.A. and back again a couple times a month for a few thousand bucks each time. Dave never described the cargo and Phil jumped at it. He said he was surprised when the cargo was a couple of girls, but he said Dave told him they were new hires for the company he worked for. He swore he never hurt any of the girls and made sure they had plenty of food and water along the way. He even installed a little plastic toilet in the back of the truck so they could pee. He said the girls didn't seem too unhappy; he knew they had been living south of the border and were probably dirt poor. And they never objected to exchanging a little of his kindness with a blow job or more."

"I've got news for you, Meadows. This isn't just two college boys that got mixed up in a shady venture. This is big business . . . and we are just at the tip of it."

CHAPTER 20

I knocked on the door to the LT's office. "You're not going to believe this." I went over the details of the case. By the time I was through he was on the phone with the FBI. They were clearly interested. Our little sting may have uncovered a vast network of organized crime they had been trying to stop for years. And not just sex trafficking, but the whole spectrum of human trafficking. It was their "job to investigate any matter where a person was induced to engage in commercial sex acts through force, fraud, or coercion, or perform any labor service through force, coercion, or threat of law or legal process." I got that right out of their manual. They even had a special task force labeled "Sex trafficking of International Adults and Children." They were obviously serious about this.

Two FBI agents were soon dispatched to our precinct. They wanted to speak to our college "guests." The started with Phil. Meadows and I watched through the glass.

"Okay, Phil. What's your last name?" The big guy spoke first.

"Lighty."

"Okay, Mr. Lighty. My name is Agent Simmons and this is Agent Smith. We're from the FBI. No more first names. You are not our friend. You are in serious trouble. In fact, I think you are so stupid you don't even realize how much trouble you are in. Do you understand what I am saying?"

"I think so."

"I know you were read your rights earlier and you waived them. Do you still waive them?'

"I think maybe I need a lawyer."

"Great! That's what I wanted to hear. You just added another ten years onto your time in jail." He looked over at his partner. What does that make . . . thirty? I told you he was stupid."

With that he got up and left. "I'll go tell the DA you're not only stupid but a coward."

Agent Smith sat down across from Phil.

"Don't let Simmons get to you. He's pissed. He's been working on stopping this human trafficking business for over a year now and has gotten nowhere. We finally have a witness, you, who could crack this wide open. Too bad you won't cooperate. Usually the first guy to crack gets the deal."

"What kind of deal?"

"Look, Phil. I can't talk to you any more without a lawyer present. If you want to give me information in exchange for possible leniency, you need to forgo the lawyer."

"Okay, forget the lawyer. I don't know anything anyway. I changed my mind."

"You'll need to sign this paper attesting to that Phil. You're making the right decision, believe me."

They started talking.

Lighty really didn't know much more than what he'd already told Kelly and Meadows. But he did shed a lot of light on Dave. Not so much on the operation but the knowledge that Eustace was the key to it.

"Like I told you before, I met Dave at a fraternity party we had at San Diego State. He's a junior at USC, I'm just a sophomore at State. Dave said a professor of his taught a business course which was like an internship. All Dave did was drive a van taking women who the business hired to work in massage parlors in L.A. That's all he said he knew, but the money was unbelievable and the girls didn't mind putting out if we were nice to them. Dave needed someone to help him drive."

"Weren't you the least bit suspicious of this? I mean, come on. This is a young man's dream come true. You deliver some girls to a job site, get paid for it, and laid in the process. I mean, really . . ."

"Honestly, I don't know anything else. I've never been arrested before for anything. This is a nightmare!"

"It's going to get worse, believe me, son."

Dave was still sitting in the other interrogation room. He'd been sitting there for hours. He was tired, scared and worried. Why did he mention Jake?

Jesus . . . He was about to ruin everything. Should he get a lawyer? Should he just tell them what he knew? Maybe they'd let him off easy. I mean, how much did he know? He was just a mover. He never hurt anyone; yeah, he fucked a few girls who were probably under eighteen; okay, way under eighteen, but it wasn't exactly rape. They never said, *no.* Maybe if I just come clean, tell them a few details, make up a few, I'll be okay . . .

The two agents entered the room. They were each carrying a container of coffee and a notepad of paper. They offered Dave a plastic bottle of water. It was warm.

There were no pleasantries.

"Mr. Eustace, I'm FBI Agent Simmons and this is Agent Smith. You are under arrest for sex trafficking." He read him his rights again.

"We just finished interrogating your buddy, Mr. Lighty. He was very cooperative. In fact, he was so cooperative that we don't really need you at all. You, my friend, are looking at a minimum of twenty years behind bar."

With that, they both started to get up and leave.

"Wait a minute. What did he say?"

"That's information you'll hear at your trial. Unless you waive your rights to us and we get your side of the story. Why'd you kill that guy anyway?"

"I already told the other guy I didn't need a lawyer! I didn't kill anybody! Jesus, what did Phil tell you?"

"Are you waiving your rights to talk to us, then?"

"Yes, sir."

"Why don't we just start with your version. We'll compare the two stories and see which one makes more sense."

It began as before. They listened, asked a few questions they already knew the answers to, and waited . . . to hear about Jake.

"So, who's this Jake guy?

"His name is Professor Whitmore. He teaches several business classes at USC where I go to college. The most popular one is called Entrepreneurship. It's really hard to get into. You need be referred by a previous student in the class. I got in the class through my fraternity, Zeta Eta Theta. The class size is only twelve and it covers two semesters.

"Which is it? Zeta Eta Theta or Theta Eta Zeta? Who ate who?"

"Sorry, I was just trying not to implicate any of them. I'm actually a Theta Chi; Phil's a Sig Ep, but they're not involved."

"Too late for that . . ."

"Anyway, the course curriculum is already established. We're basically interns. That is, we don't really have to develop a new business model, just learn how the existing one works. By using this as an example, we could start our own enterprise after we graduated.

We learned about everything: what products are marketable, where to get them, how to transport them, trucking regulations, government restrictions on transporting goods across state lines, hiring personnel, distribution centers, and most importantly, R-O-I: return on investment. It didn't matter how good your idea was if it didn't net a profit. We were governed by a marketing tool he called the SWOT analysis. Strengths, Weaknesses, Opportunities, and Threats. A technique for assessing things. Our strength was the organization itself. Business was booming. We had a constant source of product. Our weakness centered on the law. To what degree were we at risk. Remember, we didn't bring these girls across the border; they were already here. We just drove them to L.A. Jake said a good lawyer would beat that charge. The opportunities were endless. Women were eager to join us and we could diversify with other products. Threats were real. We were warned numerous times that competition could try to drive us out of business. As we got bigger, we'd become a bigger target and our weaknesses and threats would compound. We were not encouraged to carry a weapon, but were not told we shouldn't."

"Okay, we're not here to get a business degree. What does your professor have to do with this business?

"He runs it . . . with his wife."

"Here's how the business model works. It's brilliant. First, he starts us out with some cash . . . startup money. We each get three thousand bucks. For that we have to agree to use it exactly as the protocol dictates. If we vary at all, we are out of the class and will forfeit any remaining money we may have. We are divided into three teams of four and each given a different assignment. Each team is given a vehicle to use. Two good sized vans and a large delivery truck. Dr. Whitmore owns the trucks."

"Wait a minute, I read in your earlier statement that your fraternity owned the trucks."

"Oh, yeah. I wasn't entirely truthful the first time I spoke. The fraternities are not really involved at all."

"Keep going. But you keep lying to us and any deals that transpire will be off the table. What do you do with the women once you get to L.A."

"That's where the professor's wife comes in. She goes by Anita. She is the nicest person you'd ever meet. I think she's from the South. Every time we meet and talk, she tilts her head a little and blesses me, you know, like, 'Bless your heart, honey.'

"Anyway, when we have eight to ten girls, we drop them off at an apartment complex in Pasadena. She greets them all with a hug and a kiss, gives them all box lunches and shows the girls where they are staying; two to a room. As far as I can determine, she treats them really good. Two of the guys from my team are always there to help her plus two from the other two teams. They told me Anita had a string of massage parlors all over the country. Those girls were making her a fortune. One of the guys told me that Anita asked him to come home with her one night. He wasn't sure why, until she told him Dr. Whitmore was going to be at a conference for the weekend. She said she didn't feel safe in L.A. without a man in the house. He said he was confused at first; there were at least eight men he had seen already. Anyway, he said her place was like a movie star's. He'd never seen a house so big or so beautiful. They entered through an eight-foot-high iron gate with a guard out front. There was an eight-car garage. Out back was a twenty-five-meter pool with a ten-foot rock waterfall at one end. There must have been five-or six men doing yardwork and maintenance throughout the grounds . . . at least several acres. She even had a tennis court! The whole thing was surrounded by an eight-foot wall covered in ivy. A maid met them at the door. He saw armed guards by the doors. He and Anita had dinner served to them on a table on the veranda overlooking the pool. Afterwards they had some drinks and then she fucked his lights out. He said it was his first time with an older woman. He's not sure he'll ever date a younger one now! I wasn't sure I believed him. But our routine was to collect our pay for the delivery and head back to San Diego to await another shipment."

"I thought you said you delivered the girls to a big six-foot-eight black guy with a gold tooth?"

"Again, I was hedging a little. That big guy *was* in the house, but Anita was clearly in charge."

I thought both of them had been 'hedging' a little.

"Okay, Mr. Eustace. I think we've heard enough. You know what I think? I think you're just a spoiled college frat boy that thinks he can get away with anything. It's been like that your whole life, hasn't it? Well, Daddy's not going to get you out of this. You may just be a pawn in this 'entrepreneurship', but you're not so innocent. I find it hard to believe that you didn't know what was going on. Massage parlors? Come on. Those girls were slaves. They left home to get away from their poverty, their hopelessness. They had nothing. All they wanted was a chance . . . and you took it away from them."

"Human trafficking is the most heinous crime in society, Mr. Eustace. You were an integral part of it . . . and you will pay for it."

"What about our deal?" he begged.

"There was never a deal. But you did cooperate. That will certainly be in your favor during sentencing. You're still going to jail." They forced a big grin and got up and left.

KELLY

The agents were all smiles when they approached us outside too. Agent Smith crowed, "We'll take over from here. We owe you guys a depth of gratitude for uncovering this operation. This will take down hundreds of traffickers. And I think Professor Whitmore just lost his job . . . and his wife."

"What's the chance we could be with you when you take them down?" I asked.

Smith, whom I now assumed was the leader, thought for a moment, then said, "Since you guys started this, it's probably only fair that you get to see the end of it. The only thing you need to remember is, it's our show. Don't get in the way; cooperate fully with any information you get."

We jumped at the opportunity. Simmons said he'd give us a call when they were ready to spring the raid. It might be a couple of days.

We still had a murder on our hands . . . and two severed heads that were unaccounted for, but we hoped they could wait awhile.

CHAPTER 21

The first problem, the most recent murder, didn't cooperate. We got a call from the police that they had found two bodies in a motel in National City. They had called for the ME and he had asked them to call us.

We took Meadows' car over to National City. It was getting dark. Bob was already there. He was checking the bodies. There were two of them—a male and a female. They were obviously dead: their heads were missing.

As he looked up at us, I asked, "Why did you call us in on this?"

"Take a look on that table. The white cowboy hat and mask of Richard Nixon. Looks like payback to me."

Meadows started looking around. She went into the kitchen. Opened the refrigerator door.

"I found the heads!" she yelled.

So, it begins again. Always with a body. In this case, two. The ME checks the victims, determines what caused their deaths. Were they killed before they were decapitated, or after? Were they killed here in this room, or moved. How were they killed? How long ago were they killed? Who were they? Did they have identification on them? Why were they killed?

"They were shot. Each one twice in the back with a high-powered revolver. Notice the shell casings by the sofa. They've been dead less than 72 hours. Rigor mortis is still present. There's only a little pooling of blood due to gravity. I can give you a better idea of the time when I examine them in my lab. They were dead before their heads were cut off. Probably with a hacksaw or machete of some kind. Notice the serrations around the throat."

"How do you know they weren't still alive when they had their throats cut?" asked Meadows.

"Because there's no blood spray. That means the heart had stopped beating and wasn't pumping any blood. No pump, no spray."

I looked around. No signs of violence in the room. Everything neat and tidy. But the door had been broken into. It looked like maybe the victims were caught unaware, and before they realized it, it was already too late. Escape was no longer an option. They had been made to kneel in the middle of the living room and each shot twice in the back. Who knows why they had their heads cut off? More than likely a warning to others. Because of the mask and cowboy hat, I was pretty sure this was payback for putting their noses in that sex trafficking business.

We talked to the manager of the motel. It was a seedy dive rented mostly by the hour. The furniture was old and the bed well-used. There was a kitchenette with a microwave and refrigerator. The microwave didn't work. He didn't remember who rented the room. He was sure he'd never seen the dead guy before and was not even sure he was the one who rented the room. He paid cash and there was a woman with him. She looked like all the other women who used that room. Curiously, they paid for two nights. The only reason he called the cops was the "patron" next door heard gunshots from the room. When he opened the door for the cops, he saw the bodies.

He said it sounded like these victims were hiding from somebody.

I asked him, "Why?"

"Who rents a room for two nights when you just need a blow job?" he smirked.

CHAPTER 22

It was now very late. I told Meadows I was going home. To my house. She said she was tired as well. We weren't going out for dinner. I considered where we'd begin tomorrow and decided the best place was at the ME's. Maybe he'd have some fresh information on the new bodies and a lead on the severed heads. It was worth a try. Right now, we were at a dead end.

She drove me home and said she'd be back in the morning to pick me up. I wanted my own car but figured I could pick it up later.

Surprise! I got a good nice sleep. Meadows came by at seven. She brought a coffee for each of us. I was up, just getting out of the shower, and told her I'd be right out. "Make yourself at home," I yelled.

She did. I guess women by nature are nosy . . . maybe men are too, but she immediately started looking in my refrigerator for . . . who knows what? A head? There wasn't much in there. She opened the carton of milk and sniffed. She jerked her head back, made a funny face, and emptied the contents into the sink. The two bottles of Bud were fresher, as was a half empty carton of eggs. I read somewhere that you didn't need to put eggs in the fridge. Makes sense; chickens don't put their eggs in the fridge either and they do all right. I just do what my mom taught me. Meadows opened the cupboards: maybe three or four plates. Two glasses; neither matched. How many did you need? I did have four wine glasses. I think someone gave them to me with a bottle of wine once. There was a cereal box, opened, on the counter and not much else. I tended to eat out.

Not satisfied, she headed for the guest bedroom. That's what I called it anyway. I had a four-room condo: living room, kitchen, master bedroom, and another room. I ate at a table in the kitchen. There was one bathroom, but I don't include it in the description. The other room I used for storage. It did have a bed in it so technically it was a guest bedroom. There were no sheets or pillows on the bed, just a lot of dirty clothes. It also had a lot of boxes, and my bicycle, and some suitcases, and . . . well, you get the picture. It had a small closet, too. The kind with the folding doors. I hated it. It was always coming off the track in the middle. After a quick look around, she headed right for that. Just what one would expect: lots of clothes in no particular order hanging neatly on the rack and several pairs of shoes scattered on the floor beside some more boxes. She slid her thumbs between the hangers and started to separate the items. She stopped when she came to my Service Dress Blue uniform. It had two gold stripes at the end of both sleeves: Lieutenant. I stayed in the Reserves for a while when I first got out, but I hadn't worn that since. I don't know why I kept it, but I had clearly forgotten about it. She pulled it off the hanger and was holding it up high in front of her just as I entered the room.

"Impressive," she offered. "I've never seen so many ribbons."

Five rows of three ribbons, with one above the rest, in the middle. She was talking about the colorful decorative devices each service awards their personnel for various achievements. They're not really ribbons. They're devices that are pinned in rows across the uniform worn on the left side above the chest pocket. Three in a row, as many rows as needed. They're worn in place of medals they represent.

"My dad had a lot of these, but not nearly as many as you have. And he was a Vice Admiral. Tell me about them."

"Well, the large gold device pinned directly above the ribbons is called a Trident, and it instantly identifies me to all who see it as a Navy SEAL. There are other devices that signify the wearer as Surface Warfare qualified, Commanding Officer, Submarine qualified, and others. I didn't have any of those. As far as the ribbons, most of them are for places I have been, or campaigns I was a part of. Just by virtue of where we went, we earned more ribbons. They don't mean much. Heck, the joke is the Air Force gets a ribbon just for showing up . . . at least I think it's a joke. The only meaningful ones are the ones farthest to the right, or to the left if you are facing it, in the upper row, and the one on top in the middle. Those are personal ribbons, and they stand for something you did or made happen. Those, I don't usually talk about. Maybe someday over a beer, if I'm drunk enough, I'll tell you. I earned them, but I'm not entirely proud of all of them."

She put the uniform back, laughing. "I never understood why all you servicemen keep your uniforms once you get out. My dad could lose fifty pounds and still not get into his! One of these days I'll take you up over that beer. I really do want to know what those ribbons are all about."

We headed to the precinct to get my car and we both drove over to Doc's. He was just getting in . . .

CHAPTER 23

"**Good morning, Bob.** Hopefully you've got some decent news for us. We've reached a dead end. The FBI has taken over our trafficking case. They think the extent of the stench stretches from California to Ohio. The good news is that they know who's running the show and who killed our two unknowns. We can't discuss the fine points yet. We're waiting for the start of their arrest phase. We've been invited to tag along."

"Well, at least you've got good news. The only thing I was able to pin down, by the internal body temperature, was the time of death: between sixteen and twenty hours before we found them. I don't think it matters much now since you seem to know who the killers are, or at least who ordered the killings. I sent the fingerprints over to your guys for processing. I was also able to retrieve one of the slugs from the male's body and sent it over too. Maybe they can match it with bullets from a gun used some other time."

"Thanks, Bob. This case may be just about a wrap but we still have some other deaths we have to investigate that have nothing to do with this one. I'm still completely puzzled about those severed heads we found. Nothing explains how the head was found in the suitcase at the plane crash. There were dozens of persons at the scene though, even before the police arrived, and anyone of them could have planted it. I still think it was on the plane when it left Newark.

"The murderer of those girls in Chula Vista and that severed head in the closet was probably the work of our dead guy we found yesterday," volunteered Meadows. "I doubt if we'll ever know who they were."

I've never been patient. I need to complete my agenda. But I have to be careful. If I'm not, someone is going to screw up all my plans. I'll find another body. I'm not going to wait any longer. Where to look . . .

I'll just go for a ride. Maybe that will calm me down. The road along and off Highway 8 isn't always well traveled at night; especially between El Cajon and Alpine. Maybe I'll hit a deer. That might cheer me up.

I hate driving at night though. There's always some idiot who forgets to dim their bright lights. It's really blinding.

Shit! Right on cue. I think he's' drunk as well. Christ! Stay over on your own side . . .

Too late, the drunk swerved, crossing the center line, and narrowly missed him. He yanked the steering wheel over to the right. He was going too fast but managed to miss a tree before hitting another bump and coming to rest on the side of the road. The drunk continued on, oblivious.

Now what? What did I hit? God help me if I have a flat. There's no one else on the road and it's pitch dark. How will I get a tow out here this late at night?

He got out and inspected all the wheels. No damage. He looked back along the road to where he had narrowly missed the tree. Then he saw it.

A body? Did I hit somebody? Calm down. Take it easy. Take a look. Yes, it's a teenage girl . . . and she's quite dead. She looks Hispanic. I need to get her into the car before someone else passes by. I'll take her to my place: The cutting room.

She lay there. Nude on the table as before. The only difference was this time she was already dead. Not a big deal, he thought. The end result would still be the same. Too bad he wouldn't get to talk to her though. He found that comforting just before he cut their head off. They needed to know the why . . . certain people also needed to know . . .

CHAPTER 24

We got the call early in the morning. FBI were in place and ready. We were invited to ride along with Agent Simmons in the mobile van the FBI used for monitoring and surveillance. They had established the whereabouts of Anita Whitmore's apartments and knew the time that the professor held his entrepreneurship class. They were not sure they knew where the initial pick-up of the women was. The college boys had clammed up and their lawyers were insuring they not say anything further. They were going to proceed anyway. The plan was to hit the Whitmore's all at once so there was little chance of an errant warning.

The massage parlors were a problem. They didn't know where all of them were located and they couldn't count on assistance from other law enforcement agents for help; especially in the San Francisco area. It was unlikely that we would be able to find them all or catch their managers. A lot of girls would still be at risk.

We were told that back in 1971, the city of Berkley had become a "sanctuary city." The Viet Nam War was not popular during that period. Not only to the city of Berkley, but to many servicemen as well. When the Navy's aircraft carrier, USS *Coral Sea*, was returning to port in Alameda, over 1000 sailors out of a crew of 4500 protested against its return to Viet Nam once it had off-loaded its cargo of Vietnamese refugees. They formed an organization called "Save Our Ship." Their goal was to stop the ship from returning to Viet Nam. It got lots of publicity. Sympathetic to their pleas, the regional council in Berkley decided to "recognize the inherent human dignity and worth of every person," their words, by granting safe haven to anyone seeking protection. When the *Coral Sea* left days later, 35 sailors did not re-board and were declared UA; that is, on unauthorized absence. Some of them sought sanctuary. Unfortunately, since the end of the Viet Nam War, or the War Against America, as the people in Viet Nam now call it, sanctuary sometimes impedes our efforts to halt illegal immigration and all human trafficking. When law enforcement personnel catch illegals in the course of a crime, they will not always turn over that information to us; that is, federal officials. Some people feel that sanctuary cities sometime serve to help traffickers and other illegals escape prosecution.

We were headed for the campus of the University of Southern California. Actually, Meadows was. I was going with Smith to see the missus. They didn't notify the administration we were coming. The area around the school is much like anywhere else except that since 1965 when riots broke out in the neighborhood of Watts, law enforcement personnel have not been exactly welcomed with open arms. Watts was only a few blocks northeast of the campus. We were quiet. We didn't want to raise a ruckus.

Agent Simmons entered Dr. Whitmore's class quietly, while his team sealed off all the exits from the outside. He sat down in the back of the class and listened to the topic at hand. After a minute, he raised his hand, signaling he had a question.

"Yes, sir. Did you have a question?" asked the professor, confused by the intruder.

"What will happen to anyone who is apprehended by police at any phase of this enterprise?" Simmons posed.

"I'm sorry, who are you? I don't understand the question and I don't believe you are a member of this course." He sounded agitated.

"Well, maybe I can make the question clearer. If someone gets caught transporting any of your product, which is determined to be illegal, will they go to jail?"

"Sir, I think I've heard enough. If you will excuse me, I'm going to go make a formal complaint to the administration citing your interruption of my class and unwarranted accusations. The class is dismissed."

"Actually, I've heard enough as well, Doctor. Please remain where you are . . . all of you. You are all under arrest for sex trafficking, contributing to the delinquency of a minor, probably rape, and a few other offenses I can't think of off of the top of my head. By the way, here's the answer to my question: yes, you will go to jail. Some of you for life!"

With that, the doors opened and in walked several agents armed with plastic cords to handcuff everyone in the room. Other than a few shouts of "What the hell is going on?" there was no resistance. We had a big bus waiting for everyone right outside to take everyone to booking. It was a good day for us.

CHAPTER 25

It didn't go as smoothly in Pasadena. Agents raided the apartment complex where the girls were kept. The only guards were college boys. They did not resist and played dumb like the others. Lovely Miss Anita was not there. After a little intimidation, one of the boys did volunteer where she might be. He said he'd been there. She had a large lot in Sunland, northeast of here. We rounded everyone up and booked them. We put them in two busses. One for the women, and one for the college boys.

Then we headed for Sunland. The house was definitely in a large lot, surrounded by a wall. A long driveway led up to a gate. As we approached, a guard stepped out of a small guardhouse. Before the FBI even showed him their badges, he was on the phone and was able to warn the house. He told us there were some college boys inside, but we knew they would be no help to her. Our first threat was the armed guards in the house and stationed along the wall. Fortunately, there were no dogs. No one likes to shoot a dog. He said she also had a lot of stored ammunition.

There were ten agents on the ground and a helicopter above manned with two sniper teams; plus, Agent Smith and me. We were all prepared. When the agents burst through the gate, one of the guards stationed on the porch was foolish enough to open fire on them. A sniper bullet silenced him quickly. A couple of nearby guards surrendered without a shot, but several fled into the house. This is when it got dicey.

Agent Smith used his bullhorn to address the house and, specifically, Mrs. Whitmore.

"Anita, This the FBI. We've already apprehended your husband. He is in custody right now, along with the students involved. They're already in jail. We know all about the business you two have been operating and it is over. Your only course of action is to lay down whatever weapons you may have and surrender peacefully before any more people get hurt."

There was no reply and no movement from within the house. The FBI brought up a bullet proof vehicle and approached the front door. Shots rang out. "Y'all can just turn that thing around, honey, and get off of my property. I know my rights. You need a warrant to come on my property. You can't just waltz right in here and start demanding anything."

Actually, they did have a warrant. Further, one of her men had just taken a shot at them. They probably didn't even need the warrant.

Another shot, and then one of the agents shot a teargas grenade into the front window. Then another along the side. Two agents rushed the house from the side. Two others from the other side. Two ran around back. The helo covered the whole area.

It didn't take long for several of the guards to come out, coughing and rubbing their eyes. Their hands were empty. Whitmore refused. When another guard started out, she screamed, "Coward, what am I paying you for?"

Smith grabbed one of the surrendering guards. "You! Who's in there with her? How many are there?"

"I'm not sure, man. I saw a few of those college kids. They're harmless. They're scared shitless. But I know for sure there are four of her personal guards. Those guys are mean. The big guy, he's the killer."

"What do you mean?"

"He takes care of problems. Last week he shot and killed a guy and his squeeze down in National City in retaliation for a hit they did on one of our safe houses. And that's not the first time. They've all got automatic weapons . . . and they know how to use them. Three of them were former marines. I know they've got enough ammunition to equip an army."

He called back as he was led away, "I think they have gas masks too."

Smith looked at me and said, "This is not going to end well. The thing is, we really need Whitmore alive. She is the key to the whereabouts of her massage parlors and her distribution centers. Without her, we've still got a lot of digging to do and we may never uncover all them."

Well, right now we felt time was on our side. They weren't going anywhere and we could use it to plan our mission. *It's SEAL time again*, I thought.

That was the great thing about the SEALS. They never did anything without it being well thought out. Before we went anywhere we all knew our roles, we all knew where we were going, and what our objective was. We knew where the trouble was most likely to occur and if need be, we knew three different directions to get out. That's why I joined the Navy SEALS. If I was going to put my life on the line, I was going with the "A" team. I'd be well trained, well equipped, and well informed.

I had a friend who told me that was a major difference in his army experience. He was an eighteen-year-old enlisted; a draftee. He said they would go on patrol and all they were told was they had to take some hill, or some piece of territory. They didn't know *why* and they didn't know *what* was on that hill. They were told that there would be a whole lot of shelling before they went that would obliterate anything alive. They would be needed just to mop up. He said a lot of young boys died taking that hill. When they finally did, someone accidentally called in more shelling: on top of them. Friendly fire, they called it. They lost a lot more until they beat feet back down off that hill. A couple days later, the VC just walked right back in. "What a waste . . ."

That brought back another memory. *Waste.* That was the most used words I remember hearing back then. "What a waste of time. What a waste of money. We wasted them . . ."

"Listen up, gentlemen, "Anita was yelling again. "I've got three college boys right here beside me. They're good boys. Right now, two of 'em are tied up and I've got a gun up against the head of the other. They are going to be our ticket out of here, y'all hear?"

"You can't use them to bargain with, Anita. They're just as guilty as you are. They're going to jail too."

"Well, you start anything dumb and they're gonna be dead. You think their mommas would like to hear them words? You know just as well as I do that they just watch my 'employees' around the grounds . . . make sure they're still working and not trying to run away. They ain't worth shit to me."

"What do you want?"

"I want transportation out of here. Safe transportation to the airport. I want a jet lined up to take me and my crew to any destination I choose . . . to be named later. I don't need money. I got plenty of that. And I'm not stupid. I know it will take some time. I'll give you four hours. In the meantime, don't go itching your britches and trying something stupid. These boys would appreciate that."

"Let me see what I can do," shouted Smith.

"Oh, and one more thing, Mr. FBI. Don't you go telling my husband when I leave. He'll be just fine where he's at." She actually cackled.

Now what? We had four hours to comply with her demands or come up with a plan to eliminate the problem. We surely had enough guns to overpower them, but that would cause a lot of dead bodies; and we needed Anita alive.

It wasn't my show. This was the FBI's mission.

But I *was* a Navy Seal. This was the kind of thing we trained for. What would I do?

First on the agenda was to understand the environment. The place was walled in, and we had law enforcement personnel stationed everywhere. The occupants inside were staying there. They could not leave until we let them . . . or we carried them out.

Next was the house itself. Could we get any plans of the building? Could we get information regarding exits, basements, or roof landing areas from one of the guards who surrendered? Could we gain access from the roof without being seen?

What kind of training did the guards have? Are their names known to the surrendering guards? If so, and they had been in the military, we could easily get access to that kind of information.

Assuming the second question is answered, can we create some kind of distraction while one or two agents gain access into the house?

Finally, how do we get the weapon away from Whitmore, protect the hostages, and keep her alive?

How long do we wait?

The FBI was slightly ahead of me. That had already begun questioning the guards.

They said there was no basement and they did know the guards still inside. Three were from the same unit. Army rangers. Their records were quickly obtained. They weren't from the elite units. Still, not to be taken lightly. A fourth guy, the leader and most dangerous, had no military record, and was Mexican. He was definitely big. Six-eight and way over 300 pounds. They called him Chico. He was just a bully, but the others accepted his authority. For some reason Anita liked him . . . and she paid well.

I suggested putting a man in the helo and dropping him on the roof. I also suggested that with my background and training, I should be the man. Smith wasn't excited about my plan, but upon reflection, decided he didn't have anyone more qualified.

He called the helo. When it landed outside the gate area, I traded places with one of the snipers. Back up we went. The existing sniper was a former marine. He was a graduate of the first USMC Scout Sniper Class of 1977 in Quantico, Virginia.

I looked at his weapon: an M40A1 rifle discharging a chambered 308 Win 7.62 NATO Match caliber cartridge. I was familiar with this weapon. SEAL's used them occasionally in Viet Nam. It is extremely accurate in the right hands. This one would be. It mounted a UNertl 8X scope and had a suppressor to reduce the sound intensity. At the helo's low altitude over the roof, he would have to try hard to miss. He was now my new best friend.

Agent Smith tried creating a diversion. He used his bullhorn to call Whitmore. He wanted her engaged while I was being lowered to the roof. "Anita, we need more time and more information. I'm in contact with the airport and they need to know more about your destination. They have to file a flight plan, gain clearances, determine fuel requirements, and a lot of other things I don't even know about."

"You're just stalling, and you know it. Tell you what. You've now got three hours and then I start shooting the college boys; one every half hour. So, you still have four hours, but you won't need as big a plane . . ." And she laughed. "I'll only have one kid left."

I couldn't hear much of it between rotor blades and the distance to Smith. As many times that I'd made a descent like this, I always knew what I was going to meet down below. I didn't know anything about this rooftop or if someone had been positioned on it just to eliminate this kind of threat from above.

I should have known they were not stupid.

As I was dangling about 20 feet from the rooftop, a guard stood up and took aim at me. He was almost immediately dispatched by my new sniper best buddy. There was hardly a sound. Maybe the guard was more stupid than I thought. Didn't he notice the helicopter? One down, three to go.

I dropped to the roof and signaled the helo to haul the line back up. I did not have a blueprint of the house but one of the surrendering guards had explained there was only one way up to the roof. That was through a skylight up in the attic. The now deceased guard had left it open when he was stationed up there. Once in the attic, there was a pull-down door attached to a ladder into the garage. It was an eight-car garage and the door to the attic was in the far side of the garage. To get to the main door into the house, I'd have to cross around eight vehicles. I quickly dropped into the attic and backed down the pull-down ladder, surveying the immense garage. It's amazing how quickly the mind processes what the eyes see: a huge garage supported by two large pillars in the middle; in between, a Caddie, Porsche, Beamer, two empty spaces, then a white car, a pickup truck and an SUV. As I looked for any guards, I was also struck by how clean and neat this garage was. My garage hardly had room in it for one car. Where did I get all that junk? *One of life's great mysteries*, I thought.

As I made my way past a couple of the cars I heard a door open.

It was the big guy. He was loading up the SUV on the end with a lot of bags.

I don't think he saw me. Evidently, he was planning some kind of escape if the negotiations went sour or was preparing to move everyone to the awaiting plane if the FBI blinked. I didn't see a weapon, but he might still be carrying a revolver. I moved around a couple of cars until I could see him clearly. He had his back to me.

"Stop right there," I yelled. "FBI." Okay, not officially, but I was authorized to say that, I thought. After all, I was carrying the semi-automatic rifle an agent handed me. So, there was a link. This weapon was new to me but looked sufficient to intimidate folks.

"Turn around slowly; raise your hands. It's all over, Chico." I walked closer. It was difficult to move around the parked cars and maintain constant sight of him. As he turned, he realized my dilemma and ducked down behind a car.

"You screwed up, amigo," he boasted. "You should have shot me. You're not giving the orders any more. It's my turn. In a couple of minutes another guy is going to come through that door and he's going to fill you full of holes. And then I'm going to piss on your dead head!"

I didn't respond. He couldn't see me. I had ducked down when he had and I was slowly inching my way around the rear of the third vehicle from the door leading into the house. It was a large four-door Ford 150 pick-up truck. Plenty of cover. I kept going. I kept looking under the vehicles to see if I could spot him. Maybe I could shoot his feet out from under him. No dice. Where was he? Was he still in the garage? Did he get into that first car? Where would I hide?

I was now at a critical juncture. I had moved behind the rear of the first vehicle in the line of eight; the SUV. That witness was right: it *was* a Toyota. Is he waiting for me to show my head . . . so he can blow it off? I figured waiting didn't solve the problem . . . we could be here all day . . . or until one of his buddies showed up. Then my problem would compound. "In for a penny, in for a pound," as my dad used to say. Actually, I think he said, "Get off your ass and move!"

I got up, looked around, failed to find anything else, so I took off my shoe and heaved it over to the far side of the SUV, hoping it would cause a distraction. I quickly rushed around the corner of the car, preparing to fire at what I was sure was the end of a gun barrel.

The big guy was sitting on his ass up against the front wheel of the car. There was no gun. He turned his head and laughed. "You threw your *shoe?*"

Followed by, "What took you so long?" He smiled so wide his gold tooth popped into view. Then he started to get up. I told him to stay put. He ignored me, stood up anyway, and faced me.

Shit, he really was a giant.

"I don't have a gun. I don't need one to take care of you anyway. Why don't we settle this the old-fashioned way, amigo? Like real men. Or are you afraid of me, Mr. FBI?" He laughed, "Right now, you're dead and don't even know it."

For some reason I was fixated on that shiny gold tooth.

He took another step towards me. The distance was about eight feet. I knew I couldn't let him get any closer or he would rush me. This guy was a killer, but I wasn't afraid of him. I doubt if he had ever faced a SEAL before. I'm not stupid, and I was itching to show him who was boss. So, I did . . .

I shot him.

The first bullet hit him just below his nose. That damned gold tooth! He never felt the next round that hit him in the forehead; he was already dead and didn't know it. He collapsed on his back. I didn't feel a thing. He was just another piece of meat to me. How many times had I heard that?

Work to do. I was sure the occupants in the house had heard my shots. They would be on alert. Of course, they wouldn't know who fired the shots. Big Guy? Nope. I opened the door of the garage leading into the house. Where was I?

The hallway in front of me stretched out over twenty feet. One door five feet away on the right and an opening at the end on the left.

I peeked around the door on the right. It was open. Stepping inside I could see it was the laundry room. Empty. I returned to the hallway. As silently as I could, I reached the end and entered the kitchen. Empty as well. Where was everyone? There were two paid guards left, Whitmore, and at least three college boys. Were they all in one room? Not likely. The guards would be posted at entry points. Whitmore was threatening one boy with a gun and the other two more than likely tied up in the same room.

I started with the entry points. There had to be a back door . . . maybe several. Adjacent to the kitchen was a good-sized eating area and to the left a large room, probably the main living area. It connected to the veranda outside overlooking the swimming pool. Mostly glass. A view to die for . . .

Lying on his stomach, facing the pool was one of the guards. He was concentrating on a couple of FBI agents who had taken cover outside by the large concrete planters on either side of the steps leading to the pool. A stand-off for now.

I snuck up behind him and put the barrel of my rifle on his back. He flinched, but didn't turn. I didn't have to say a word. He pushed his rifle out in front of him and stretched both hands over his head to lay flat on the ground. Faced with how I was going to secure him, and not having any cuffs or ties, I motioned for him to get up. I pointed to the door and with the end of the rifle gave him a nudge to start walking. He hesitated, but understood. I saw the FBI agents begin to come out to receive him.

Where was the other guard? Shots rang out and suddenly I was on the ground.

Then, it was dark.

CHAPTER 26

Then someone turned on the light. What the hell just happened? A lot of pain. I was looking up in the face of Meadows. Where was I? What was Meadows doing here?

Of course, I must have been shot. It wasn't the first time, but this was different. I had actually been unconscious. Seriously?

Meadows spoke. "Good afternoon, Detective Kelly. Did you enjoy your little nap? I've been waiting beside this bed all morning for you. How do you feel?"

"Confused and embarrassed." Again, "What the hell just happened? A minute ago, I was in a house. All I remember is pushing that guard out the back door . . . and then I must have blacked out."

A nurse came in just as Meadows was about to explain. She checked the IV bag to see if I was still getting fluids and how much it contained, looked at the machine I was hooked up to and proclaimed I was doing remarkably well. Blood pressure was normal, heart rate and rhythm normal, and more gobble-de-gook. She emptied a bag of urine at the base of my bed and said, "I'll be back later to take your catheter out."

Meadows blurted, "Can I help?" They both laughed. The nurse looked at me and smiled: "Glad you're awake. I'm told your surgery went well and you should be up and around in a couple of days. Are you in any pain? I can give you a little happy juice if you need it."

I didn't. Before she left though, she added, "We only have one shoe in your belongings bag. Any idea where the other one is?" Then she left.

"You missed all the excitement. After you went down, the agents out back rushed the building and took out the remaining guard. Whitmore was holed up in a bedroom upstairs. Taking her out was easy. She really didn't want to die. Confronted by many armed men and no one to protect her, she surrendered without a fight. No one hurt the college kids. They're all in custody right now and Whitmore has been very cooperative. Her operation was quite extensive. She had massage parlors all over California and Arizona. Professor Whitmore wasn't really a doctor, or a professor. He used fake credentials to get the position at USC. He was a con man, and a good one. Before this he had conned a wealthy widow in Italy out of millions. Probably more before her. He went to jail for a year but they never recovered the money. That's how he said he fronted the entire organization. The FBI arrested over a hundred people engaged in their operation. I'm sure it won't stop sex trafficking any time soon, but it certainly put a dent in it for a while. You did good, Kelly."

"Yeah, but I don't feel so good. Where was I shot? The whole right side of my body aches."

"The first bullet just grazed your head. No damage there, but it caused you to lose consciousness. The second bullet hit you on the right side, just below your clavicle. You were lucky. It went through your lung, nicked your scapula, and exited out your side without hitting any more bones or major blood vessels. They got you to the hospital and they operated to repair your wounds yesterday. I'm not sure what all they did . . . it obviously worked. But like the nurse said, you won't be going anywhere soon."

But I did go home. Finally. Three days later they discharged me and wheeled me out in a wheel chair. I don't know why they do that. I could walk just fine. Something about falls . . . and lawsuits. Silly. Why would anyone sue a hospital that had just saved their life?

Meadows was there to drive me home. She asked if I'd rather go to her place or mine. I chose mine. I could walk okay but I wasn't up for much more. My right side still ached.

We stopped at a Starbucks for some coffee. I asked Meadows what she was doing now. "Any leads on our case?"

"Nothing. In fact, we're at a dead end. We've got two severed heads; three if you count the one at that PSA crash site in '78. We don't know the names of any of them and we don't know how they got there. Every turn we take leads us nowhere.

We have nothing to indicate they're related to our sex trafficking case. Right now, I'm on a couple days of earned vacation. I thought I might spend some time with you to make sure you were okay."

We headed for my house.

Opening the door, I lost my balance and started to fall. She quickly grabbed my arm and walked with me into the kitchen where I found a chair.

"Thanks. I just got a little dizzy for a second. Maybe I just need to rest for a while."

"Okay, I get the message. Let me help you into your room. You get some rest. I'll be back with your lunch. What are you hungry for?"

"How about a hamburger and fries? Make sure they put tomatoes on it and no onions. Ever since they made me wear a raw onion around my neck going through a fraternity initiation I feel nauseous just thinking about one. They called the onion a "happy apple." Take a bite . . . don't be sad, be happy . . . all night long. There was nothing happy about it."

"Okay, you can have my tomatoes." She left. I slept. I think the two oxycodone tablets I took helped.

She was back around one o'clock. I was still in bed but awake. I was feeling much better. I got up, shuffled slowly into the kitchen, and sat down at the table across from her. She had also bought me a chocolate milkshake. Wow . . . I liked her more all the time.

"How are you feeling?" she asked. "You've got a little more color in your face now."

"I'm much better, thanks. Not ready to run a marathon though."

"Were you ever?" she laughed.

"Actually, I did run a marathon once. It was on a little island called Diego Garcia. Ever heard of it?"

"Sure. My father's ship was once anchored out in its bay many years ago. It's a British Island, I believe. Located about two thousand miles from nowhere in the middle of the Indian Ocean."

"Correct. We, well my SEAL team and I, flew out there once to reconnoiter the area for one of our operations. The problem was there was only one flight arriving on a Saturday and then nothing until the next flight departed the following Saturday. That meant we had to spend a week there. Let me tell you, in 1969 there wasn't much to do. The island itself is about 33 miles long from tip to tip. It's shaped like a big "V" with a large bay within the "V." The bay is about 9 miles across. I think the widest section of land isn't over a mile and a half wide. At the mouth of the bay are two little islands, called Bird Islands. They are off-limits to everyone. Three British officers are stationed on Diego to provide legal jurisdiction, but the U.S. uses it for communication and sometimes submarine repairs. They station a repair ship there occasionally to provide that service. While we were there, B-52s were flying in and out daily."

"What's that got to do with your marathon?"

"Hang on, I'll tell you. Bored, and tired of the same old exercise routine, we cooked up a race. From one end of the island to the other. Turned out to be just under a 32-mile race. Did I forget to tell you, the temperature at that time of year averaged 92 degrees Fahrenheit? Well, we only got 11 guys to enter the race, even after we each put in a hundred dollars to the winner. I thought I was a shoo-in for that eleven-hundred bucks. And I would have been except for the heat . . . and the humidity. We started early in the morning and I was pacing myself. At the 23-mile marker we'd put up, I was far ahead of the closest competitor when I felt really bad . . . like I was going to puke. I was hot, really hot. My head was suddenly spinning and down I went. I didn't know what was happening. Fortunately, there were corpsmen along the run and one was on me almost immediately." "Heat stroke," he yelled, and he actually began to start an IV right there where I had fallen. He hooked it to a bottle of saline solution or something, placed a cool towel over my forehead and I soon began to feel better. At least I didn't come in last. Three guys dropped out after about ten miles. Unfortunately, I lost my eleven-hundred-dollar prize money. They didn't give out participation awards to everyone back in those days either.

"So, you never really ran a marathon, then," she laughed.

"I said I ran a marathon race, I never said I finished."

"What were the SEALS doing in Diego Garcia?

"Look, all of our SEAL missions are classified. You know that joke, 'If I tell you, I'll have to kill you'? Well, it's not that lethal, but it's true. We were bound not to divulge our missions . . . ever. I still believe I am."

"Can you tell me more about all the ribbons I saw the other day? They really intrigue me." With that she got up and retrieved my set of Blues.

"Start with the last one."

"Okay. The last two, actually, are expert sharpshooter's medals. One for pistol and the other for rifle. The next one is for Viet Nam Service. If you were there, you earned one. Then there is the Viet Nam Campaign ribbon. For every major campaign the U.S. waged, you got one. Notice I've got three little bronze stars on mine. Instead of getting another ribbon, you got a star. Once you got four stars, the next one you earn replaces all of them with one Silver Star. The red and yellow one is the National Defense ribbon. Everyone who is in the military in a time of conflict gets one. The day I graduated OCS I got one. That one is known as a Gedunk Medal in the Navy. You just happened to be alive at the wrong time. The next bunch are just for places I have been. After that, the rest are personal awards. They are the most meaningful to folks on your promotion board. The more of those one gets, the better chance of being promoted. It's all about competition. The least impressive is Navy Achievement, then Navy Commendation, then Meritorious Service, then Legion of Merit. Those are given in peace time operations. In a combat zone, those would merit a "V" for valor. You might also be awarded a Bronze Star, Silver Star, Navy Cross or the Medal of Honor, our highest award. To get that, most men, or women, have to die."

CHAPTER 27

"You've got a lot of those personal ribbons. What did you do to earn them?"

"That's the thing, it's difficult to talk about. For me, they often represent a time when one or more of my buddies were killed. Or, I had to kill someone, or more than one. They are not pleasant memories or times of great accomplishments, to me. Yeah, mission accomplished, but I nagged over the cost. Even one death was too much."

"Can you talk about the Silver Star?" she persisted.

"Okay, I'll give you the highlights. It was on my second tour. 1970. Four months before my initial obligation of service was up. We were sent on a mission to rescue a downed Air Force pilot shot down south of the DMZ between North and South Viet Nam. We weren't the first to be called. Earlier, the army and the air force had tried. It was just too dangerous for helos or other aircraft. The enemy was everywhere. We had an idea where the pilot was located, but reaching him would be impossible by land. The only way was by the river near where he was. The current was too swift to swim and going by boat way too dangerous. VC would be hunting all along the riverbank. But I had an idea.

"I remembered what one of those tunnel rats I mentioned earlier told me. Some of those tunnels were actually dug right up to the edge of a river. The VC would dig down several yards and make a horizontal hole which actually connected into the river. If the VC were surrounded, they could make their escape by dropping into the hole connected into the water and swim away. It was ingenious." I said.

"You lost me. I'm no engineer, but it seems to me that the river would just flood their entire tunnel all the way back to the original entrance. What am I missing?"

"Okay, maybe I didn't explain it correctly. Let me try again . . .

"The VC would dig a horizontal tunnel right up to about 6 feet away from the edge of the riverbank, and about 6 to 8 feet above the water. Remember, the bank was about 15 fifteen feet high above the river surface. Then they would dig down about 8 to 10 feet below the surface of the water and dig horizontally again the remaining 6 feet into the river itself. That way the water only flooded that 6 feet and maybe a little of the vertical dig. Does that make it clearer?"

"Yeah, but I don't think I'd ever want to jump down into that hole filled with water." Meadows scrunched up her nose.

"You would if your life depended on it."

"So, I brought up the idea to my commander." He wasn't impressed. 'I think you've been smoking dope too much. Do you even know where the entrance to that tunnel is? How do you know if it isn't occupied . . . and not by us?'

'I don't,' I replied. 'But I know who might.'

'I'm listening,' and he got out his map.

My tunnel rat friend was still in Na Trang. I tracked him down and gave him a call. His answer surprised the heck out of me.

'Lieutenant Colonel Chu, how may I help you?'

LCOL? I didn't realize he was in the U.S. Army . . . and a Colonel? He was just Brian to me; I had mistakenly thought he was a Vietnamese soldier recruited to help us. That was a mistake I wouldn't make again. He and his team had cleared miles of tunnels and were pretty sure those were clean. He also knew of the branch near the river I described and he would be glad to show me the way. He said we'd have to hurry. The VC were coming closer and closer and they would have to abandon this watch very soon."

"I can't believe you would risk your life on such a risky mission," Meadows interrupted.

"Well, we departed the next morning. I can tell you one thing though, I could never be a tunnel rat . . . besides the fact I am too large. It's dark down there! And there are right and left hand turns every fifteen or twenty feet or more. You don't have any idea what's lurking on the other side of that turn: a rifle, bayonet, booby trap? Your mind tells you to go back; your duty tells you to press forward. It's a wonder all of these guys don't have serious mental problems. These guys are true heroes!"

"To make a long story shorter, we found an exit into the river. It was upstream from the pilot's last known location. When we got to the end of the tunnel I stopped. I was looking at a hole in the ground about three feet in diameter.

"Now what? It was a good thing Brian, the tunnel rat, was behind me. He kind of chuckled. "This is going to be a little tricky for you. That hole in front of you is about six feet deep. The water is up to about one to two feet. That means when your feet touch the bottom, standing upright, your head should be about four feet above the river. You need to jump down with an air tank clutched to your chest and your mask on. The escape tunnel into the river is about six feet long and four feet high and four feet wide. Bend down and put the tank and regulator you are holding out in front of you into that tunnel. I will then hand you your scuba tank and the additional mask. Put the tank and regulator on, bend down and swim out the tunnel into the river pushing the spare tank ahead of you. Got it? It's a piece of cake; I did this once before without using scuba gear. Ready?"

"Was he kidding me? Was I *ready*? I asked him to repeat everything he just said, slowly. I thanked Brian for his help. He said he was going back the way he came. He laughed and said, 'You wouldn't catch *me* going down that tunnel again.'

"Turns out I was a good listener. When I dropped down I could see light at the end of the tunnel and swam/pushed my way forward. The river water was much clearer than I anticipated, and I was able to quickly orient myself. I soon started to drift downstream with the current. I hadn't brought fins; too cumbersome and not really needed. I surfaced slowly every few yards, looking for the pilot. I hadn't drifted along the shore line far when I surfaced again to have a look-see. There he was, clutching a large tree root half submerged in the water along the bank. He spotted me almost immediately, and motioned me over. With his gear on, we dipped under the surface and drifted with the current several miles until we were caught by a net suspended below the surface by my SEAL team buddies.

"That would have been the end of the story, but several VC spotted us and opened fire. That was their mistake. We had team members stationed on the east side of the river with heavy weapons. There was a heated exchange of gunfire before they eliminated the enemy. Unfortunately, one of our guys was killed. To make matter worse, we were sitting ducks and the pilot we had just rescued was also shot and almost killed. He got the million-dollar wound: he got sent home. I heard later that he got a medal too. He earned it.

"I got a Silver Star and a Purple Heart out of it."

"You were shot?"

"That's right. Took a bullet in the ass. Nothing serious. Earned me another trip to Subic Bay."

"Holy shit! How do people do what you do? I can't imagine volunteering for something like that."

"I told you, it was either that or get drafted. You don't see fifty-year-olds joining up. Poll the politicians. How many of them were ever in the military or served in Viet Nam? They're always quick to cite national defense. But it's always about power or more territory or more resources; it's pure greed. They *start* the wars; they *don't* fight them. That's what they need the young guys for."

"What was the Bronze Star for?" She changed the subject.

"That's kind of ironic. We were heading into the jungle on a mission to ferret out a POW camp. We usually went via the jungles because the roads were too dangerous and the paths made by the Vietnamese locals were too well known. That made for tough work in the heat and humidity. We all carried machetes. Well, our guy on point was ducking under a tree limb, when a snake dropped down and latched on to his hand. That was about the only part of his body that was exposed. We had been briefed extensively when we landed in Nam on the kinds of dangerous critters we might encounter. The most lethal was a bamboo viper. But they are a small snake and don't inject much venom. Most folks just find the bite uncomfortable but no one ever dies. This guy bitched for a second, then threw the snake to the ground and stomped on it. He then turned and continued on. The rest of us didn't think much of it until he started choking a while later. I went over to him and his face was swollen and he was having a hard time breathing. I asked him if he was allergic to anything and he shook his head, like . . . I don't think so. As the swelling continued, I was pretty sure he was. It only took another couple of minutes and he was down and turning blue. Usually we had a SEAL team member who was also a corpsman but this time he wasn't with us. We were not supposed to engage the enemy, just mark their position. In college I had majored in Biology and Physical Education. One of the courses I took was Care and Prevention of Injuries. It included how to perform a tracheotomy on someone suffering from anaphylactic shock. Technically, it's really a cricothyrotomy. Feeling for his Adam's apple, I made an incision in the notch right below it with my knife about a half inch deep. I had already grabbed a long piece of bamboo and cut it down to a size where I could insert it into the hole I'd made. The inside of the stalk is hollow so it allows air to pass through. Immediately our man took a deep breath and smiled. I'll tell you, these guys are tough hombres. He never panicked, waited patiently for someone to help him, and smiled like nothing had happened. We sent him back with a buddy just the same."

"So, I was put in for a medal . . . and got my Bronze Star. I said ironic because I always thought that medal was just as important as the Silver Star. Maybe more, he was my teammate."

"I think you earned both of them." She sounded impressed.

She stared at me for a second, I wasn't sure what she was thinking. Then she took a bite of her hamburger.

"What's on your mind?" I asked.

"I was just thinking about what I was doing here in California while you were risking your life a world away. About that time, late '60s and early '70s my Dad was stationed on an aircraft carrier out of Alameda, across the Bay from San Francisco, on the Oakland side. He was the commanding officer. That was not a good time or place to be in the military . . . they were not welcomed with open arms. Demonstrations were held almost weekly. Despite my dad's position, I often joined them. It didn't make for a happy conversation at the dinner table. I was actually glad when he deployed."

"What were you doing? I asked."

"I was in college at the University of San Francisco. I'm really ashamed to say I was pretty vocal about our involvement in Viet Nam . . . but took my anger out at the wrong people. A bunch of us would camp out at the airport and scream at the military guys returning home."

"Yeah, I remember those days. I was never spit on, but I was called a baby killer more than once passing through the L.A. airport."

"Why did we do that? You said yourself you didn't want to go over there. You didn't even want to join the military. You had no choice. We were yelling at the wrong people. Nixon, and Johnson, Westmoreland . . . those are the ones we should have called baby killers. I'm sorry. We were young and stupid. I think we all owe you a debt of gratitude."

"Tell you what: you just bought me a hamburger and fries . . . and a milkshake. Let's call us even." I grinned, and continued . . .

"Besides, I probably would have done the same thing you did if I had been in your shoes. I never resented your behavior; I didn't like what we were doing either.

I used to think, though, that what you should have been demonstrating against was the inequality of the draft. It looked like to me that black kids and poor kids were the predominant draftees—especially those in Nam. The rich guys, the kids with influence, somehow avoided going. In my fraternity of over ninety men, only a handful went into the military . . . and those were guys like me that had no other option. A few joined the National Guard, most got medical deferments. It was unfair."

"Let's not forget: Women weren't in the draft selection process either. Now that's really discrimination," I laughed; she didn't.

"I'm curious. Did you ever meet Doc Hughs while you were in Viet Nam?"

"Yeah, but only for a little while. His ship actually anchored in the bay in Diego Garcia while we were there. From what I remember, their crew got liberty after 1730 every day. They would shuttle one of their motor-whale boats every half hour back and forth to the pier. There wasn't much to do once the crew landed though. Water was warm and the sandy beaches gorgeous. We'd go snorkeling in the bay. I swear you could see over 120 feet underwater, it was that clear. There was one big hammerhead shark that ruled that bay. He was at least 18 feet long. They named him Hector. You know, they never had a shark bite in that bay; there were so many fish that the sharks didn't bother us. One of the guys our team found a huge helmet shell. Must have weighed at least ten pounds. He rigged up a rope between two trees, put a fish hook with a line attached into the meat of the shell and hung it up by the fishing line on the rope. Next morning the shell was lying on the sand, clean as a whistle. The weight of the shell had pulled that snail right out. The snail was still hanging on the rope. Neatest thing I'd ever seen. If that island was off the coast of California, there would be million-dollar hotels on every square inch of it.

"Doc ended up at the Officer's Club out on the point of the island right on the beach. That's where I was holed up as well. Plenty of beer available. Before we left the next morning, Doc might have had one too many. He regaled me with stories about his life after Newport. After Naval Justice School, he was ordained as the ship's Legal Officer onboard a large Naval Amphibious ship called the USS Paul Revere, a troop transport. Their job was to haul a thousand marines around to various landing points according to their mission. He said it wasn't very exciting. I told him it was better than being shot at. He agreed. Basically, we just told stories the whole evening. Some were memories of OCS and some about our current jobs. I remember one story he told that we really cracked up over: As the legal officer he had a legal yeoman who worked for him. His last name was 'Forks.' And he hated it. People were always making fun of it and referring to him obscenely. He came to Bob one day and asked if there was any way to legally change his name. Bob went to the Navy's Uniform Code of Military Justice book, and looked it up. Yes, he could. He just needed to fill out some paperwork, enclose some money and a certified copy of his birth certificate, and wait. So, Forks did. A month or two later, when they were in the P.I. and getting mail, Forks ran into the administration office of the ship and showed Bob his letter. Bob said he was beaming. Forks had legally changed his name . . . to *Forker*."

They both laughed. It was hard not to.

"What does a legal officer do? Is he a real lawyer?" She asked.

"No, they basically handle non-judicial punishment, Summary Court Martials, Captain's Mast, and administrative discharges. None of these things result in any jail time. About the most severe sentence is correctional custody. That can be up to 45 days in a facility usually run by the marines. It's given to 'adjust' one's behavior. Administrative separations were a big issue for Bob. They can be for a variety of reasons. Drug abuse was rampant over in Nam. First offense might result in Mast, but ship captains usually didn't want to fool around with abusers. There were too many lives at stake on a ship. Recommendations for discharge were common. Offenders usually were released with a General Discharge, vice an Honorable one if they hadn't committed a crime. Not too significant because they didn't lose any benefits earned, but the reason for discharge was listed on their discharge paper, their DD214, and sometimes that hurt their chances for employment. Felonies might merit a Bad Conduct Discharge or even a Dishonorable Discharge."

"I've never heard of a Summary Courts Martial," she interrupted. "Is that different than a General Court Martial?"

"Didn't your father ever talk about the Navy? He was an Admiral, after all."

"My father never discussed his job. Of course, he was never home to discuss it. He was a Line Officer. His career involved two years at sea, two years at a school training him to go back to sea, two more years at sea, etcetera, etcetera, until he finally qualified to be the captain of his own ship. This took eighteen to twenty years. Then he went to the Pentagon. He was divorced from my mom long before that. So, no, I don't have a clue about the types of Courts Martials or anything else."

"Okay. Sorry I asked. There are actually three types of trials; Summary, Special, and General. The differences are the severity of the cases tried, the number of members on the court, and the severity of the sentence. Summary Courts have a single judge and jury. The sentence is not much more than at a Captain's Mast. Special and General Courts are for felony cases and the worse the offense, the higher the court, the more severe the sentencing.

Bob told me most of the time he was standing watches. Even though he was the legal officer, he was primarily a junior line officer in training to one day become captain of a ship, like your father started out. That meant standing Officer of the Deck bridge watches, Engineering watches, and Combat Information Center watches. He had a four hour watch every eight hours; 24 hours a day, 7 days a week. In between, he did his collateral duties, which included legal. Free time, whenever available, was reserved for sleep. Bob said he could fall asleep as soon as his head hit the pillow and he'd catch 15 to 20 minutes of shut-eye like that throughout the day.

Bob had lots of stories. The legal business was a challenge. Drugs were a problem, moral was low. Remember, the deployments were six to nine months long. Tough on relationships back home and at least half of the sailors were there because they enlisted rather than get drafted. No one wanted to be in Viet Nam. Anyway, I never saw Bob again until I became a police officer here in San Diego.

I finished my burger. "Can we call it a day? I'm really tired and my conversational skills are waning."

"Of course, let me help you into your room." She got up and helped get out of my chair, and assisted me into my bed. She even kissed me on the cheek. "Good night, Kelly. I put your phone right here on the night stand. If you need anything, please call me. Otherwise I'll be back around six with your supper. Anything special?"

But I was already asleep. Oxycodone is wonderful . . .

CHAPTER 28

I dreamt about Viet Nam. Waste. There was that word again. It seemed like it was the word of the day. I didn't understand why . . . until I had been there a while. After I landed in Nam I was billeted in a little place called Camp Tienshaw. While I was waiting for the rest of the team to show up I met an army Captain. He was occasionally in camp and we had a couple of beers one night. He said he was going into Da Nang tomorrow with some of his troops to get some supplies and I'd be welcome to join them.

He showed up the next morning with three of his guys driving a three-quarter-ton truck.

"Come on, we're heading for the supply warehouse. I'll show you how the system works."

We stopped in front of a building bigger than any Sears store I'd ever seen. One story . . . but it must have covered two acres of ground. He and I stepped inside to a wire cage cubicle, probably 8 × 12 feet in size. From what I could see through the wire, the building was stocked with millions of items, literally.

"Good morning, Sergeant," the captain explained. "I'm here to pick up a fan. I've got a little generator where we're at, and it's hot."

"No problem, Captain, we've got dozens of them," spoke the Sgt. "Just get this paperwork authorization signed and you're in business." With that he handed the Captain three sheets of paper. "You'll need all three signatures on those forms, government regulations."

"Okay, where do I get the signatures?"

"The first one is right across the street. The second guy is now on leave . . . and the third one is on a mission somewhere. I don't know when either of them will be back. Sorry, sir."

"I understand Sarge. I'm government issue myself. We'll come back later."

With that, we both walked out.

"Are you kidding me?" I blurted. "How is that right? There's a whole warehouse full of stuff that no one can use?"

He just laughed. "Let me show you how the system really works." We headed back into the cage.

The captain was now irate. He proceeded to tell that sergeant exactly what he thought of his "system" using colorful language and even veiled threats. The sergeant just stood there, not saying a word. This went on for over ten minutes before the captain looked at me and winked.

"Sergeant, I know it's not your fault. You are only following orders. I apologize for my outburst. But there's got to be a better system." We turned and left, again.

Outside his men were waiting by their truck. One of the men was holding a fan. The back of the truck was heavily laden with everything and anything it could hold. It appeared that while we were in yelling at the sergeant, they were out back raiding the place.

"That's the way the system really works, Kelly," the captain laughed. "And that sergeant knew all the time that's what we were doing." It's quite an efficient way of doing business."

Waste. When the war ended we just left everything there.

I talked to a friend of mine who got drafted right out of high school. Eighteen years young. He told me after boot camp he went straight to Nam. He barely knew how to use his weapon. He knew nothing about war or killing. On his first patrol they *wasted* a "gook." They took my friend aside and made him smash the enemy's head in with his rifle and his boots until the head was unrecognizable. That was the intention: it wasn't a human anymore, it was a piece of meat. That's what they all were . . . waste.

CHAPTER 29

MEADOWS

Meadows was at her desk. The phone rang.

"Meadows? How's Kelly doing?" It was her LT.

"He's been out of the hospital for a couple of days now but still under the weather. I doubt he'll be able to come back to work for at least a week."

"Okay, you're on your own for this one. There's been another plane crash. And they found another head."

"Another PSA plane crash? Another head? What's going on?"

I was told this time it crashed just after take-off. The main runway at Lindbergh Field runs north and south. Planes take off to the north and veer west over Point Loma and out over the Pacific Ocean before turning north again and heading up the coast. The depth of the water around there is between 120 and 320 feet. It's usually a beautiful view for the passengers seated on the left side of the plane. They can see Coronado Island, the city of San Diego, and the Coronado Bridge, as well as all the Navy ships and yachts along Harbor and Shelter Island. If San Diego was known as the most "livable city," Coronado was known as the "Crown City" within. Twenty-two thousand residents strong, there wasn't room for any more. Their most famous landmark was the Hotel Del Coronado, a presence in the city since 1888 when it was the single largest resort hotel in the world, known for its Victorian architecture, modern luxuries, and beachfront recreation. It had hosted presidents, royalties, and celebrities through the years and been featured in numerous books and movies. In 1970, it was designated a California Historical Landmark and then a National Historical Landmark in 1977.

At that moment; however, the passengers on this particular flight could not have cared less. Something was wrong. Instead of climbing, the plane seemed to be leveling off, and actually dropping. One of the flight attendants yelled, "Brace for impact!" There were screams, then panic, as the plane plunged nose first into the frigid waters.

Both engines had failed.

It didn't take Meadows long to get there with her siren and lights blaring. Doc Hughs was waiting. He was standing on the beach in back of the Hotel Del, as the locals called it. The police had herded hundreds of looky-loos back from the beach and behind the wooden rail of the hotel deck. A more water-resistant suitcase had washed ashore on the beach. One of the cops at the scene had pulled it out of the water, floating among a ton of other debris. Doc had been called when they found the head inside. It was severed just like the others. This time there *were* bodies: lots of them, scattered among the waves. Fortunately, there wasn't much chop and the waves were small: one to two feet. The bodies kept rolling in.

The suitcase was tagged; just like the other one, with the same name. Dean Meritt.

Was this a game? What was going on?

Doc Hughs was just as confused as Meadows. He said he'd try to get some identification on the head but doubted if it would be more than he got on the others. Age, race, marks, if any. That name again, Dean, was puzzling, but not helpful.

Meadows was looking out at the water when she noticed a lone figure standing at the edge. His feet were getting wet when the larger waves rolled in. It didn't seem to bother him or he was too absorbed in thought to notice.

"Hey Doc, who's that guy standing over there? I don't recognize him. I thought they were supposed to move all the bystanders back up on the deck."

"Oh, they did, that's my brother, Jim. Some of the funeral homes were called to help transport the bodies to the morgue. He's a driver. Haven't you met him?"

"No, I haven't, but maybe I'll introduce myself."

I walked over to him. He was about my height. A little pudgy; could stand some exercise. Needed a haircut, big time. I never liked hair extending over the ears and down over their collar in the back. And get rid of the sideburns and the mustache. What's with that? Hasn't that hippy look gone out of style?

Extending my hand, I said, "Hi, I'm Detective Linda Meadows, Joe Kelly's partner. I understand you are Doc Hughs' brother."

"Yes, ma'am. Jim Hughs at your service." They shook hands.

"Tough night, huh?" She queried.

"I guess. I see bodies every day. Not this many at once, though. I wonder how it happened."

"I heard that the pilot radioed to the tower that he had lost an engine right after takeoff and he was getting permission to re-land. According to that transmission, as he was making his turn over Point Loma, he lost his second engine. At that point, the plane went down. So far, they haven't recovered any survivors. How'd you get here so quickly?"

"I was already in the area. I had to pick up a body at an assisted living residency near here. I got a radio call while I was there from Mr. Anderson, my boss, directing me to come here."

"Must be a difficult job. How long have you been doing it? Seems like it would be awfully depressing."

"Sometimes, but there are benefits. It can't be any more depressing than being a cop. I mean, nobody likes you guys. You're always chasing the scum in our society, and half the time you can't even solve their crimes. My job is much more satisfying. The dead can't talk; they're at peace. You might be surprised how that puts me at ease. I started doing this a year after I graduated high school. I think 1969. My brother was over in Viet Nam. I had wanted to enlist but failed the physical. Asthma. Go figure. Bob was a runt and I was a pretty good athlete. Bob told me he didn't think it was possible to fail that physical. He said you just needed to be breathing. That hurt me worse than failing the damn thing. "

But he laughed and said, "Bob and I were really close growing up, but when he went away to college, our relationship changed. I don't know why. Probably just the fact that we were so far apart. I can blame the Navy for that . . . and that stupid war. And then he was always so busy: medical school, internships, and the rest. I never saw him much. I missed that; still do."

Meadows couldn't understand why Doc never mentioned his brother. Was it just the distance that pulled them apart . . . or was it something else? Always the detective, she pried a little.

"Were you involved in that PSA plane crash in '78? That was a mess too. Did they call the funeral homes for help in transporting bodies there too?"

"I remember that clearly. It was early in the morning . . . before nine, I think. I don't go to work until one in the afternoon, usually. But I live in North Park, right around where the plane crashed. I was lucky. The plane and debris landed a block away from my house. I heard it though. It sounded like a freight train and then a huge explosion. Shook a picture off my wall. I remember running outside to see what had happened and saw smoke rising from down the street. I ran over and saw people lying on the ground, some dead, some just crying. I think those folks had been in the homes that were hit. There wasn't much I could do. The cops came right away and moved me and some others away from the scene. I saw my brother arrive, but I don't think he saw me. I watched for a while and then went back to my house."

"Interesting," she thought. "Isn't it ironic that even though you and Bob went separate ways, that you both ended up dealing with dead bodies? I mean, sure they're dead under different circumstances, but still dead."

"Wow, I never thought about that. Bob went to college, became a doctor and I barely passed high school. And here we are at the same site, picking up dead bodies together. Yeah, that is ironic."

"Well, Bob isn't here to pick up bodies. He's here because it's also a crime scene."

"What do you mean?"

"Let's just say there is a body here, or at least part of a body, that doesn't belong on that plane. That's why I am here. The plane crash will be investigated by Civil Aviation authorities. They'll eventually find the critical black box that will help them determine the cause of the crash. I've got nothing to do with that. I investigate crimes. But right now, I'm a little handicapped because my partner, Detective Kelly, is home in bed. The slacker."

"Joe Kelly. You mentioned him before." He added, "Is that the Kelly my brother knew in the Navy?."

"Yeah, did you know him?"

"No, only the name. My brother has talked about him. It's been a long time; he was in the Navy then, OCS, he called it. He wrote letters home to my dad; mother had already died. Anyway, I read some of them. Kelly must be pretty awesome. Bob said if it wasn't for him he would have gone to Canada; that's how much he hated OCS. Kelly was the rock that got him through. Talk about irony: Bob, me, you, and now Kelly are all connected in some fashion. Small world, huh?"

Yeah, small world, I thought. Is it also a coincidence that he has been to both of the sites where we found severed heads? Am I putting too much into this?

I wonder if he was around the safe house where the girls were killed . . . or the plane crash at Lindbergh Field? Leave it alone, Linda. You're really reaching now.

"Maybe we should all get together for lunch or a beer someday. Talk about what's happening in or lives. What do you think?"

"Doubt if that will ever happen. We don't have much in common. Besides, we're all too busy. Thanks for the offer. I've got to go. My hearse is filled. Nice talking to you. Maybe we'll meet again."

I had a feeling we would.

I watched him go. Was there a connection? How? I needed to talk to Manny. He wasn't telling us everything. Kelly and I both had picked up on that.

I headed back to the station. Doc was busy with bodies. Again, the only one that really mattered to him was the severed head. The others would all have to be identified and he would be involved like the last one; but they probably wouldn't be that difficult to identify: they were all mostly in one piece.

On the way to work the next morning, my thoughts were running wild in my head. Should I stop and talk to Kelly before I rushed headlong into something that was only a nagging feeling? I decided to stop at his house, but first: Starbucks.

Kelly was still in bed, propped up on two pillows watching TV. I knocked, but entered without waiting for a response from him. "It's only me," I yelled. "Are you decent?"

"Would it matter?"

"I guess not. I was hoping I'd get lucky," I laughed. "Coffee?"

"You are a mind reader," as he took the cup and smiled. "My guess is, that's not the only reason you stopped by. You're not on vacation anymore, are you?"

"No, surely you've been watching the news regarding the plane crash off Point Loma?

"Yeah, this is getting serious. Three plane crashes out of Lindbergh Field in less than three years. What's going on?" He sat up in bed, taking a sip of his coffee. "Don't tell me you found another head?"

"Doc's probably processing it right now. I spoke to him down at the beach off the Del. He said it was the same as the others, Latino girl in her twenties. But get this, she was found in another suitcase with the same ID: Dean Meritt."

"Well, that pretty much confirms this is the work of a serial killer, but either he or she is getting careless, or sending us a message: they're better than we are."

"It's definitely a taunt of some kind," I agreed.

Kelly thought for a moment. "I've got an idea. Maybe this is more than a taunt. Maybe this is all about publicity. We find the head; the perp gets recognition once we publicize the picture in the newspapers and on television. Maybe that's what gets him off. It's not the killing, it's the exposure."

"I think you may be right," I continued. "Let's not air the picture this time. Maybe we can get a response."

"One more thing. I met Doc Hugh's brother last night . . . out at the beach by the Hotel Del. I got a call about the plane crash and the fact that they had found another suitcase with a severed head inside. Doc was examining the bodies as they washed ashore but it appeared obvious they had all died in the crash before being drowned. At any rate, I noticed a guy on the beach and Doc said it was his brother. Have you ever met him?"

"I don't think so. I think Joe mentioned him once or twice in some of our conversations at OCS, but nothing rings a bell. I think he said he was much younger . . . four years or so."

"How old is Doc?"

"Same age as yours truly: thirty-five."

"Well, we got to talking and he mentioned that he lived in North Park and was a witness to the carnage in '78 when that PSA plane crashed. Now here he is at the scene of this recent crash and . . . another severed head. I just have a strange feeling that this may be connected. There's something else that bothers me. Do you remember when we first talked to Manny? He said those college boys came once a week and always brought two girls, like clockwork. They did the same thing every time."

'Your point?"

"We only found three bodies in the fire. If they came twice, what happened to the fourth?"

"Holy shit! That's right," Kelly blurted. "I knew Manny wasn't telling us everything. Where is he, anyway?"

"I suppose he's still in lockup. I was on my way to inquire when I thought I'd better run it by you first."

"Don't wait for me, Meadows. You're way ahead of me. I don't think I'll be ready to travel for a couple of days anyway. You also need to talk to Lt. Hill. See if he thinks we need to alert the public that we have a serial killer at large. Of course, the downside to that is we just give the perp more publicity."

Lieutenant Hill decided we would not air this picture. But we would have to alert law enforcement agencies throughout the area and in L.A. He also warned us, "If we continue to find more heads, we'll *have* to give the media a head's up. We don't know for sure who this sicko is targeting. The public should be on guard.

CHAPTER 30

The county jail isn't the nicest place to stay. I suppose it was never intended to be. There are three types of lawbreakers that stay here. One: those that are arrested pending a plea agreement, a trial, or sentencing. Two: those who have been convicted of a misdemeanor and serving a sentence of less than a year, and finally those who are just awaiting transfer to a prison or elsewhere.

In California, a prison, or penitentiary, is usually reserved for those convicted of a felony offense and are serving a sentence of over one year.

Our jail is a busy place. Arrivals come in daily. Many arrivals. Some for only a few days. Some are released after posting bail or placed under supervision on probation. The lucky few are released on their own recognizance under an agreement to appear in court at a later date.

Like most states, California correctional facilities are overcrowded. Sometimes prisoners are even released early to make room for more. Right now, there are two prisoners sharing a one-person designated room with bunk beds. Imagine being in a 6 × 8 foot room with a small table and perhaps two chairs. In the corner is a toilet that doesn't flush. I can smell the urine just thinking about it. It's no wonder there are uprisings by the inmates.

Jails are not a democracy. It's their way or the highway. Even when I show my credentials, they make me surrender my weapon and stamp my hand with some ink that is invisible to the naked eye. I guess that's so they can make sure I've got the stamp on when I leave. I would imagine that some cagey folks have tried to trade places with someone and sneak out in the past . . . won't work now. Anyway, I passed through the metal detector and requested one of the guys at the desk to see a Miguel Rodriguez.

He looked through his files. "Not here," he said. "He was released on $15,000 bail four days ago."

"You're kidding me. Where'd he come up with that kind of money?"

"You'll have to ask the court for that. We don't keep those kinds of records here."

That's going to be a problem, I thought. Chances are he was bailed out by whoever was running the trafficking operation. Maybe I can subpoena the court to give me the name of who bailed him out. If I didn't find him I'd bet we'd never see old Manny again.

I headed to the courthouse. According to their records, Manny was released when a gentleman named Lawrence Reynolds posted his bond and gave them fifteen thousand bucks in cash to guarantee his return. Miguel Rodriguez was to appear for trial in three weeks.

I was able to get the address of Mr. Reynolds. Nice address. He lived in Coronado. Next to La Jolla, that might have been the most expensive neighborhood in San Diego. I headed over there.

Crossing the Coronado Bridge was a treat, all in itself. Over a mile long, it wasn't a straight line from one end to the other. It was actually shaped like an elongated 'S' with the large end on the Coronado side and a small 'S' curving up and around to the mainland side. Of course, there was a toll booth. A dollar each way, both located on the Coronado side. This was California, after all. I think they taxed the seagulls. Once on the island, there was a golf course on the left and soccer field on the right. Then, very expensive old homes along the coast on either side with views of the city and harbor. Living in La Jolla, I couldn't complain, but I had wanted to live in Coronado ever since I could remember. Never could afford it; still can't. I couldn't afford the property taxes on the house I own now. Fortunately, I didn't have to. My lawyer was smart enough to include those annual taxes in the settlement.

His house was on the left, on Glorietta Boulevard. I had to go a couple of blocks further before I could get there because of the one-way street but I was able to circle back to Glorietta. It curved all the way around the south-eastern portion of the island almost to the Del.

He lived in an old Tudor style home. Looked like it had a thatched roof. The lot was at least a third of an acre: large for Coronado. I pulled into his driveway. He had a two-car garage. As I was about to walk up to his door, a cab pulled up behind me. A man got out, paid the driver, and walked over to me as the cabbie unloaded his suitcase. He looked to be around 60. Average height. He was wearing an expensive suit. I really liked his tie.

"Can I help you?" he asked.

I was in an unmarked vehicle, so he had no way of knowing I was law enforcement. I showed him my badge.

"Perhaps. Are you Lawrence Reynolds?"

"That I am, Ma'am. "I live here with my son, Arthur. I don't know if he's home or not. He's probably working. I just returned from London, on business. Why don't you come in and you can tell me what this is all about? Are we in trouble?"

"No, I'm investigating the disappearance of someone. Perhaps you or your son could shed some light on it and maybe I'll able to locate him."

I followed him inside. "Sir, someone using your driver's license and paying a cash guarantee bailed a suspect in a murder case out of jail last week. Do you have any idea how that may have happened?"

"None at all. I keep my license in a drawer in my office when I travel. I never drive in London and only use my passport for identification. I'll show you." He went into his office and returned with his license. Sure enough, it was the driver's license of one Lawrence Reynolds on Glorietta Blvd.

"Would you check to see if your son is home?" I persisted.

"Sure, follow me."

We entered a room that appeared to be solid oak or mahogany in color and furnishing. At any rate it was impressive, but too dark and masculine for my taste.

"Arthur, I'm home. Are you here?" he yelled. "He works odd days, today may be one of them."

"Does he work around here? I could just drop by to see him. Save us both a trip later."

"He works at the airport, as a baggage handler. His hours are usually eight to eight, four days a week. The days vary. I'm not sure which days he's on."

"Do you know which airline?" I asked.

"I think it's PSA, but I'm not sure. Sometimes when it gets busy they help each other out."

"Does your son drive his own car or does he use yours? I assume he's over sixteen?"

"Oh yes, he's thirty now. My, how time flies. He's got an old Chevy, a '57, I think. He says it's a classic. He's had it since he was in high school. I remember it was a big deal for him to drive a bunch of the kids on his soccer team to games. I've offered to buy him a new one, but he said his drives just fine. I took him down to my Porsche dealer to see if anything interests him, but no sale. I'm sorry, I'm rambling. Ever since my wife died, it's just been the two of us. I guess I spoil him."

I didn't see anything further I needed from Mr. Reynolds, so I apologized for any inconvenience I may have caused and handed him my card. "When your son returns, would you please have him give me a call?" I was planning on driving to the airport right away but I didn't want the father calling to give him a head's up.

Getting back in my car, I began to assess the information I now had.

Manny knew something he didn't share with us. What was it?

There were only three bodies found at the safe house. Based on their routine, there should have been four. What happened to the other one?

Jim Hughs was at the site of two severed head findings. Was he connected? Was he ever at the safe house?

Did Jim know Manny? How?

Manny was bailed out of jail by someone using Lawrence Reynold's license and a lot of cash. Why?

Who other than the son, Arthur Reynolds, would have access to that license?

Another connection: Reynolds worked at baggage handling for PSA and Jim Hughs collected bodies for a living. Coincidence?

Who had fifteen large available to bail out a pawn in that sex tracking racket? What did Manny know that made him so valuable?

Why did Arthur loan Manny his car?

One more thing: Manny, Arthur and Jim Hughs were all around thirty years old and all played soccer in high school. Were they all team mates on the same team?

My head was spinning. I headed for the terminal at Lindbergh Field.

CHAPTER 31

For a city as large as San Diego, Lindbergh Field wasn't that large. It only had one terminal. I parked outside, showed a cop my badge, and headed for the information center and asked if I could speak to someone in charge of employment. The young lady there asked me if I was looking for a job. I showed her my identification and she told me where I could go.

I wanted to tell her where she could go . . .

It was upstairs on the left.

This time I showed my ID first. The man was very helpful. Yes, Arthur Reynolds was scheduled for today; however, he left suddenly less than a half hour ago claiming to be quite sick.

"Do you know if he went to the hospital, or home?" I asked.

"I'm sorry," He replied. "He came up here, said he didn't feel well and had to leave. He didn't say where he was going or when he would be back. We've never had any trouble with him and he was always here on time so I had no reason to question him. Funny thing, though. As he was leaving he said that if his dad called *again*, to tell him he loved him." *Again*, he said. Dad had alerted him to my visit.

And now, another dead end. I'm batting a thousand. I need to talk to Kelly. Tomorrow. It's too late now and he said he'd be ready to go then.

Where is her picture? This is important. Nobody cares about her. Nobody misses her. Only I care. I don't want her to die without anyone seeing her picture. She is my messenger. How could they do this? I've waited for days and nothing. Do they know something? Maybe I shouldn't have used the name Dean Meritt again. Not many people knew that name. It was only important that a certain detective knew . . . that was the whole point. Was I getting too cocky? What's wrong with me?

119

CHAPTER 32

I was just leaving my desk to head over to see Kelly when I got the call. It was from the police dispatcher. Someone found a body at the end of Ocean Boulevard in Coronado. It was in the weeds just before the back entrance to the Naval Air Station. Police are on the scene. The ME has already been notified. We need a detective ASAP. That would be me. It was less than ten miles from headquarters to the scene. Of course, in San Diego, distance is measured in time, not miles. At 0630, the traffic crossing the Coronado Bridge is sometimes backed up to I-5 and even onto Highway 163 through Balboa Park. Crossing the bridge and paying the toll is often the easy part. Navy personnel are heading to the air station and the three aircraft carriers parked there. Twenty thousand sailors, usually one per car. I could have used the siren, but it wouldn't have done any good. There was no room for anyone to pull over.

I arrived at the scene at 0720. *Not bad*, I thought.

I showed my badge to one of the officers posted just inside the yellow tape barriers. I knew him, but it was protocol. He told me the 'body' was found by an early morning surfer. "That's him standing right over there," he pointed.

I went over and identified myself.

"Can you tell me how you came to be involved in this?" I asked.

He said the only reason he was even looking up there was because his dog was barking like crazy at something. He kept calling his dog to come back but he refused. When he approached, he almost gagged.

"I've never seen a dead body before, at least not a real one. The movies are one thing, but this . . . and the smell . . ."

I told him to stick around, I may have some more questions later. I went over to the body. It really was gross. Blood everywhere . . . and no head.

Doc Hughs was already here, examining the body. He looked over at me when I approached. "Caucasian male, decapitated with a very sharp instrument, but not cleanly . . . while he was alive. I'll have to look closer at the lab, but it looks like someone used an axe or a large saber. Rigor still present. I'd say he hasn't been dead more than 36 hours. I'll get closer to the time of death later. The hands are still intact so I should get good prints. If he's in the system, we'll identify him."

Just then, one of the other police officers came running up.

"Detective! Doc Hughs! You need to see this."

He motioned for us to follow him around the side of the iron fence along the shore. Perched on top of one of the poles of the fence was the severed head.

It wasn't enough to kill the guy; whoever did it was also sending a message.

Ever the clinician, Doc volunteered, "If it helps, I'd say he was under thirty-five years old."

There were no other clues. The area around there was sand and weeds. Lots of footprints; no help. No weapon found.

A severed head? Was there a connection to the others? But this one was a male.

Another piece to add to the puzzle.

I really need to talk to Kelly. I wrote down the surfer's name and address and told him he could go. We appreciated his help. Doc would continue with his investigation and let me know the pertinent details when he could. I told him to call Kelly. The coroner's ambulance was just arriving. So was the media. I was heading to Kelly's house.

CHAPTER 33

JIM HUGHS

"Manny, what the hell is going on? Where are you? Things are really spinning out of control!"

"Hey man, I'm just trying to stay out of sight. Did you know they put a hit out on Arthur last night? Them guys are serious, man. I think we got way in over our heads."

"Yeah, I know, but the money was serious, too. I don't know how much you've got stashed but I've got at least a couple hundred thousand of Arthur's money. He told me the setup was too good to pass up. All you had to do was housesit those girls, it was like hitting the motherlode. That was the perfect setup. Those stupid college kids thought they were just moving girls . . . it was really all about moving drugs . . . big time. And you got laid as a bonus! What was Arthur's role, anyway? He never told me why he was getting paid. Seemed like you were doing all the work."

"I recruited Arthur a long time ago. He was the eyes and ears on the street. His job was to monitor the competition. Gangs and local drug dealers were not anxious for us to move into their territory. We had an agreement that we wouldn't interfere in the San Diego business and they agreed to leave us alone. Our distribution went to L.A. and San Francisco and Phoenix. Unfortunately, he was watching the wrong groups. He should have been paying attention to the sex trafficking part of the operation. That's the group that finally nailed us when they sent that guy over to kill the girls."

"Arthur was stupid. Why did he use his dad's name to bail you out? As soon as the cartel guys found out who bailed you, he was as good as dead. They were watching you. Arthur was the only one beside me that knew how to get in touch with you. They needed to make sure he wouldn't . . . or couldn't. We both need to be careful now. They may need to eliminate us too."

"Come on man. How would they connect you to me? The only thing we have in common is high school. Soccer, really. We didn't even go to the same schools."

"That's true, but don't forget the girl who died at the safe house. I know that wasn't your fault; you said she was sick. But you called me to pick up the body so no one would know. I'm sure those drug guys were watching and they saw someone pick up that girl. They don't know who. If they find you, I could be in trouble. They won't find the girl, she went straight to the crematory . . . when I was through with her."

"Man, you are really sick. Why do you do that?"

"Who cares? Nobody knows her. Another unknown. A nobody. She's dead. At least she was good for something."

"Look, I didn't call you, Arthur did. You have no connection to me and as long as the cops can't find me, you've got nothing to worry about. Man, I'm scared shitless of the cartel, though. They mean business. I'm going to use my money to get the hell out of Dodge. After this call, you won't be able to reach me. I'm history, Bro. It's been real, Man, I owe you one."

"Wait a minute," I interrupted. "What if I need to warn you or get a message to you that's really important? Isn't there anyway I can reach you?"

"Okay, but you can only use this if you think I am about to be killed. I'm heading to Frisco. I have a friend of my mother's that said I could stay with her. She's no relation, so it will be difficult to trace me. Her name is Diana Mendez. Her number is 415-232-1212. Don't write that down, memorize it. I hope you never need it."

With that, he hung up. I wrote the number down along with the name. Fuck him . . .

The phone rang . . . It was my brother. He needed to talk again.

"I just returned from the scene of a ghastly murder over in Coronado. The deceased has been identified as one Arthur Reynolds. Didn't you play soccer with him in high school?

"Maybe. There was a rich kid named Reynolds that was on our team. He wasn't that good. Most of the really good players were Mexican. I wasn't that close to Reynolds. His family was out of our league."

"If I remember correctly, you use to hang out with him and a Mexican kid. What was his name?"

"I think it was Miguel. But I'm not positive of that. Everyone called him Manny, though. He had a habit of saying 'man' all the time. It was a nickname that stuck. Why?"

"Because someone cut off Arthur's head. I'm sure you have read about the recent spate of unexplained severed heads that have been found over the last few years. The Police are convinced there is a connection. They are very thorough and I am sure they will start interviewing anyone and everyone that knows this Reynolds guy. If they really start checking up on you, they may discover something we both know would get you into a heap of trouble. I am just trying to give you a heads up. I won't be able to protect you forever."

"Okay. Thanks for the warning. I hardly knew Arthur." I hung up. There really wasn't much more to say to Bob. I think he's just as strange as I am; he's a coroner, for God's sake.

Besides, I had other things on my mind; specifically, the warning Manny just gave me: 'They may need to eliminate us too.' Shit! What did Arthur tell them before he was killed? Did he mention me? They already knew about Manny and I'm sure they were already hunting for him. How could they know about me? The hearse . . . it had no markings, but it would indicate a funeral home. There must be tons of them in the San Diego area. Maybe I should run too. But that might make me an obvious target if they canvassed funeral homes and discovered an employee who recently quit. I'll stay, but I have to be careful. Fuck! I didn't really know what either of those guys were doing. Sex trafficking. Drug running. What the hell did I stumble into? All I was trying to do was do a favor for Manny by picking up a dead girl. I wasn't really involved. I did hold Arthur's money. He didn't want his dad finding it at his house and he was afraid to add it to his bank account. He was right about that. At first, it was only a few thousand dollars. Over time though, his take had increased exponentially. I now had well over two hundred thousand of his money. Plus, he paid me ten per cent to hold it for him. I guess it's all mine now . . . but getting involved with a cartel was stupid. I'm going to buy a gun. At least I may be able to protect myself.

CHAPTER 34

MANNY

Poor Jim. He's clueless. He has no idea the trouble he is in . . . and he didn't even do anything. I wish I hadn't had to kill that one girl at the safe house. She just kept screaming and yelling. It was the only way to shut her up. Arthur wouldn't have called Jim, and Jim would never have been involved. Everyone thinks I'm just a stupid Mexican. If they only knew I was the kingpin of this operation, not just some house-sitter. I'll try to keep him safe, but if the cops get too close, he'll have to go the way of Arthur. I should kill him anyway, but I owe him one. I wouldn't even be here if it wasn't for him. I wish Arthur hadn't told him about the drugs. That really screws up the works. Fortunately, he doesn't know how to reach me. He doesn't know my real name either. That phone number I gave him was bogus and I'm sure not going to San Francisco. The fake IDs I've had since I was twelve should make it difficult for the cops to find me. I'll get new ones very soon. I doubt if the cops even know the real reason for the scam was not sex trafficking but drug trafficking. They will eventually find the tunnel; that's too bad, but I can dig new tunnels. Fortunately, they think it was used to move girls. The unfortunate thing is that we're going to have to establish a whole new way of delivering our product. Putting that con man Whitmore in place at USC and his stupid wife running the massage parlors was brilliant. They didn't know we were running drugs either. I'm glad I thought of it. Those college boys took all the risks, and we only paid them a fraction of our profit, which came from the drugs. It was brilliant. I did hate losing Chico, though. He was the best hitman I had. He was a true soldier to the end. He knew he couldn't get caught alive. He knew too much. I'll make sure his family is well compensated. So, Fermin, maybe someday you'll be known as a Drug Lord yourself. Of course, then I'll have to stop saying, 'man' all the time. Miguel . . . Manny. I'd almost forgotten my real name: Fermin Lopez. My mother had read that Fermin was the name of a Bishop and saint who the running of the bulls in Pamplona, Spain honored. It means, 'strong', in Spanish. I think my mother was the saint. But everyone called me *'rabbit'*, back home. I wasn't very big, but I was fast . . . "quick, like a bunny" . . . my older brother said. The name stuck: El Conejo . . . the rabbit.

CHAPTER 35

DOC

Shit! What's my brother gotten into now? I have a feeling he's into something big . . . and it's going to get him killed. I'm going to have a talk with Joe. There's more to that safe house then meets the eye . . .

I called Joe. Meadows answered, "Detective Meadows."

"Good morning, Linda. I'm glad you are there. I was calling Joe. How's he doing?"

"He's much better. In fact, he tells me he's going back on the payroll today. I'm not sure he's fully recovered, but he's stubborn. How can we help you?"

"I think we need to go over the investigation of that safe house again. Perhaps we overlooked something. Remember how you were curious why there were only three bodies, not four?"

"Okay," It was Kelly on the line now. "Let's go over the notes the police made. I wrote down that a Patrolman Peters interviewed most of the people on that street to see if there were any suspicious vehicles or person frequenting the house. I really didn't look that closely at that once we discovered the sex trafficking operation. Meadows and I will go down to the station and have a look. We'll let you know if we find anything."

"Great. Maybe it will amount to nothing, but my gut tells me otherwise." I hung up. I still had my coroner's work to do. Deaths, murders, and criminal activity don't stop while you're still investigating another crime in a city as large as San Diego.

What am I going to do with this head? I sure as hell am not going to bury it, as difficult as it was to get. I had gone down to the San Ysidro port of entry and headed east towards Nogales. I didn't have to go far. Smugglers were escorting a bunch of illegals into the desert when I spotted them. I didn't see any border patrol personnel. I got out of the car and ordered them to halt. I held up a fake police badge. In the dark they assumed I was law enforcement. I told the smuggler I needed to see the women. I told them there was an alert for a young woman for which her family had offered a reward. He did not argue or try to resist. There were nine individuals in the group . . . six were men. Of the three women, one was about eighteen, the other two much older. I had a picture of a women in my hand and I compared it to the woman. I did not show it to anyone else. Surprise! It was a match. At least that's what I told the smuggler. I told him I would let him go on with the others and give him a C-Note if he would keep his mouth shut and get lost. He was only too happy to comply.

I took the girl back to my place and eventually to the cutting room. She was supposedly no different from the others. A nobody; unknown and uncared for. Destined to live a life of poverty and prostitution. Did they really think their life would be so much different here in the States?

But somebody needs to see her and I need to ensure that she's given her due. I've got to make sure she gets her picture plastered over the news and newspapers. I've got an idea. Maybe I should get the press involved. Someone must be curious. But I must wait for the right time. The head goes in the refrigerator. It won't stay long; accidents happen every day . . .

Joe called. "Bob, you may be on to something. We went over the notes taken while interviewing residents. Several of them noticed the pizza van coming and going once a week. They didn't think much of it. People were always ordering something in the neighborhood. There were a couple of things that were different. An older widowed lady noticed a strange car parked a couple of houses down from the house that caught fire. It was always there on the days that the pizza truck came. She didn't get a good look at the occupants, but she did write down the license of the car. She also said she saw a black hearse stop at the house one night and watched as two men loaded what appeared to be a coffin into it. I don't know why that never caught our attention. But that may explain why there was only three women found murdered at the scene. We need to find that hearse driver. Thanks for the tip, Bob."

Crap, I was afraid of that. It's only a matter of time before they find Jim.

CHAPTER 36

KELLY

"I think we may have a lead. Someone picked up a girl who had died at the safe house in a hearse. Who do we know who works for a funeral home and has access to a hearse?"

"Jim Hughs! The same guy who was at the scene of both airline crashes and the safe house . . . where three severed heads were found," added Meadows.

"That still doesn't explain the United flight. As far as I know, Jim was never at that scene."

"True, but wasn't Arthur Reynolds working as a baggage handler at the airport. Could he somehow have gotten that bag on the plane. Maybe he smuggled it earlier. I checked. The plane originated in San Diego, flew to London and was headed back here when it crashed. It's a stretch, but feasible."

"You're assuming Jim knew Arthur," I posed. "Do we have any evidence of that?"

"No, but I have a feeling Doc does. That's why he asked us to take a look at the evidence log."

"Let's go see Doc Hughs," I said. "Then we have to track down that license plate number our widowed lady gave us and see why someone was so interested in that safe house!"

I gave the plate number to a clerk on duty and asked him to give me the name and address of the owner when he had it. I'll be on my radio. We stopped for a late lunch and then headed for the morgue.

The County Morgue in San Diego looks very similar to any other commercial or medical building except it has a big sign over the door identifying it as the morgue. It has a large loading and unloading dock around the back.

We found Bob, that is, Doc, inside a large room containing two large walk-in refrigerators. Bob was standing beside one of the several rolling exam tables in the room. He had a knife in his hand. On each table was a body, covered in a sheet. Only their feet were visible. Around one of their toes was a label that contained the essentials of that body: time of death, whether an autopsy was needed to be conducted, name and social security number. There were two others, assistants I assumed, standing by other tables. The tables were slightly tilted toward the feet of the deceased where there is a drain. Blood and other fluids would be emptied into sink by the side of the table. There was a scale under the sink. On the other side was a surgical light. Doc was busy with a dissection.

"Bob, can you talk while you're working? We only have a few questions."

"Yes, I've only just begun," he said, not looking up. He knew who it was. No one else called him Bob in this building.

"You'd think the city was just overrun with homicides looking at this place, wouldn't you? After all, that's usually when you and I meet. Actually, most of the cases we get here are from overdoses. It's getting worse, too."

He had already made the incision which began from the pubic bone and ran all the way up to the throat. He was removing the abdominal organs when we arrived. Meadows asked if she could be excused for a moment.

She put her hand up to her mouth and hurried out of the room.

"Okay, I'll make this quick. Do you know if your brother knew either Manny or Arthur? We're pretty sure he knew either one or the other. We think Manny is the key to the entire sex trafficking operation we discovered and Jim may be involved and not even realize it."

"I'm afraid you may be right, Joe. Jim is a little weird, but he's not a criminal. I don't want to see him get hurt, and if my suspicion is correct, he may be in great danger. That's why I asked you to re-exam the investigation at the safe house more thoroughly." He put the knife down and finally looked up at me.

I didn't tell him our thoughts regarding Jim's possible connection to the severed heads. First things first.

"Do you know the name of the mortuary where Jim works?" I asked.

"Yeah, Heavenly Gardens. It's off Interstate 8 near Del Cerro."

Meadows returned, looking a little green. "I don't know how you cope with dealing with all these bodies, day in and day out. Doesn't it get to you, Doc?"

"You know, if you think about it, dying is really just as natural as being born. The sad part for me . . . is the young ones, the ones who never had a chance to live."

With that, we said we'd get back to him later. Thanking him for his help, we headed over to see Jim.

We didn't get very far. The radio interrupted just as we were getting onto I-8. There was a major crash at the junction of I-8 and I-15. Just south of the stadium. They weren't sure what happened, but there were bodies everywhere. We were near, so we volunteered to investigate.

CHAPTER 37

The school bus was traveling west on Interstate 8. There were forty-two souls on board coming back from an afternoon swim tournament in La Mesa. Heading south was a large semi-tractor trailer, loaded with mail-ordered products. The driver was going way too fast into the intersection. It was rush hour, and folks were trying to get home. Some wouldn't make it.

The bus abruptly stopped, waiting for traffic to clear in front of it. The truck couldn't stop and T-boned the bus on the right side near the rear. It damaged the suspension and punctured the fuel tank. The explosion was almost immediate. The driver of the semi was killed by the force of the crash. The passengers in the car behind the bus were engulfed in flames and died shortly after. Of the forty-two passengers, twelve were killed by the impact. Unfortunately, the rear exit was rendered useless because of the collision and fire, which left only the front exit for the remaining thirty people to escape. That was partially blocked by falling luggage and some coolers that were in the overhead. Everything was compounded because the bus had wide rows of seats, leaving only twelve inches for the aisle. Nobody wore seat belts.

In the confusion and rush to escape the flames, only fifteen people managed to escape. The rest died from smoke inhalation.

Meadows and I were already near the intersection and proceeded to the collision. Cars started to pull over immediately; either to steer clear of the fire and debris on the road or to render assistance. That proved to be futile. We pulled over about thirty yards from the crash and rushed over on foot. There was little we could do. We helped the few who escaped the flames over to the side of the road and waited, like everyone else, for the firetrucks and ambulance to arrive. Make that plural, ambulances. Police were arriving in droves. Meadows ran back to the car to get something; I assumed a fire extinguisher. Not that it would do any good.

I talked to one of the surviving boys to get a head count; he wasn't sure. Meadows noticed the driver sitting by the side of the road. She walked over to him and he told her there were forty-two passengers: thirty-seven students, four adults, and him. He saw the semi barreling down on them but couldn't do anything. He was hemmed in by cars in front and back of him. He yelled for the passengers to hang on to something, that they were going to get hit. He managed to open the front door just before impact. Fortunately, the bus did not roll over. There was immediate panic. Students were scrambling to get away from the flames and there just wasn't enough room. He saw several students crawling over the seats and others were pushing and shoving from the rear and ended up knocking the ones in front down. He waited as long as he could to exit, but the smoke was just too thick and he literally fell down the stairs trying to get out.

I began walking around to see if there were any witnesses to the crash. There were a few, but the most informative was the driver in the car who had been following the tractor trailer. He said traffic was heavy and a line of cars had been behind a driver in front of the trailer for some time. He was going way too slow. Actually, he was probably traveling close to the speed limit. That was way too slow for California drivers. He had thirty or forty car lengths of open space in front of him. I can imagine the truck driver was getting irritated, as were the rest of us, and seeing an opening in the left-hand lane, decided to pass him. He got up a head of steam and pulled beside him to pass when suddenly the slower car decided he didn't want to be behind a truck . . . and he speeded up. Ridiculous. Two pissed drivers, now going way to fast, rapidly approaching the intersection. The slower driver put on his brakes, the truck tried to, but too late, it crashed into the bus.

"Do you see the car that impeded the tractor-trailer?"

"Yeah, it stopped right alongside me. I think it was an old Corvair. I use to have a '64. Never did care for it. The driver got out holding something. He was carrying it in front of him. I never saw it, but it may have been a fire extinguisher. I thought he might have been trying to help someone. I got out to help passengers exiting the bus. I never saw him again, but I noticed his car turn around and head back north on I-15. "

"How about the driver? Could you describe him?"

"Maybe six feet, looked to be in his early thirties. He had a beard and long hair. I really never got a good look at his face. Sorry."

"You're welcome. You've been a big help." I started to leave when he said, "I did get the license number of his car." I wrote it down.

I shook his hand and turned to look at the rig. The entire front of the truck's cab was still in flames, but the trailer was pretty much intact. I walked around the rear and noticed that the two large doors were open. There was no lock. I didn't think the impact of the collision would have sprung them and wondered if someone had tried to steal some of the contents. I looked inside but it looked like everything was packed tightly and no one had taken anything. They would have to inventory it later. The firetrucks had arrived, along with the ambulances. Doc Hughs was here as well, talking to Meadows. He had all his equipment with him, but it didn't appear he would need anything until the fire was out and they could extricate the victims. He started walking around the tractor-trailer just as I approached.

"Anything pertinent?" I asked Meadows.

"The lady in front of the bus said the traffic was crazy. As they approached the intersection, everything just stopped cold. She said she thought someone was in the wrong lane and just stopped until another car was nice enough to let them move over. The back-up on the freeway had already jammed. People were honking their horns impatiently."

Bob came back around. "It will be days before we can positively identify the most badly burned bodies. It may be similar to the charred women in that safe house. The others we can get with fingerprints and of course, we will have a roster of who was on board and the name of the truck driver. He's toast as well. We'll test him for any impairment."

The state police were here as well as the city police and they were directing traffic and isolating the crash site. Both lanes on I-8 west were closed, but one southbound lane on I-15 was open to allow west bound traffic onto I-8 down from the crash site. Lots of frustrated people. It's always difficult to move a huge tractor-trailer after a crash. The fire department called for a back-up trailer to come and unload the cargo before any effort to remove it. We waited about 45 minutes before another trailer pulled up and a couple of guys got out to start the off-load. The contents of the trailer were all packed in boxes of assorted sizes, all carrying the logo of the company and shipping labels. As they started to move the boxes, one of the men, in passing, noticed that a box about the size of a microwave oven was not labeled and did not have any markings on it.

"Where did this come from?" He seemed to be talking to himself.

Meadows overheard him and walked over and showed her credentials. "What are you talking about?"

"Well, everything we ship would be marked. They all came from our mail-order distributing plant so they would be packed in our own boxes. Each would have our logo and the name and address of the buyer. When they get to the end warehouse, they would go out for delivery. No box would be shipped this way without a recipient address."

"So, what's the problem?" She asked.

"This box is not ours. It has no logo and no address. Someone added it to the cargo either before it left the plant or right here."

"May I see it?"

"You can have it."

He gave it Meadows. She opened it. The driver almost gagged.

Inside was a severed head.

CHAPTER 38

Another female. Probably Hispanic from her looks. Another mystery. How did it get here? Who put it here?

We headed over to Doc Hughs and handed him the box with the severed head. We had the guy who found it sign for it, then we signed for it, and gave it to Doc. A female reporter ran over to us, paper and pen in hand. She was covering the scene of the accident, but overheard our conversation with the truck driver and witnessed his reaction. She was quite attractive.

"Pamela Raines, here with the San Diego Union. Can you tell me what happened here, Detectives?"

"You really need to talk to the Highway Patrol. They will have the big picture."

"I'm not talking about the crash. I'm talking about what you found in the box."

"That may involve a crime, Ma'am. It's something we'll have to investigate. That's all I can say at this time."

"I understand, Detective . . . Kelly?" She was staring at my badge. "If you don't mind I'll just have a word with the driver. Thanks for your cooperation."

I couldn't stop her, but I knew this was going to cause problems. "No problem, have a nice day." That's all I could think to say.

Doc was standing there holding the box. He started to leave. Not fast enough. Raines directed her attention to him. She knew who he was. Plus, he was wearing his jacket which had the letters ME stenciled on it. "Why are *you* here? Just what *is* in that box? Is this a crime scene?"

"Well . . . miss . . . ?"

"Raines."

"Ms. Raines, we are in the middle of an investigation. Unfortunately, I can't give you any information at this time."

"You can at least tell me if there is a crime involved, can't you?"

Doc smiled. "We won't know if there is a crime involved until we complete the investigation."

He turned and walked over to us. "Nosy, isn't she? I doubted if you wanted me to share this yet . . . am I correct?"

"Absolutely. This is yet another piece to our puzzle. I think I'm starting to see the picture."

Our work here was done. Doc and the police would handle the rest of it. We continued to our meeting with Jim.

As I glanced back, I could see Ms. Raines was becoming very interested in the driver's story.

We stopped at the mortuary and found Mr. Anderson inside. He was discussing a funeral arrangement with a patron. I asked him where we could find Jim Hughs. He said he should be at the crematorium. "Let me make sure." With that he excused himself and picked up the phone.

Four rings later: "Jim Hughs, can I help you?"

"Jim, I'm here in the funeral home. There are a couple of detectives that would like a word with you. Would you please come up here?"

I interrupted him and said we'd go see him. That might be easier.

"Never mind, Jim. They'll drive over to you. Just sit tight. Thanks." He looked over to us and said, "I hope this is nothing serious. Jim is such a good employee. I'd hate to lose him. He's worked for me a long time and he's never been in trouble."

"We just want to talk to him. Nothing for you to be concerned about. By the way, do you own more than one hearse?"

"No, just the one, and Jim is our only driver."

We asked for directions; it wasn't far. As we were walking out, Meadows said, "Are you kidding me? Nothing to worry about? We're talking murder, Kelly."

She drove. It only took a few minutes to the crematory.

"You seem hell bent to implicate Jim Hughs for something, Linda," I warned. "What's your theory?"

"Think about it, Kelly. He lived in the vicinity of the PSA plane crash. He was at the beach in back of the Hotel Del. That witness described a man similar to Jim driving the same kind of car as he does at the school bus crash. I'll bet he was at the safe house at one time or another. He was friends with Arthur and a Mexican on their soccer team. Could that have been Manny? One more thing: his friend Arthur worked as baggage handler at Lindbergh Field. Who better to add an additional bag tagged back to San Diego via London?"

"Okay, let's pursue your angle. But it's still very circumstantial. A good defense lawyer could even make a case that YOU are the serial killer. You were at all the scenes just like he was, except for the United crash. But if Jim will admit to being at the safe house, you've got a pretty good case for something. Here's what we'll do: we confront Jim with the knowledge that we already know he was at the safe house scene. We have a witness that saw him and another guy put a body in a hearse. They got the license number of it and it matches yours. Maybe he'll confess to something else . . ."

We entered the crematory. It was a modest-sized room housing a large cremation chamber. It looked like a pizza oven in a commercial kitchen. The outside was stainless steel with electric panels which I assumed were for regulating the temperature as well as exhaust fans and circulating pumps. There was also another machine that I later learned was for processing the remaining bone fragments to a consistent size before placing the ashes into an urn. There was a small refrigerator in the corner. Jim was standing beside a long table next to a body wrapped in a plastic sheet and bound with tape. There was another table on wheels next to that, holding a cardboard box. It looked like a coffin.

"Jim, I'm Detective Kelly, and I think you've already met Detective Meadows." We showed him our badges. He hardly looked at us, or our badges.

"If you will excuse me, I need to get this body into this box and into the retort, sorry, cremation chamber, while the fire is blazing." With that, he lifted the body into the 'coffin' and wheeled it over to the oven. He tilted the table, and the box slid into the chamber. I noticed that the flames came from above, not below as I had imagined. He closed the heavy door.

"What can I do for you detectives?" he asked.

Trying to put him a little at ease, I asked some simple questions. "Is this crematory part of the funeral home owned by Mr. Andrews, or does he contract out the service?"

"He and his family has owned this and the funeral home for many years. I've been working here since I graduated from high school."

"If you don't mind me saying, it seems a little depressing to me. How do you cope with all this death? Particularly the burning of bodies."

"I hear that all the time. People sometimes tell me that this process seems a little gruesome and disrespectful of the body. Not for me," He explained. "Unlike a burial, the cremation process is actually more pleasing than the slow decay of a body underground. To me, *that* is gruesome."

"Do you own a Corvair?" I asked. It was blunt and served to jolt his thoughts.

"Uh, yeah. Why?"

"Well, one was seen at the scene of an accident—possibly even a murder, if you will—this afternoon. The driver matched your description and the license plate number matches your car. In addition, what looked like a body was loaded into a hearse at the scene of a murder, or murders, several days ago. The license plate of the hearse also matches the license plate of the hearse you drive. Can you explain why you were at the scene of these incidents?"

"Yeah, I was at the bus accident. That stupid tractor trailer was trying to run me over. I was driving the speed limit, and he tried to pass me. I saw all the traffic up ahead and sped up hoping he would back off and slow down, but he just kept going faster. He looked over and gave me the finger as he was passing but when he looked back ahead he knew it would be too late to stop before he ran into the slow-moving traffic. To make matters worse, a school bus moved forward and stopped right in front of him. It was horrible. I got out to see if I could help, but the fire was too intense and there were many others around so I just turned around and left. I didn't think I did anything wrong."

I changed the subject. "What were you doing at that house in Chula Vista a couple of weeks ago?" He hesitated, and I knew he was thinking. Probably trying to put a spin on his actions. People always try to tell a story with a few details of their own. The word *embellish* comes to mind. I was anxious to hear Jim's.

"I got a call from Arthur, a friend of mine who said he needed some help. He said a friend of his was partying with a couple of girls and one of the girls got sick. Really sick. She started throwing up and coughing and then she passed out. The guy tried to revive her, but he knew she was dead. He thought about calling 9-1-1 or calling the cops, but he's an illegal immigrant. He knew when they checked, he would be picked up and deported. The girl was homeless, also illegal, and no one would know if she just disappeared."

I didn't interrupt. This was going to be good.

"I didn't know what to do. Arthur was my friend, and he was helping Manny."

"Manny?" I couldn't help myself.

"Oh, yeah . . . Manny. He was the guy partying with the girls. That was his nickname. I never really knew his real name. Anyway, I debated and argued with Arthur, but he finally wore me down and I agreed to come over, pick up the girl, and cremate her. Listen, I know it was wrong, but no one was supposed to know, and what did it hurt? The girl was some unknown, a nobody, and I didn't want to see my friend deported."

"How did you know Arthur?" I changed the subject again, to keep him off balance.

"Arthur?"

"You know, Arthur Reynolds. You mentioned his name earlier. You used to play soccer with him and Manny back in high school. Of course, back then Manny was Miguel. Don't you remember? You gave him the nickname, Manny." Jim was already confused. He had forgotten he had already mentioned he got a call from Arthur, a friend of his.

"Oh, that Arthur. We hardly ever saw each other after that."

"Too bad. Did you know that Arthur was murdered the other night? He told his dad that he thought someone was trying to kill him because he had gotten involved with transporting women from Tijuana into the U.S. He didn't think anyone would get hurt but now some girls had been killed and the only ones who knew about the operation was him and Manny and Jim Hughs."

I had him now.

"Jesus, I had nothing to do with that! All I did was pick up that dead girl. Arthur told me it was all Manny's idea. The whole operation of transporting girls to that safe house to L.A., San Francisco, and Phoenix. They were just a go-between. You need to talk to Manny. He gave me his number and contact in 'Frisco. Here, I've got it in my billfold."

I wrote the name and number down, but I doubted it was real.

"What did Arthur tell you about the drug operation?" I baited him. "Quit playing dumb. We already know all about it. Maybe you can fill us in on more of the details."

"Okay. Listen, I'll tell you everything I know. But you have to believe me, I had nothing to do with the sex trafficking or the drug running. I picked up a dead girl for Manny, and I held a little money to cover for Arthur. That's it."

"Let's start with your arrival at the safe house. Who called you?"

"Arthur actually called me. Manny must have called him. I met Arthur at the safe house and he helped me load the girl's body into the hearse and then he rode with me to the crematory."

"Was Manny there?"

"Where?"

"At the safe house."

"Yes, but he was just guarding the other girls. They were upset about the dead girl. I asked Manny how the girl died and he said she was sick. He didn't know why, but he wanted her out of there in case she was contagious."

"Did you talk to Arthur on the way to the crematory?"

"Yeah. But I swear I had nothing to do with this and if I had known what was going on I would never have picked up that girl."

"Go on."

"Okay. Arthur said the sex trafficking was just a cover for the drug operation. The girls served as the distraction. I don't know how that happened, but Arthur said it was ingenious. He thought Manny was the boss. Arthur's job was just to monitor the gangs and drug running in the San Diego area. He'd lived there all his life and knew the drug areas and where the buys were made. He had friends who kept him informed regarding where the drugs were coming from . . . for a price. They never interfered. There was a mutual understanding about their business and the business at the safe house. No one wanted to cause a disturbance or get the police or media involved. Moving the girls only two at a time in a van that could hold ten meant there was plenty of room for drugs. It also didn't overload the truck if it had to stop at a weigh station somewhere. Arthur told me the girls and the drugs were transported together using a tunnel between Tijuana and an industrial area across the border into the U.S. They hired their own mechanics to create spaces to hide the drugs. The vans the college kids drove carried 600–800 pounds of cocaine, heroin, or marijuana hidden in the tail lights, compartments under the seats and altered glove compartments. The bigger truck's entire undercarriage contained compartments for the drugs. Arthur laughed because he thought the FBI hadn't even checked the vehicles they confiscated from the sex trafficking bust. They're probably still packed with drugs in some holding lot."

"Do you know where the industrial area is in that they pick up the girls?"

"No. Like I said before, the only involvement I had was to pick up that one dead girl. I made a mistake. I'm sorry."

"How do you know all this?" Meadows asked. Jim was starting to sound like he was a bigger part of this operation than he let on.

"Like I said, Arthur drove with me to the crematory. After we had burned the body and disposed the ashes, I drove him back to his car still parked at the safe house. We stopped for a beer along the way. After a couple or more, he got more talkative. He even joked that Manny's little enterprise was so successful and efficient at moving drugs across the border that he was even thinking about building more tunnels and adding features like ventilation systems and electric lights in addition to the track and carts. The tunnel he was currently using only stretched about a hundred yards, but he was thinking about tunneling even farther."

"Anything else you can think of?" Kelly asked. "I know you think you were just a pawn in this whole thing, but I'm not totally convinced. Right now, we could arrest you for secretly transporting that body without notifying proper authorities. With what you just told us, you'd probably just get a slap on the wrist and a fine. You might also get fired. Look, I don't think you are a crook. I don't think you were involved in the sex trafficking or the drug business. I've looked up your record and the only offense you've ever committed was an illegal turn. As a favor to your brother, Bob, I'm going to give you a break. You only get one. Keep your nose clean and if Manny ever contacts you again, notify us immediately."

With that, we left.

I don't know who was more surprised, Jim . . . or Meadows.

Meadows didn't say a word, out loud. She just stared at me. She looked, to put it mildly, incredulous.

MEADOWS

They walked, in complete silence, out the door. Kelly got into the driver's side; she had already chosen shotgun. The only sound was the door closing. Kelly started the car. The silence didn't last long.

"Are you shitting me? You let him off? Jesus, he's clearly guilty of transporting a body illegally, but aren't you forgetting about something else? What about the severed heads? Circumstantial, sure, but enough to prosecute. Why are you protecting him? Again, are you shitting me?"

"You're right. I mean, no, I'm not shitting you . . . as you so delicately put it. The mystery of those heads is exactly why I let him off easy. I think we should give him some rope. We really don't have enough evidence to hold him for the murders. In fact, we don't even know he committed the murders. Those heads could have come from dead bodies. Lord knows, he's got many to choose from. And we're not the only ones protecting him. Bob is too. Remember how he directed us back to the safe house? He wanted us to clear him from that operation. Bob knows something about Jim that we also don't know. Too many unknowns. I think we should keep a close watch on Jim and go from there. Besides, our first order of business is to contact Agent Smith and the FBI again. Drug smuggling is definitely right up his alley."

"All right. I take back all those nasty words I wasn't calling you out loud. But I'm sure you heard them."

"That I did, Linda. My ears are still burning." They both laughed. I was thinking, "Maybe we should talk to Doc. He might be able to tell us whether the victims were still alive when the heads were cut off. If they weren't, that would give further credence to Jim's involvement."

"Great idea. Tomorrow, we notify the FBI."

CHAPTER 39

Unfortunately, the shit hit the fan before that. Lt. Hill decided, rightly I'm sure, to release the photo of the severed head Doc had sent over to him. An hour later, an example of what was about to displayed prominently on the front page of the *San Diego Union* was sent over. The message was clear, the reporter wanted more information or an inflammatory article like this might be published creating a whirlwind of bad press.

> **"SERIAL KILLER?"**
> *Another severed head. How many more will have to be discovered before the police department intends to notify its citizens of the danger. Within the last three or four months, three isolated heads have been found, "that we know of." Yesterday the head of a young Hispanic female was found in the back of a delivery truck at the scene of that tractor-trailer/school bus accident. There was no body, just the head. Our investigation has also discovered a severed head was found in a suitcase amidst the horrific PSA plane crash months ago. Yet another was found at the end of Ocean Boulevard in Coronado. There have been no explanations for any of them. These are clearly not accidents. This paper is calling on our police department to give us answers. Is this the work of a serial killer? What are they trying to hide?*

LT got a call soon after. "Lieutenant, this is Pamela Raines. Did you get the copy of the article and picture I sent to you? We haven't published this . . . yet. I sent that as a courtesy to you. I didn't want this to be blown out of proportion before I completely understood all the facts. We have always had a good relationship with the police, and I do not want to do anything to jeopardize that."

"I appreciate that, Ms. Raines. I really don't like talking over the phone, though. I will be happy to make my lead detective available to you if you'd like. He is currently handling this issue."

"Thank you, Lieutenant . . . his name?"

"Kelly, Sergeant Joe Kelly."

"Is he available today? How can I reach him?"

"Not sure, I'll radio him and try to set up a time for you to meet. I know he is busy. What is your number?"

"She gave him her office number and then warned: I can wait a day or two . . . but we can't sit on this much longer. As far as I know I am the only one with this information. Television crews were at the scene of the school bus crash too. I don't know if they were aware of the severed head. If they sniff that out, they may not be so accommodating."

"I understand, let me give him a buzz." He hung up swearing to himself.

We put in a personal call to FBI Agent Smith. Was that his real name? Anyway, after a short hold he came to the phone.

"Smith here. Is this Detective Kelly?"

"No. It's Detective Meadows, but Kelly is standing near."

"That's okay, what can I do for you, Detective?"

"We think that bust we had of that sex trafficking operation was just a cover-up for a much larger drug running scheme. That's beyond our scope of business. We're turning it over to you guys."

"Thanks for thinking so highly of us, but that business falls squarely in the hands of the Drug Enforcement Agency. Let me put you in contact with someone I know there that can help you. Maybe he can grease the wheels a little to make things happen. By the way, he is already aware of it. We found a ton of dope in the trucks we confiscated."

He searched in his wallet for a card and finding the one he wanted, read the name and number to Meadows.

"Make sure you tell him I referred you. By the way, I really want to thank you and Detective Kelly for all your help in bringing down those trafficking folks. I put Kelly in for a citation with LT. Hill. He surely deserves it. Hopefully, he is fully recovered from his wounds."

"You're welcome. Kelly has healed nicely. He's his same old grumpy self again," she laughed. "Say, what's your first name? Agent Smith sounds a little too convenient to me."

"It's John." And he hung up.

They called the DEA. The agent's name was Mendez. Roger Mendez. He told them he had been with the agency a long time and was quite familiar with the various drug cartels running drugs. At the present time, most of the drugs were coming in from the Gulf Coast, but they were starting to see an uptick from Mexico. He said we may have uncovered this early operation. He agreed to meet with us at our police station tomorrow around nine. He had business in that area tomorrow and would already be near us.

I gave him our names and numbers and told him we looked forward to the meet.

We hung up at the same time.

We decided to talk to Doc Hughs and headed over to the morgue.

I drove. I was in a talkative mood today.

"Do we really think Doc's brother severed all those heads? He could have. He has the bodies already. If Doc tells us they've all been dead for many hours before they were found, we have a pretty good case, don't you think?"

Kelly paused, "I don't really know what to think. I'm not even sure Manny, or Miguel, or whatever his name is couldn't have planned the murders himself. He might not have done it himself, but one of his henchmen could . . . just to cause further distraction of his main business: drug running. You've got to admit; the sex trafficking was pretty ingenious. If it hadn't been for Jim picking up that body, he'd still be in business."

"Wow! I hadn't even considered that. Even so, Jim's hiding something. He's still too evasive with his answers."

We pulled into the loading dock. It was the fastest way into the building from the parking lot. Doc wasn't there. One of the attendants told us he was in his office.

"Good morning, Doc. We've got a couple of questions we need to clear up."

"Good morning Detective Meadows, Joe. Glad to help. Pull up some chairs and get comfortable. What's on your mind?"

"The severed heads. Can you determine whether the heads were cut off before or after they were dead?"

"I wish I could, but I can't. It would be possible if I had the body and it was still at the scene of the incident. If the head was severed while alive, the heart would be beating and blood spatter would be everywhere. I think I mentioned that when we found the two bodies earlier. Regardless, once the head is decapitated, the blood will drain; either alive or dead. I can already guess your next question: How long were the heads kept before you found them? Right?"

"Right. It would be helpful to know if the heads were severed awaiting an accident or if the body was kept alive until just an after accident happened."

"That I can help you with. Although without the entire body it is unlikely I can give you a firm date as to the severing. Let me give you some background in the way a body decomposes. There are several processes. When the heart stops beating, blood stops flowing and it tends to gravitate to the lowest points of the body. That's called Livor Mortis. We can get an idea of how long a body has been laying somewhere by the density of the color. You already know about rigor mortis. Once the dying process begins, almost immediately, oxygen is deprived to the cells of the body. Without it, a process called anaerobic fermentation begins which produces a byproduct called lactic acid. That's what causes rigor mortis. Within ten minutes to several hours, the joints and muscles begin to stiffen. The face begins first. When the body is present, bacterial cells in the abdomen rapidly break down flesh which releases digestive enzymes which in turn are free to digest other tissue. Four to ten days later, gases are produced, causing a terrible smell, bloating, insect infestation, and so on. That leads us to algor mortis. The body usually loses about 1.4 degrees Fahrenheit every hour from the ambient temperature. That can vary according to the weather. So, depending on the state of the body and the temperature of the organs, we can pretty accurately determine the time of death. Without the body, the head is not exposed to those digestive enzymes; blood has been drained; body temperature if difficult to assess, and it is much more difficult to pinpoint death. If Rigor is present, we can assume death occurred within 36 to 72 hours. If is not present, death would have occurred sometime after that . . . or before rigor began: ten minutes or so. I don't think that pertains in this case. Does that help?"

"The biology class was helpful, but . . . can you tell us when our heads were severed?"

"They were all dead for at least 36 to 72 hours."

"You realize, Doc, that all the evidence we have so far really implicates your brother. It's only circumstantial though, and Kelly has been quick to point out that the evidence could also be explained differently to implicate others as well."

Kelly interjected. "Bob. We believe that Jim is not telling us the whole truth about his actions. He is hiding something. I don't want to see you get hurt in this. If Jim has told you something that you are not sharing with us, you need to come forward. If we do find out that Jim is guilty, and you have not been forthright, you could be guilty of abetting a crime. We don't want that to happen."

"I know, Joe. But I'm just as perplexed in this as you are. I don't think Jim is involved in murder. If he *is* cutting off the heads of corpses, I can promise you I am not aware of it; I cannot guarantee that he isn't. He's my brother. I've been protecting him my whole life; I won't protect him from murder."

"Let's hope we're wrong and the evidence leads us elsewhere. For now, it's pretty strong in Jim's direction. Thanks for your help, Doc, we need to head back to the station. Sorry if we upset you . . . and you're right, it could be someone else."

CHAPTER 40

"What do we do now? I'm in favor of lunch and then heading back to the station and going over the case, once again. It always seems to stimulate another thought when we do. Besides, we've got nothing going on until we meet with Roger somebody in the DEA tomorrow."

"You're driving." Kelly was too absorbed in thought.

We stopped at a Subway. Neither of us was particularly hungry. He had a six-inch BMT on Honey Oat and I had the same. Only I made mine into a salad. No bun; chopped. With oil and vinegar dressing, not bad. We got them to go. At the station, we got coffee from the shared pot. Usually hot. When it wasn't, we heard about it.

KELLY

"You want to recap, let's start with what we know: First, we have four severed heads, not counting the two you found in the refrigerator, or Arthur. According to Doc, all the heads had been severed at least 36 to 72 hours before they were found. That might indicate that the victims were killed awaiting an accident or incidence to occur, not killed just after the incident. Perhaps they were placed in a refrigerator or something to preserve them. Why were they only placed at the scene of accidents?

Second, there are at least two persons, and maybe more, that we can, with a little imagination, place at the scene of the discovery of the heads. You . . . I know . . . I know, and Jim Hughs. There is a valid possibility that Manny or Miguel or whomever is also responsible, and the more we dig into this, the more I get the feeling he is.

Three. Manny, Arthur, and Jim were all involved in the sex trafficking affair at that safe house. Arthur is dead, Manny is nowhere to be found, and we just exonerated Jim . . . for now.

Which brings me to four. Manny said he was sorry to lose his best man, Chico, at Anita's house. Was Chico part of Manny's sex trafficking or one of his hitmen in the drug business? We know the drug smuggling is still going on. Will Manny need to replace him? I think finding a new face might lead us to Manny.

"We definitely need to talk to Roger Mendez."

"What now?" asked Meadows.

"Good question. Let's go home. I think we're in for a long day tomorrow with the DEA."

I can't imagine that they suspect me. Still, I'm not going to be able to hide what I'm doing much longer. Maybe I can distract them with a more credible suspect. I hate doing that to an innocent person, but I may have no choice. I have an idea. It's time to alert the media. They've only seen two female heads and male over in Coronado, but neither of the two PSA crashes. I think I'll give them a hint about the second one . . . the one they didn't put on the news. They must be curious now. And still no comment from authorities. It's perfect, but I need another girl. Then they'll start digging. Where to look this time . . .

I was half way home when my radio buzzed. It was LT Hill. "Yes sir."

"Why do you insist on calling me, *sir*? How about boss, or your highness . . . anything but sir. For some reason, it makes me feel old."

"Sorry, sir. It's the Navy in me. I'll try to remember that from now on, your holiness!" They both laughed.

"Kelly, we've got a problem. A reporter for the Union just called me. She knows about the head you found at the tractor-trailer accident. To make matters worse, she researched the PSA crash in '78 and the discovery of *that* head and she somehow got wind of a solitary head found off the coast of Coronado after the second PSA crash. I think it's safe to assume she was at the scene of the Reynolds' murder in Coronado as well. She smells a story. I told her she could reach out to you to get the details but she is impatient. We need to give her something soon or the picture of a head is going to make the front page along with some op-ed that will not make us look good at all."

"I was afraid of that. Was her name Raines?"

"Let me see; I wrote it down . . . just a second . . . yeah, Pamela Raines."

"She was nearby when we found the head. I didn't give her much information, but I'm sure the truck driver was more than obliging. Okay, I'll talk to her. How much info are we sharing?"

"Well, she already knows about the PSA crash of '78. I was hoping we could keep that under wraps. The male in Coronado could easily be discounted as an isolated event . . . *or* . . . we could lump them all together as part of that sex trafficking operation we just put an end to. I don't know if she knows about the male and female killed in National City. Their heads were severed too."

"Let's go with the retaliation angle. Somebody snitched and ruined their business running girls. A message was sent for everyone to see. Media exposure made the message even clearer. What better message than a severed head of your competitor?"

"Sounds reasonable. Unfortunately, I really do think the severed heads found without the bodies are the work of a serial killer. I'm not sure how much longer we can keep this controlled. I am going to tell her about the two heads we found in the refrigerator in National City, though. Giving her a little more information might make her trust our story more. What's her number?"

Writing it down, the mention of the press triggered a thought: "By the way, how much exposure did we get for putting an end to that sex trafficking ring?"

"Oh, that's right . . . I forgot about your *fake* injury." He laughed. "You were taking a few days off in the hospital when that came out. Front page stuff. Made us look pretty good. We got some good press out of that. The FBI was more than generous with their praise and they even mentioned your name in passing. I think Agent Smith even put you in for some kind of citation. Fat chance of that ever happening." He laughed again, and hung up.

I called Raines. She picked up on the first ring. Was she waiting by the phone for my call? *She's anxious . . . and impatient*, I thought.

"Pamela Raines. How can I help you?"

"Good afternoon. I'm Detective Kelly. I believe Lieutenant Hill gave you my name. How can I help *you*?"

"Well, I'm sure he briefed you on the matter . . . but there are far too many holes. I need more detail. I was hoping you could fill in the holes before I had to run an incomplete and not particularly complementary article questioning your police tactics in the paper."

"He did, and I'll be happy to give you what I can. You know the drill. Some details are confidential while the investigation is still in progress. Perhaps you would like to meet me later and we could discuss filling in your holes?"

She laughed. "You make this sound exciting, Detective!" She paused, then . . . "Forgive me, where and when?"

"This afternoon is good. How about we meet around four. I've got some business near Point Loma . . . do you know where that coffee house called 'the Living Room' is?"

"I think so. The two-story building on Rosecrans? That's been there forever."

"That's the one. How about we meet there at four?"

"Meet you there," and we both hung up together.

She got there first. As I walked in she signaled me with her hand and I sat down across the table from her.

"I haven't ordered anything. Do you want something or should we get right to the point?"

A waitress came over. "Coffee, black." There went the Navy in me again.

"Just a glass of ice tea, unsweetened, please. Thank you."

"Do I call you Detective, or Sergeant?"

"Call me Kelly, please. It's easier and far less intimidating than detective. No one calls me Sergeant. I was in the Navy, not the Marines. Why don't you tell me what you already know?"

"Okay. There have been a rash of heads without bodies being found in this area for some time. I know you know I am aware of the man found headless in Coronado. Arthur Reynolds. I also know about the United Airline's crash where the coroner found a head in a suitcase and now we have the head found at the school bus accident. I've been looking at other accident scenes as well. In our archives I found notice of a severed head discovered at the scene of that PSA crash over in North Park in 1978. That got very little press and I could not find out if that head was accounted for. What's going on? Who's doing this? Is this the work of one person or gang related? I'm starting to think we have a serial killer at large. What do you think?"

"I'm not sure. How much can I trust you? I can't reveal my conclusions without assurance that you won't publish them. The most probable explanation is that these murders have been made by organized crime. There are huge profits to be made in illegal drugs and sex trafficking. Competition among smugglers can lead to violence. Your paper did a nice article about the sex trafficking operation we put out of business a few months ago. That resulted in bodies as well. A man and a woman were shot and decapitated in National City in retaliation for them killing three women in a safe house in Chula Vista.

These gangs do not just kill people to eliminate competition . . . they also want to make sure no one wants to forget. What better way than by cutting off their heads. That gets television and newspaper coverage."

"So, you think all these severed heads are related to gang or cartel activity? It's all about publicity?"

"That's one theory."

"You have another?"

"Let's make a deal. If I tell you another theory, you have to agree not to run with it. In return, *if* and when we solve this case, I will give you an exclusive interview with all the details. What do you say to that?"

"I don't like deals. I *will* agree to publish only what you have said about the murders and severed heads being gang related retaliation. I can surmise your other theory points to a serial killer. That I will keep under my hat . . . but if there is another head discovered, I'm going to have to let people know. They need to be aware and vigilant. Their life may depend upon it."

"Well, that's the deal. Take it or leave it. It's the best I can do right now."

I finished my coffee. There didn't seem to be anything more to say. For the first time, I looked at her . . . I mean really looked. Nice figure . . . and teeth . . . and eyes. She was between twenty-five and thirty years old. Pretty. Brown hair . . . she wore it down over her shoulders. Five-six, maybe; I remembered her from the school bus scene. Definitely shorter than Meadows. An eight out of ten. I pushed my chair back, laid ten bucks on the table, and started to excuse myself.

"What's your hurry? Got a date?"

"Actually, I do. Tomorrow morning, with a DEA agent. Boring. Nice meeting you." And I turned to leave.

"Kelly . . . remember, we have a deal!"

CHAPTER 41

Agent Mendez met us at the precinct at 0930. He had just finished investigating another bust of cocaine distribution in the city. He told us the environment was changing. "Since the '60s, the majority of drug smuggling involved marijuana and occasionally heroin. True to form, the government didn't see cocaine as being as much of a threat as the aforementioned drugs and we lost our focus on all the other drugs. Money and manpower dried up. Cocaine then became the drug of choice during the late '70s. Columbian cartels are now bringing large quantities of cocaine into the country making the drug more available and less expensive. To make matters worse, they are circulating false rumors that the drug is not addictive. Coke basically makes you feel invincible. It also heightens sexual enjoyment and arousal. That has helped spread its image as the *party drug*. The problem is that it only lasts a short time, and then you crave more."

"Do you know where the cocaine is coming from?" I asked.

"No. We do know from various sources that a drug lord from the state of Sinaloa, Mexico, a man named Pedro Aviles Perez may be the major distribution of marijuana. But knowing his name and apprehending him is another matter. First, you have to find him. Second, you need the cooperation of the Mexican government. Unfortunately, many of the politicians have either been paid off or have had their families threatened. They are no help. The local police are worse. Many of them actually work for the cartel. These cartels are vicious. The amount of money to be made in illegal drugs is staggering, and the United States is a major buyer. If people want to use drugs, there will always be drug smugglers. Because of this, there are competing smugglers and tariff wars leading to many killings, both here and in Mexico."

"We haven't seen a rash of killings related to drugs here in San Diego," interjected Meadows.

"For good reason. It's important to remember, these cartel leaders are not uneducated Mexican laborers working in the fields. They are sophisticated businessmen and they are extremely resistant to interlopers. There's a new player named Lopez who has already made a name for himself as one of the most violent. He's known in Mexico as El Conejo . . . the rabbit. He's not even forty years old yet."

"We're pretty sure either he or one of his hitmen killed a man named Arthur Reynolds a while ago. I'm sure Arthur knew too much and knew who 'Manny" really was," I interrupted.

"Manny?"

"Sorry. The guy who was actually running the sex-trafficking operation went by Manny. He had fingerprints that matched an ID we had to the name Miguel. Obviously false. Jim mentioned the name Fermin Lopez. We weren't aware of the connection you mentioned."

"Understood. El Conejo doesn't take prisoners. I would imagine the other guys running drugs in San Diego do not interfere with his operations. Smith told me about the guy who killed the girls and burned them at that safe house. He probably didn't realize it involved drugs and was just trying to eliminate competition to his sex trafficking operation. Unfortunately for him, the Rabbit didn't care. Notice he cut their heads off. That's a sign that the victim is inconsequential. Was Arthur shot?"

"No, they cut off his head."

"If it had been a higher up, he would have been tortured, beaten, and shot in the head . . . more than once. It sends a message . . ."

"And to think we had him in jail already . . . and let him go. Unbelievable." Meadows again.

"Look, don't blame yourself. This guy is really good at disappearing. And he killed the guy that bailed him out so he wouldn't talk! I'm really surprised he didn't kill everyone associated with that safe house operation because I'm sure he tortured Arthur and got lots of names before he cut off his head."

That thought troubled me . . . I wasn't sure why. Did Arthur confess that he had told Jim about the drug operation? Jim may be as good as dead . . .

"The guy just doesn't take chances. People are like pawns in a game of chess to him. He will sacrifice everyone to insure his business succeeds. He probably got it from his father, who started out as a rancher but soon discovered how lucrative drugs were and began growing opium.

Here's what we know: Lopez dropped out of school in the third grade and with few opportunities to earn money, started his own business growing marijuana. That must have pissed his father off because he kicked him out of the house. Lopez, perhaps fearing for his safety, fled with his brother to the U.S. Being short, he was able to pass for ten or twelve, and after getting a fake ID, became Miguel Rodriguez. He was also a pretty good soccer player. He became friends with a few boys on the area traveling soccer team. You just told me they nicknamed him 'Manny.' It wasn't long before he saw an opportunity to transport his drugs into the U.S. across the border."

"I don't get it. If you know all of this, why haven't you been able to stop it?"

"Mainly, because we didn't know all this until you uncovered the sex-trafficking operation. But that's not it entirely. I'll give you two more reasons: One, up until now, our concentration on smuggling has been on the East Coast. That's where most of the narcotics are coming into. There's one particular drug lord, a woman, no less, who is believed to be the key to the cocaine distribution in the East. She's known as the 'Godmother of Cocaine'; drug lord of the Medellin Cartel. She started in Queens, New York City, and has recently moved to warmer climes in Miami. I think she is as vicious as they come. Since she's moved, the streets of Miami are covered with blood and cocaine.

"Two, we didn't have a firm grasp of the drug smuggling operation here in San Diego. It appeared to us to be just a few locals, so we only concentrated our efforts at stopping the smuggling at the border. As you know, that has been proven to be all but impossible. We use dogs who are very efficient and reliable, but it's too easy to avoid the traffic stops at the borders and utilize the vast areas that are unguarded between vehicle crossings."

"But now you are aware they are using a tunnel, or tunnels. And you've got to admit, combining the drug smuggling with sex trafficking and hiring that con artist to use college boys to do Manny . . . or Lopez's . . . dirty work, was pretty smart."

"No objections there. We are just lucky your good detective work was able to uncover and put an end to that so-called *entrepreneurship*. With your help, we have pinpointed the location, or at least the area, of the tunnel they used and should be able to ferret out any still existing operation. We can't be sure they are still using the same tunnel since you stopped the distribution via the sex trafficking route, but they may not be aware that we know of the tunnel yet.

We are pretty sure the tunnel originates in an area just south of the border called Garita de Otay. It would be chosen for two reasons. First, it's in the middle of buildings and infrastructure on both sides of the border which could facilitate secretive construction and has heavy industrial activity which helps to conceal other activity. Secondly, Otay Mesa, a suburb of San Diego, sits on a plateau that stretches across the border and is made up of a kind of clay that is self-supporting and workable like wax. This makes it sturdier than typical soil so you can dig down into it and carve out a tunnel without bracing to reinforce the passageway. We've had our engineers studying it."

We're planning a raid in a day or two. Unfortunately, you cannot not be invited . . . but we will keep you informed."

I was about to object, when Agent Mendez interrupted, "Officially. You are both welcome to be with us in an *unofficial* capacity. Kind of like when you tagged along with the FBI . . . but we know how that ended up, don't we?" He smiled. "Tomorrow, you are invited to come to our DEA headquarters and listen in on our planning for the raid. Nine o'clock sharp. That is, if your boss will give you the time off. I don't think this will amount to more than a couple of days. I'll leave your names at the information desk at the entrance. The security guard will direct you to our conference room. We're on the second floor."

Lt. Hill was all in on the raid and our participation. If this was successful, we surely would see a decrease in drugs in our area and the crime associated with it. We were told to take the next day off and prepare for the raid. It would probably begin after nightfall and might take several nights before any smuggling occurred.

Meadows and I were both okay with that. We had been going strong for several days now and I was still sore from the gun-shot wound. We were all smiles as we headed out of the station to our respective cars.

Meadows spoke first. "I heard you had a meeting with that female reporter we spoke to at the school bus crash. What was that all about?"

I filled her in.

"What was she like? I mean, the way she flipped her hair when she was talking to you made it pretty obvious she was impressed."

"You're kidding me. I didn't even notice."

"Most men wouldn't . . . but believe me, women notice those things."

"Are you jealous?" I laughed. "She's a reporter. She wanted to know all about the severed heads. That's it."

"Right. Are you going to see her again?"

"Say good night, Linda. It's time to go home."

162

CHAPTER 42

"Ms. Raines? We need to talk." She was standing outside the coffee shop she frequented most mornings before heading to her nearby newspaper's office. A short man had approached her. "It's about Detective Kelly . . . something you really need to know about him."

She was confused. "What do you mean? Is he in danger . . . did he do something wrong? What's this all about?"

"Let's just say, what I know will put you on the map. It may be the story of the year. Come with me where we can talk. I promise you, you will not be sorry."

"I can't just hop in a car with you. I don't even know you. Tell me here . . . right now. I'm not going with you anywhere," She wasn't going to be intimidated.

"No problem, señora, there are other reporters." He turned and began walking away.

"Wait! Maybe we can meet somewhere. I have a car." The reporter in her overtook her wariness.

"As you wish. Meet me in the parking lot of Jack Murphy Stadium . . . the southeast section. Thirty minutes. Come alone." The man turned and left.

Jack Murphy Stadium was close. The San Diego Union was in Mission Valley, only a mile or two away.

He was standing by his vehicle as she approached. Theirs were the only cars in the lot. She parked alongside his and got out. "Okay. What's this all about? Why all the cloak and dagger mystery?"

"I'm about to tell you, Ms. Raines. Can I call you Pamela?" With that, he pulled a gun out of his jacket and pointed it at her. "But we really need to go somewhere more private. Please get into the car."

"I'm not going anywhere with you. That gun doesn't scare me. You wouldn't dare use it out here. Too many eyes and ears in this area."

Unfortunately, she hadn't noticed the other man who was in the car. He was walking near her now . . . he had a gun as well . . . and he stuck it in her back. The first man quickly grabbed both of her arms and jerked them together before tying them with a piece of rope.

"In the car . . . now."

She was feeling a little less brazen now and did as she was told, sliding in the back seat with the gun holder beside her. The original man got into the driver's seat and they drove away.

She had a thousand questions, but was told just to shut up. She complied.

What seemed like thirty minutes passed and they came to an old house off of Highway 15 North. She didn't know if she should be nervous because she had seen their faces or relieved because there was nothing to be concerned about. Maybe the guns were only needed to overcome her initial resistance. She was scared; none the less.

As soon as she entered the house, she was taken into a back room, where a man was standing on a large plastic sheet. "You talk too much. It's bad for business." With that, Manny shot her in the head. "Undress her and put her in the trunk. We'll put her body somewhere where it will be easy to find, but I'll take her head . . . maybe we'll give it to someone who will appreciate the irony."

CHAPTER 43

DOC

The phone rang. It was the lieutenant down at the precinct. This was getting old. "Don't tell me you found another severed head."

"Yes . . . and no."

"That's confusing, what's up? "

"A patrolman found a body, but the severed head . . . is missing."

"Where is it? I'll be there as soon as I can."

"It's over by the stadium, near the school bus collision. It's just north of I-8 maybe 100 yards onto I-15. You'll see the police vehicles. Meadows and Kelly are already there."

I got there fairly quickly. The traffic wasn't too bad, for a change. There were two patrol vehicles and Kelly's car parked along the road. They had blocked off one north bound lane on I-15. Yellow tape outlined the crime scene.

"Where is the body?"

"Over there, Doc, in the weeds."

It was a female body. Obviously dead. The missing head was my first clue. She was nude, lying on her back. Her arms were folded neatly in her lap. It was also obvious that they were staged: she was holding a note pad and pen in them.

I tried to lift her arm; it was stiff. Rigor. There was little pooling of blood. I was pretty sure she had been killed elsewhere and dropped here.

"Any idea who this might have been? Surely this wasn't from the bus crash."

"Not a chance, Doc. I think the notepad is the clue. Who did we see recently with a notepad and pen?"

"Raines? The reporter?"

"Just a guess, but I think fingerprints will confirm it. I've already had our LT contact the newspaper to see if they had hers on file. They told him all of their employees have had background checks. They would have hers."

"Okay, let's get her back to the morgue. I'll be able to better pinpoint time of death there, now that we have a body."

The ME's transport ambulance soon arrived and the body was carried inside.

"I'll give you my results as soon as I get back to the morgue. Get a hold of the Union and tell them to deliver her prints to my office. It's possible it's not her. Has anyone called her home or place of work to determine if she's missing?"

Meadows answered. "When I radioed our LT and asked him to call the paper asking for her prints they told him she had not appeared for work this morning. That wasn't all that unusual, though. She often was out researching a case or following up on a lead. She also does not answer her home phone."

"Got it. Call you later . . ."

I followed the ambulance to the morgue.

The fingerprints arrived about the time we got there. It was a definite match. Why would anyone kill Raines? Did it have to do with the severed head case or was she too close to another investigation? At any rate, somebody wanted to silence her.

I checked her body temperature. Usually from the liver or other internal organ. The ambient temperature outside was a warm 73 degrees which wouldn't affect the cooling process significantly. Normal body temperature is around 98.6 degrees. Her internal temperature was now 94.8 degrees. She'd been dead for about 2 and a half hours. It was now 11:00 A.M. Sometime around 8 A.M. this morning she'd met her demise. There was very little blood splatter so unless she'd been washed, she was dead before she was beheaded. I looked for signs of trauma, but could find none. Her hands had been tied at one point, you could see the imprint of the rope around her wrists. Perhaps she'd been shot in the head.

I called the police station. Kelly and Meadows were both there. I gave them all the information I had obtained.

"Thanks, Doc. This is a real puzzler. Meadows and I have been trying to figure out who and why someone would want her out of the way. I'm going to head over to her office and see what cases she was working on. Maybe that will give us a lead of some sort."

Meadows interjected, "Maybe this is another taunt: we get the body this time, but no head. Could this still be the work of our serial killer? "

KELLY

The newspaper didn't offer much. The main thing she had been working on was the case of the severed heads. To me, that meant either the killer thought she was getting too close, or he was taunting us as Meadows suggested, or . . . it was the work of the cartel again. Another message?

I headed back to the station. Meadows was at her desk.

"What did you find out?"

"Nothing we didn't already know. I don't know where to look either."

"Okay, no more questions . . . what are your plans? I'm going home and take a long soak in my hot tub, have a glass of wine, and listen to the surf."

"I really hadn't given it much thought. I'll probably head on home. I need to clean the house, vacuum the rugs, and wash the car. That escapade I had up north also reminded me how cluttered my garage was. I think I'll clean it out as well. And I need to get more milk."

She looked at me strangely. "Tell me you're joking, please!"

We both laughed. "Actually, I had been hoping Pamela would call." She gave me a dirty look and half smacked me across the shoulder.

"That's not funny. "

"Or . . . maybe a friend of mine would invite me over to her house . . . maybe have a glass or two of wine, soak in a nice warm hot tub, and watch the sunset. I wouldn't mind listening to the surf either."

She got in her car and rolled down the window. "I'll meet you there."

CHAPTER 44

She beat me handily, partly because I stopped for some Chinese along the way. I got my favorites: Moo goo gai pan, cashew chicken, beef with broccoli, and chow mein noodles. I am definitely not a connoisseur. But I won't go hungry, either.

When I got there, the front door was open. I yelled to let her know I was here and closed and locked the door behind me . . . force of habit.

"I'm out back, by the hot tub. Put on your suit and join me."

What suit? I put the food on the kitchen table and walked out onto her deck. She was standing next to the hot tub, her back to me, completely naked. She stepped over the edge and slowly sank into the warm water. She slid down the side of the tub and turned around. Her breasts seemed to be floating on the bubbles. The nipples were erect. So was I . . .

"Come on in, she beckoned, the waters' fine."

I took my clothes off, down to my boxers, and climbed in. The water was not just warm, it was hot. I winced as I eased my balls into the water. She laughed and pulled my boxers off. As I sat down, she crawled over and straddled my lap and we embraced. She kissed me softly, using her tongue; she was so warm and tender. I'd forgotten what it was like to have feelings for someone. I kissed her back, a little harder. With one hand I put my arm around her and with the other I caressed her breast. She inched up a little higher, placing the nipple of her breast close to my mouth, begging me to kiss it. As I did, and flicked my tongue over it, she reached down and grabbed my member while manipulating her hips just so, allowing me to enter her. She moved sensually, slowly, until the lips of her vagina were soon touching my belly. We were totally connected. I sat still, letting her enjoy her movements. She continued for a while, then sat up, and climbed out of the tub and lay on the soft cushion alongside.

"This is much easier, out of the water," she said. I wasn't going to argue and got out of the tub, still quite erect. She rolled over on her stomach, got on her knees, and I entered her from behind. "My favorite position," she cooed.

I was really hot, and try as I may, I couldn't contain myself and ejaculated inside her way too quickly.

"You needed that," she said. "You've been too wound up lately. I thought a little 'in-and-out' would do you good." And she laughed.

"Now, after you've had a little rest, it's my turn."

She got up and re-entered the hot tub. She lay there, soaking in the warmth. Then she started to caress herself. Her hands knew just how to touch . . . and where. She spread her legs slightly and rubbed her fingers over the lips of her vagina, slowly parting them. She rubbed her self, slowly at first, then faster. She was totally in the moment, but when I thought she was going to climax, she quit. She got out of the tub again, and lay on her back. Spreading her legs, and bending her knees, she looked at me and said, "I need your help, please."

I lay between her legs and spread the lips again with both thumbs; her sex was red and enlarged. I gently kissed her thighs and slowly inched my mouth into her vagina. I sucked on her clit; I flicked and massaged it with my tongue. Two fingers found their way inside her. As my tongue toyed with her clit, my fingers moved in and out, working deeper into her body. Her hips were heaving and when I could tell she was on the verge of climaxing, I stopped. I crawled forward and kissed her gently on her mouth, and started working my way down her body again, kissing both of her breasts, her naval and the area just above her sex. She was still moving her hips up and down slowly . . . begging me to continue. I moved between her legs again and put my thumbs on either side of those lips, so inviting. I spread them open and placed my mouth inside. This time, I was more aggressive. I sucked her clit hard, inserted my fingers deeply and continued until she gasped and screamed. She bucked and shuddered. She wasn't done. She yelled for me to fuck her . . . now! I spread her legs and bent her knees forward, entering her completely. As I fucked her, in and out, she grabbed her hair and screamed again. I came again, as well.

"Ooooh, that was nice. *Really* nice! . . . Were you ever a toy boy?"

We lay there for a while. "I wonder if the neighbors were listening?" I chuckled.

"I hope so. That old coot next door needs some excitement. I'll bet he hasn't gotten his rocks off in years," she laughed. We both got back into the hot tub.

I was enjoying just feeling the hot water, my arms around her, my eyes closed when she said, "What's a BBC? You mentioned it was a drink I might like."

"It's a mixture of Baily's Irish Cream, bananas, and coconut rum. If you have the ingredients, I'll make us one."

"Look in the liquor cabinet in the den. My ex had all kinds of alcohol in there. I know there are bananas on the kitchen counter."

"Okay. Give me a second, I'm not sure I can walk right this moment." We both laughed.

I walked into the kitchen and found the ingredients. "Where's your blender?"

"In the pantry. Middle shelf on the left." Impressive. If she had asked me where something was in *my* kitchen, we'd still be looking.

I mixed the drink: two bananas, a half cup of coconut rum, and two cups of Baily's. You really can't put too much Baily into it. Sometimes I say, Baily's to taste. Put it all in a blender, fill to the top with ice, and crush. Makes two to four drinks, depending upon the size of your glass.

I handed her a glass. Mine was already half empty.

"Wow! That *is* good. Did you make more than one?"

"Let's eat first, I'm hungry," I offered. "How about some Chinese? There's some on your table. All we have to do is warm it up."

We ate at the table, and had another BBC. There was very little talking. There was a strange silence between us. Finally, I spoke. "Linda, I have to ask, where is this going? I think I could fall in love with you. But I'm not sure we're on the same wave length."

"Kelly, honey, you are the best thing that has happened to me since my divorce. Maybe even before that. But let's not get too far ahead of ourselves. Right now, I am really enjoying the moment. The sex is incredible. If we weren't partners, I'd ask you to move in with me. In fact, you can stay over any time you want. And for the record, I'm not seeing anyone else. But . . ."

I interrupted her, "But . . . there's always a *but*. I fell in love with a woman years ago and had my heart broken. I don't want to go through that again. I need to be on firm ground knowing what direction this relationship is going . . . or I need to move on. I need some kind of commitment."

She was silent. Then she said, "We're partners. I'm here for you whenever you need me. If you want me to say, I love you, okay . . . I *do* love you. But I'm not ready to do more than enjoy your company right now. We're both detectives working on incredibly difficult assignments: Sex trafficking, drug running, and some psycho severing heads. I think we should concentrate on those things for the time being. Don't hate me, Kelly, and don't leave me. Just give me some more time."

"I can do that, Linda. I'll try not to bother you again."

With that, I excused myself. "We have an appointment with the DEA at 9 A.M. sharp in the morning. I'll meet you there."

As I was walking to the door, Linda called out, "Kelly, please, don't go away mad. I know you may be hurt, but it really is better this way."

"I'm sure you're right, Linda. I'm sure you're right."

As I walked to the car, I really *did* know she was right. But my ego was hurt. I was also acting like a lovesick teenager. Get over it, stupid: enjoy the moment, like she said. I was smiling again as I drove off, thinking about her incredible body and the sex we'd just had.

CHAPTER 45

I called her early the next morning. She didn't pick up so I left her a message on her answering machine. "Linda, we don't need to take two cars to the briefing. I'll meet you at the precinct and we'll drive over together. By the way, I had an incredible time with you last night."

She drove into the station at 0830. I was already at my desk. She walked over to her desk. Didn't say a word, but casually rubbed the back of my neck in passing.

Good, I thought, all is well with the world.

We were early at the DEA building. We entered into the lobby and approached the security desk. Showing our badges, the guard handed us a package, a visitor's badge, and told us we were to meet Agent Mendez on the second floor; his name is on the door: second right after you get off the elevator.

"Have a great day, Detectives."

Wow! Right away, I liked their efficiency.

Linda started reading the material in the package as we headed for the elevator.

The first page listed the names of the people who were expected to attend this meeting. It began with the senior member, Boyd Robinson, PsyD. Linda told me that meant Doctor of Psychology. Psychology? What does that have to do with the sale and distribution of illegal drugs?

Agent Mendez was third on the list. He had a master's degree in criminology. The second name I was already familiar with: Richard Schmidt. He was a lawyer I knew from past trials, a prosecutor. Detectives Meadows and Kelly were listed at the bottom of twelve names.

There was a brief outline of the agenda:

Introduction of the attendees

Chain of Command

Background of the case

Mission Goals

Overview of the area involved

Plan of attack

Associated risks

Expected fallout

Questions and Answers

Well, we'd already seen a list of the attendees. The chain of command at the raid itself would be headed by Agent Mendez. There were two others listed in order next. I guess the rest of us were privates.

We already knew the background; *we* gave it to them. Everything else, we would soon find out.

We got off the elevator and knocked on the door with the name Agent Roger Mendez printed on the glass.

"Come on in Detectives, you're right on time."

He motioned for us to have a seat as we entered.

"I don't know what kind of briefings you two are used to. This one may be a little different. Kelly, you were a Navy Seal. You know how to give orders as well as take them. Today will be mostly listening. I would rather that you do not interrupt Dr. Robinson. There will be time for questions later. During the plans of the raid, there will be discussion and that's when you are both free to add your comments. We certainly value your experience."

I didn't know how to respond, so I harkened back to my Navy days and said, "Yes sir."

"Great! Let's go to the meeting. You two can sit in the front row right next to me."

The room was a good size. There was more than enough room to hold at least thirty seats. Of course, there were only about twelve there now. We weren't the first to enter, at least six seats were already taken in the back row. There was a lectern up front and a table holding a projector beside it. On the back wall was a large screen. The windows on the right wall were covered by drawn shades. There were only two pictures on any of the walls, the president and vice president. We sat down in the front row just before nine. The rest of the chairs were soon occupied. Dr. Robinson walked in at nine . . . exactly. No one stood up. Okay, it wasn't totally military protocol.

Dr. Robinson was a tall man, taller than me. He was also physically fit . . . for a man about age sixty. He was dressed in a dark blue suit and a solid red tie. His hair was short, not balding, and mostly gray, as was his mustache and goatee. I thought he might have been handsome in his youth, but now he looked a bit weathered. I guess age does that to folks . . .

"Gentlemen," and he smiled at Meadows, "and lady . . . today we are finally going to wreak some havoc on the drug runners. Thanks to the outstanding work that the San Diego Police have done in uncovering a major sex and drug trafficking operation, I believe we are going to put a serious dent in their distribution process.

"As you know, we have located a tunnel in the Otay Mesa area. It is sophisticated and capable of transporting thousands of pounds of illegal drugs every day. We don't know how many guards there are or the level of fire power they may have. Because of that, we need to go in quickly and with as little noise as possible. I am in the process of coordinating the assistance of the Mexican authorities in Tijuana who have assured me that they will attack the entrance on their end. Together we will squeeze the smugglers between us and finally close down their operation.

"We have a number of goals:

"First, we need to discontinue their link from Mexico to the U.S. That is, the tunnel. When we have secured it, we will take out any contraband and seal both ends.

"Second, we need to take at least one guard or worker, prisoner. Their information could be very valuable.

"Third, and most important, we must eliminate our casualties. Don't take chances; don't try to be a hero. Work together as a team, remember your training and come back safely.

"Agent Mendez will now go over the plans for the raid. Thank you and good luck."

Dr. Robinson started to leave the room. I couldn't resist . . .

"Sir, do you really think it is wise to alert the Mexican authorities? They have been known to leak information to the cartels. If there is a chance that that happens, the raid may go badly."

He turned to face me. "I'm sorry, who are you? I don't recognize you as a DEA agent."

"Joe Kelly, Detective for the San Diego Police Department. The agency you mentioned that was instrumental in exposing this operation."

175

"Ah, yes. Detective Kelly. I *have* heard of you. Didn't you swing down from a helicopter and single-handedly apprehend a gang of sex traffickers? Congratulations! But this operation is far more sensitive. Like it or not, we are treading on foreign soil and we cannot just go willy-nilly into their country without notification. I do realize the risk, sir, but it is one we will have to work with and overcome. But thank you for your question. It serves to remind everyone that we must be vigilant and expect more resistance than we'd like."

With that, he walked out of the door.

My face was getting red. Did he really congratulate me or make me out a fool? Well, it wasn't the first time and surely wouldn't be the last. Meadows patted me on the knee . . .

Agent Mendez got up and headed to the podium. We had more definitive information regarding the exact location of the building housing the exit of the tunnel. Money bought us a confidential informant . . . more money bought us the location.

We listened as he outlined the situation. Basically, there would be two snipers up on the roofs of the buildings adjacent to the building containing the tunnel's exit. One on each side. Agent Mendez and two other agents would then enter the warehouse, identify themselves and place everyone under arrest. That was the best-case scenario. More than likely, these guys would not surrender peacefully. Everyone was to wear bullet-proof vests and helmets with night vision goggles that can be pulled down when needed. Backup would enter from the front and rear of the warehouse to stem the situation before it got out of hand. Hopefully, our Mexican authorities will be duplicating our efforts at the entrance. We would carefully clear our end of the tunnel and meet in the middle.

He asked if there any questions. I had one. "Where do you want Meadows and I?"

"Glad you ask. While we are taking out the guards, I'd like you both to head to the tunnel exit, entrance in this case, and make sure no reinforcements arrive to help. We'll issue you automatic assault rifles to assist."

"What if the Mexican authorities are either not there or are cooperating with the cartel by not even showing up?"

"That, Detective, you can count on."

"We've brought along with us enough dynamite to blow up half of this entire building if we choose. If push comes to shove we'll blow up this fucking tunnel . . . with them in it."

We started the mission around 7:30 P.M. It wouldn't be completely dark, but we wanted to be sure of our target before then. We also figured they would be moving drugs long before that so they'd be ready for shipment when it got really dark.

I watched the snipers take position. There was no activity outside of the warehouse. Our informant, slash snitch, had told us everyone usually stayed inside so as to not attract undue attention. Most people thought the warehouse was abandoned. Mendez pointed to the men who would be guarding the exits to take position. He and two other agents proceeded to the front door. Not surprisingly, there was a chain lock between the handles. A bolt cutter quickly dispatched that. I looked over at Meadows . . . she looked cute in her helmet and SWAT clothing . . . so I winked at her. She gave me a puzzled look back but gave me a thumbs up. They opened the door and we followed them inside. We hadn't gone ten feet when the first guard spotted us.

A shot or series of shots rang out. "DEA, you're all under arrest."

I'm not sure it was exactly in that order. There were many more guards . . . many more than we expected, for sure. They were hiding behind large containers along the wall. It sounded like they all opened fire at once.

Mendez went down almost immediately. The agent next to him tried to radio the guys guarding the exits to enter. I wasn't sure he got it out before he was hit, too. The remaining agent, with Meadows and I, managed to get to cover behind an old pick-up by the door. It wasn't much, but protection is protection. I told Meadows to stay put and keep her head down. The other agent and I would try to flank them. Just then, the lights in the warehouse went out. We found out later that one of the agents stationed outside pulled the master switch. He figured we'd have a better chance than the guards inside if they were blind. It worked. I got up and sprinted to the right wall. The agent sprinted left. I yelled at Meadows: "Forget what I just said. Pull your goggles down and head over to the tunnel entrance. Make sure no one comes up. Don't ask questions, just shoot!" The blinded guards continued to shoot in the direction where we were at last. Their shots made them easy to locate. I saw one of them duck his head behind a box. Shit, he couldn't be over sixteen! "Put the gun down," I yelled. He stood up, dropped his rifle and cried, "Don't shoot! Please, don't shoot!" I didn't. I smacked him hard with my rifle butt under his chin. A classic boxer's uppercut. The concussion of his teeth coming together and jarring his brain did the trick. He was out cold. I tossed his rifle back out towards the warehouse door. I heard gun fire coming from the far corner of the warehouse and then more coming from the tunnel entrance. I could see other guards raising their hands in surrender as our agents surrounded them. They really didn't put up much of a fight when they knew they couldn't win.

I ran over towards the tunnel, stopping only for a second to check on Mendez. He was dead; shot through the neck and bled out. Unlucky. Helmet and bullet proof vest were useless.

More shots. Meadows yelled, "Kelly, I need help . . . now!"

She was definitely in trouble. As fast as she shot one guy, another appeared. It reminded me of the tunnels in 'Nam. They would have a machine gun nest rigged up at the entrance of a tunnel, hidden by brush. By the time you took out those gunners, another group would immediately take their place. Who knew how many VC were down in those holes?

I didn't have any hand grenades so all we could do if keep firing. It became pretty obvious that the end was near. There were so many bodies piled up at the foot of the tunnel that it was impossible for any more to climb up. Someone must have called a halt because they stopped coming. We reloaded and waited.

One of the other agents came by and the lights came back on. I could see about seven or eight guards being let away in handcuffs. The sixteen-year-old was among them. The agent said they had called for an ambulance and bus to transport the prisoners. They would take over from here.

"What about the mission?" I asked. "Dr. Robinson made it clear we needed to put this tunnel out of commission. Why do you think we brought all the dynamite?"

"Listen, Detective. I'm aware of the mission. But we've already lost one man and a badly wounded agent on his way to the hospital. I also remember him saying to not take chances and come back safely. That's what I intend to do."

Just then someone shouted from inside the tunnel. "*Hola*! Don't shoot! Don't shoot! I am Lieutenant Ortega of the police in charge of the de Otay area of Tijuana." He climbed up the ladder.

"What are you doing? We had it in good authority that you were initiating this raid tomorrow night. We were not prepared for your assault. If we hadn't been called by locals we would not have gotten here in time to help."

I just stared at him.

"But you have done well, my friends. We can take over from here. We will clean out this tunnel and close up your end. You can be assured it will not be used again."

"I have a better idea. Why don't you turn around and crawl back to the hole you just came from, *LIEUTENANT*? We'll clean out the tunnel and *we'll* make sure nobody ever uses this tunnel again. Understand?" I hitched my weapon up just a little bit higher. He got the message. I pointed my hand over toward where Agent Mendez had fallen. "We lost a very good man tonight, and you know why. I'm in no mood for arguments, and neither are these other agents. You could do us a favor, though."

"And what is that?"

"Pick up and transport those dead bodies at the bottom of the ladder and take them back to Mexico . . . and don't bother to take anything else. We'll be watching."

"You have no reason to talk like this to us, my friend. It was an unfortunate mistake." He yelled something in Spanish and they returned to the tunnel. We watched them go . . . They loaded the bodies into one of the wheeled carts and began pushing it back. There wasn't room for all of them and a couple of cops ended up dragging the rest back.

"You weren't exactly diplomatic to our law enforcement brothers." It was the lawyer who said he was packing up and going home; Schmidt. "Good for you. I was *this* close to shooting him myself when he gave us that phony excuse about the wrong date." He held up his right hand, thumb and forefinger about an inch apart. "Mendez knew they were crooked; as did Robertson. Still, we had to play politics. I will post a couple of agents at their end of the tunnel to discourage anyone else from entering. I don't think their police will interfere any time soon. Tomorrow I'm going to have our agents start hauling out all the contraband we can find. Then we're going to blow this thing to kingdom come." He told one of the agents nearby to follow the Mexican police to the other end. "Make sure they don't pick up anything along the way."

I reached out to shake his hand. "Thanks, I feel better about usurping your authority." I found out later that Schmidt occasionally worked for the DEA, just to ensure that all the "i's" and "t's" were done correctly and the proceedings remained within our jurisdiction.

"Just don't make it a habit, Detective. And take care of your partner. She's the brave one. I think she killed over a half dozen guards all by herself." He shook my hand, went over and shook Meadow's hand, turned, and left the building.

I walked over to Meadows. She sat down on the floor, shaking her head. "I'm not sure I'm cut out for this line of work, Kelly. That's the first time I ever shot anyone . . . and I shot six or seven of them! I don't think I'll ever get over this."

"I've lost count how many people I've killed and I can tell you this: You never get used to it. But you do get over it. You did what you had to do to survive. Plain and simple. Do you think those men would have hesitated to kill you? I'm proud of you, Linda. You not only saved your life, but the lives of the rest of us as well. When we get back to the station, I'm going to let you wear my Silver Star!"

They both laughed.

CHAPTER 46

KELLY

The fallout from the raid would be monumental to the disruption of drugs entering along that border for years. Unfortunately, the fallout for the success of the raid was to be felt even more dramatically within Mexico. It started almost immediately.

The Mexican police lieutenant we met at the raid was found beaten, tortured, and shot in the head several times. He lay in the street for hours before anyone dared to touch him. Our snitch, the one who showed us the location of the tunnel, was never heard from again. We hoped he had just skipped town, but the odds were against it. We had a feeling those two would be targeted. After all, that LT was supposed to be insurance that our raid would fail. He was a coward. He paid the price. But the massacre that followed was unexpected.

Two politicians elected to represent the Otay Mesa area were kidnapped, stripped, skinned alive, and hung from a lamp post in the center of the district. Their families were not spared either. The wives and children were gathered together in the square, bound with ropes and doused with gasoline before being set afire. Their screams could be heard on our side of the border. No one dared to intervene.

A local newspaper ran a front-page headline deploring the slaughter. It only ran once. The editor was quickly dispatched along with several of his reporters a day later. Their heads were found floating in a nearby river.

It appeared the Mexican authorities were either being paid not to interfere or they had gotten the message that to interfere was suicide.

Whatever the case, no one was ever apprehended. Yet everyone seemed to know: It was the hand of El Conejo.

It didn't stop on the Mexican side, either. Several San Diego gang members were beheaded with notes attached to their bodies warning not to fuck with the cartel operations. The biggest shock came within our own police department. One of our patrolmen was implicated. He was found in his vehicle one morning after his shift. No head; blood spattered everywhere. It appeared that someone had been in the back seat and decapitated the cop while he was still alive. He was still sitting in the driver's seat; his head was on the floor. Another revenge killing?

Was this our innocent Manny? How could we have been so fooled?

Despite the rampage in Mexico, things actually quieted down in regard to the drug trade in the San Diego and southern California area. The only tunnel they were aware of had been sealed. Thousands of pounds of cocaine, heroin and marijuana had been confiscated, and over a hundred thousand dollars in cash had been found before they blasted both ends shut. Both the FBI and DEA were busy congratulating themselves . . . with good reason.

The Director of the FBI held an awards ceremony to recognize the two detectives. It was held in a large auditorium in one of the hotels in Mission Valley. Over a hundred people were in attendance, including FBI agents Smith and Simmons, Dr. Robertson, and the attorney, Richard Schmidt. There was a special commendation for Agent Mendez. His wife was there to receive the medal. The Director cited them all for "their assistance in identifying and solving some of the toughest problems out there without waiting for someone else to fix them. The city of San Diego and a large swatch of the rest of the country is a safer place because of their efforts."

The police commissioner was beaming as he stood to read Detectives Kelly and Meadows their individual Meritorious Service citations.

When the ceremony was over and people were talking and congregating around the refreshments provided, Agent Smith approached Kelly.

"Congratulations Detective. Can I have a word with you and your partner?"

"Thank you, sir. Let me see if I can find her."

She was over in the corner, a glass of wine in her hand. She had tears in her eyes. "What's up, Linda? This is supposed to be a good day."

"I know, Kelly, I *am* happy, but I just can't help but feeling down because of what happened to Agent Mendez. He paid for our medals with his life. It just doesn't seem right to celebrate this. Plus, I had to kill people!"

"I understand, Linda. Remember: Mendez never hesitated; he knew the risks, just like you do. . . . it's our job. We do it so that many more lives are not ruined or ended by drugs, prostitution, or random criminal violence. I'm proud to be your partner, Detective Meadows."

"Thank you, Kelly. I'm okay."

"Good. Dry your tears and come with me. Agent Smith wants to talk . . . to both of us."

Agent Smith was standing by the Director of the FBI when we approached. I looked at Smith, but it was the Director who shook our hands and spoke.

"Detectives, I just wanted to say congratulations again for what you did. I couldn't spell it out in front the crowd, but stopping that sex trafficking enterprise was the key to the eventual drug smuggling operation. Both will have far reaching ripples throughout this area."

"Thank you, sir," we replied in unison.

"But enough chit chat. Let me get to the point. I'd like to offer you both a job . . . with the FBI. You'd have to go through our indoctrination courses, of course, but I think you'd make a great addition to our team."

I looked at Meadows . . . she looked at me. I think we both saw the same thing: shock and bewilderment. What did he just say?

"You don't have to decide this second. All I ask it that you think about it . . . and then give Agent Smith here, a call." With that, he said "Congratulations, again," turned, and left the building.

Agent Smith shook our hands and said "That, Detectives, doesn't happen very often. Personally, I'd be honored to work with you. Give the opportunity some thought. I'll be in touch." He handed us each his card and followed the Director.

"Well, Meadows, what do you think?"

"I think I need a drink." We both laughed.

It turned out to be a good day for everyone. But we still had a very real case that needed to be solved. So, I switched gears, reviewing the case in my mind and stated what I thought was obvious. "There's one guy we haven't ruled out regarding the origin of those severed heads."

"Who?" She asked. "You've pretty much narrowed the perps down to Jim, Manny . . . or me. Who's left?"

"Think about it. Remember when I asked why all those heads were only found at the scene of accidents?"

"Yeah, and we had a plausible explanation for that."

"Bear with me. Who has been to every accident scene? Beside the ones you've just mentioned."

She considered each accident. Then it dawned on her: "Wait a minute. You're not implicating Doc Hughs, are you?

"Not intentionally. He's a good friend and a solid citizen."

"Why would he need to do something like that? What's his motive?"

"Well, that's something else to consider. Did you know that Bob's wife and child were killed in an auto accident many years ago? His daughter was only nine or ten at the time. It was a tragedy I don't think he has never really gotten over. His daughter died without really living. She never got a chance to become someone. She really died an unknown . . ."

"I see where you're going." It was Meadow's turn. "Those immigrant women were also unknown. Literally. No one knew who they were. No one cared about them. Doc may be trying to draw attention to them in some way by getting their photos in the newspaper and on television. In his mind, they would finally receive some recognition in their life, if only by being killed. He'd have to be a little sick in the head to do that, wouldn't he?"

"It *is* a stretch, and *only* a stretch. I still think it is Jim. Bob is just too balanced to be so psychologically damaged like that. I would think he would be showing other signs of strange behavior as well. It will take some pretty hard evidence to convince me of his involvement. Just the thought is just troubling.

I got up to leave when Meadows interrupted. "I need to see the files the police have on the scenes where each of the severed heads were found. We must be overlooking something. What did you say was the name of the cop you spoke to at the safe house?"

"I think his name was Peters. He's a city cop."

"Great. Just who I need to talk to; another Peters."

"What do you mean?"

"That's my ex's last name. Peters, Sean Peters."

CHAPTER 47

I decided I needed to talk to that lawyer, Mr. Schmidt, the one we met in the DEA raid. I was going around and around in my mind about the severed heads . . . and I was *sure* we had the murderer in our sights . . . we just didn't know *who:* Jim, Doc, Manny, or Meadows. It *had* to be one of them.

While I was thinking about Schmidt, I had another thought: How much evidence do I need in order to arrest and prosecute someone . . . especially since most of it is circumstantial? We had lots of that, but did it amount to more than just a hunch?

I had posed that exact question to Schmidt after the raid. He told me that we need to talk.

I called Schmidt's office to get an appointment. I was told by his secretary that he was still in court. She wasn't sure when the trial would be over but they usually broke around noon for lunch. Perhaps I could meet him there if it was urgent or she could put me on his calendar. I didn't want to wait that long.

Schmidt was just leaving the courtroom when I caught him.

"Mr. Schmidt, do you have a minute? I'd really like to run something by you."

"Detective Kelly. Of course. I was intrigued by our conversation the other day. Tell me about the evidence you have. All you need to arrest someone is probable cause. That just means it is more likely than *not* that someone committed a crime. If I remember correctly, the U.S. Supreme Court even stated that circumstantial evidence is intrinsically no different from testimonial, or direct, evidence. Didn't you say all you had was a hunch?"

"That's right . . . but it's backed up by a bunch of circumstances that one could make a case as being tied to more than one person.

Circumstantial evidence; nothing that absolutely makes any one of them the killer in a series of murders."

"That could be enough. Circumstances *could* create enough inferences about an accused's guilt. We usually consider a number of factors. Did the accused resist arrest? Does he have a motive for the murders? Was he present at the murder or at the time of the murder? Has he denied it? Is he evasive in his answers? Has he contradicted himself? Does he have prior arrests; a pattern of criminal behavior?"

"Well, we haven't arrested him . . . or her, yet. The only thing we have to go on is their presence where and when the bodies were found at multiple accident scenes. Actually, not a body, but a severed head."

" I wondered if that was what we were talking about. I saw that young girl's head in the paper. Did he, or she, have a reason to be there? Sometimes criminals like to hang around to watch what happens when the body is found."

"They have an explanation for . . . all of them . . . and it's reasonable. The other problem we have is that there are at least two other people who are also at the discovery of all the bodies. I have tried to rule them out, but I can use the same circumstantial evidence to arrest them as I can the person I really believe did the crime. In addition, a good defense lawyer could probably make a case that these severed heads were attempts by gangs or cartels to sensationalize a message to competitors or snitchers not to interfere."

"Sounds like you've got a problem. I doubt if the District Attorney would choose to prosecute such a case until you could rule out everyone else. Otherwise, they'd probably get a not guilty verdict and the guy would go free. Double jeopardy would apply unless you caught him killing again. Do they have a motive?"

"I can't see one, but I think someone knows one but is not coming forward. At a trial, they might . . . under oath."

"Too risky. You need to get that motive on tape and make sure the witness will testify to that in court. Still might not help, but it's another piece. You could also try to get the suspect to explain their presence at the discoveries. Perhaps you can get some inconsistency in their statements. Sometimes when confronted, they may be forced to lie or change their story. One lie leads to another and before long the entire alibi is worthless."

"I guess it's worth a try. The problem is, two of them are brothers. I'm not sure I can get either of them to share secrets about the other."

"Maybe they're in it together. Have you thought of that?"

That opened my eyes to a whole new range of questions. I hadn't even considered that. It *did* make sense . . . a little. Could Bob and Jim actually be working together? If Bob killed the girls and severed their heads, Jim would be the perfect person to dispose of the bodies. Why would Bob kill anyone? Why would Jim be willing to risk disposing of headless bodies. What's in it for him? The more I thought about it, the more ridiculous it sounded. Jim's the killer . . . I'm certain of it. I just have to prove it."

I had an idea, but it was really far-fetched. "Bear with me, sir, but I've got a hair-brained idea that I'd like to run by you."

"I'm listening. I 've been listening to hair-brained ideas from the defense lawyer in this trial all morning." He pointed to the door of the courtroom. "This couldn't be any worse."

"What if we actually brought one of my suspects to trial? We use the same circumstantial evidence for her that we have on the others . . . but I *know* she's innocent. If we went to court and prosecuted her, we'd get to hear her defense lawyer lay out a case arguing every bit of evidence we had. We'd then know if we had a solid case against the others to convict with just our circumstantial evidence. It might even enable us to determine the one piece of evidence we need to convict."

He half-smiled, and said, "What if we had enough evidence already?"

"What do you mean?"

"Suppose the jury actually convicts the person you *know* didn't do it?"

"Oh, yeah. That could be a problem. Can the prosecutor say new evidence has been submitted that exonerates the accused . . . and have the case dismissed?"

"I suppose you could . . . but I'd probably be held in contempt of court for wasting the court's time . . . and then be disbarred. Not only would it be a huge waste of time and money, but I've found it's not smart to play games with our judicial system. Besides, you already know you need more solid evidence. Just keep digging."

"You're right. I told you it was a hair-brained idea. I've just reached a roadblock in this investigation. I'm grasping at straws."

I thanked the attorney and told him I hoped to be back with an arrest someday when I had absolute proof of the murderer's guilt.

"I'm betting you will," he said. "Don't worry about far-fetched ideas, it shows you're thinking. Call me when you get some hard evidence." If you will excuse me, I've got to get back in court. Nice meeting you again . . . good luck."

He walked away shaking his head.

187

I felt bad . . . he missed his lunch.

A few days later, we were sitting in Meadow's car having stopped for lunch at a roadside taco truck. I was in the passenger seat staring out the window.

Meadows interrupted my concentration. "What are you thinking about? You seem to be really perplexed."

"Actually, I was thinking about what that FBI Director offered. What do you think?" She tilted her head a little, and looked up to me . . .

"You know, I thought about it all day yesterday. It sounds exciting . . . and the money *is* better. It would probably mean I'd have to move or sell my house. I love that place. I suppose I could rent it."

"I think it's a little more than just your house you need to be concerned with. The FBI Academy is no easy school. And you're not as young as you used to be. The physical demands are rigorous."

"I don't think they'd be a whole lot tougher than what we do now. I'm in good shape, I think I could handle that. I'm more concerned with where and what the assignments would be."

"We also don't have all the qualifications," I added. "Most of the agents speak multiple languages. I speak Spanish . . . and a little Vietnamese. Did you ever learn another language?"

"Yeah, Farsi, but it's not very useful. My dad retired from the Navy after thirty years at as a Vice Admiral. He was offered and took the position as Ambassador for the United States in Afghanistan. His qualifications were impeccable and he spoke the language. For some reason my Mom could never understand, he chose to earn a master's degree in Persian studies while attending the Navy's language school in Monterey, California, when he was a Lieutenant Commander. Upon graduation, he received orders to serve as an interpreter at the embassy in Afghanistan. Of course, the family went with him. I was only seven or eight at that time. The tour was for three years. I was home schooled by my mom, but played with the local kids and picked up the language pretty easily. Farsi, well, it's called Dari in Afghanistan, is also spoken in Pakistan and Iran. Anyway, when my Dad went back to Afghanistan in 1964, I was in college, but would fly over at the semester break and during the summer. I loved the country and the people. I became pretty fluent in a language I'll probably never have a use for."

"Impressive, but I don't see how you'd be much use in Mexico speaking Farsi." We both laughed. "But I have a bigger question: Would you consider just *one* of us joining . . . or are we a team?"

"What are you getting at?"

"Well, it sounds like you are reluctant to leave San Diego. I don't have any real ties here, having moved around most of my life. Would you want to join if I went? Would you join if I decided not to?"

She hesitated. "Right now, those are tough questions. In my mind, we'd be joining as a team. I really hadn't considered the alternative. I think we both need to consider this move carefully."

"I agree. But we need to continue to discuss this . . . weigh the positives and negatives, before we come to any decision . . . about the FBI, or our future together."

We finished our tacos and headed for the station. If you really want good Mexican food, try the taco trucks. Especially in San Diego.

Lieutenant Hill was waiting for us. Crime never sleeps . . .

"A body's been found in a second-floor condo over by the Gas Lamp district. It appears to be a drug overdose, but you need to get over there to make sure. We've already notified the ME."

He gave us the address.

CHAPTER 48

I always enjoyed going to the Gas Lamp Quarter, as it was called. Most people considered it to be the center of San Diego's nightlife scene. I couldn't argue. It consisted of sixteen square blocks of Victorian-like buildings right next to modern skyscrapers. Lots of restaurants, pubs, nightclubs and retail shops competed with art galleries, symphony halls, concert venues and museums. We were headed for one of the residential lofts nearby.

There was a patrolman at the entrance downstairs. He indicated the number of the condo and shook his head. "This is really sad. Makes me want to go home and hug my kids."

We heard the screaming from outside the door. One of our female patrolmen was holding a little girl in her arms. Couldn't have been over three years old. The baby was hysterical.

"She's been like this ever since we came in. We found her tugging at her mom's arm, tying to wake her up. Then she went over and lifted her mom's head up, trying harder. She was crying, Mommy, Mommy, wake up! . . . I've still got tears running down my face."

"It looks like an overdose. You can see the fresh track on her arm. There's evidence of older tracks as well on the other arm."

"Who called it in?" I asked.

"The superintendent," she replied.

"What's her name?" I asked.

"She told me her name was Sarah."

I watched the lady cop bounce the little girl in her arms and gently smiled into her eyes . . . "Sarah Baily."

"I meant the name of her mother." I sounded irked. But I was immediately ashamed of myself.

"Her name is . . . was Jill Baily. She worked as a manager for the Strip Club."

"You're kidding me . . . a strip club?"

"Oh no, the Strip Club in Gas Lamp is a really high-class restaurant specializing in sirloin strip steaks."

Just then, Doc arrived. He just shook his head at the scene. "Why do people do these things?" he whispered, almost to himself.

He bent over, examined the body of the dead woman. She couldn't have been over twenty-four maybe twenty-five years old.

"Some signs of trauma. Have you found any evidence of a robbery or forced entry?

Did she leave a note?"

"Honestly, we just got here ourselves. We're about to look around."

"Well, be careful not to touch anything unless you are wearing your gloves." He looked at the patrol lady: did you touch anything?"

"No, I just picked up this little one. The condo supe here opened the door. There was no evidence of a forced entry. I asked her if she lived alone. She said she was the occupant of record; her name was Jill Baily. She had a boyfriend that came over occasionally."

"You got a name?" I asked the supe. "Why did you call the police?"

"Henderson, or Hendricks. Something like that. His first name is Bill. White guy, might be around the same age as her, maybe a little older." She pointed to the woman lying face down on the floor.

"She was really a nice lady. I never figured her for a druggy. You just never know these days . . .

Oh . . ." She remembered the second question: "I called you guys because I was worried for her. She goes to work every morning like clockwork . . . and brings me a cup of coffee she's brewed on the way out. She takes her little girl to the sitter on the way. Well, I didn't see her this morning and the sitter called. She was worried about her. She hadn't heard from her either and she didn't pick up when she called her at home. I told her I'd check. When I knocked on her door, there was no response and I thought I could hear someone crying. That's when I called you. Maybe I should have gone inside to check, but I wasn't sure what to do. When I called, I was told to wait; someone would be there shortly. And the police arrived within ten minutes."

We made an extensive search of the premise. Nothing to indicate foul play. The room was not in disarray, lamps were not broken, no sign of a robbery. Meadows found something interesting in the nightstand next to the bed. It was an invoice from a rehab center in La Mesa. It was dated five months ago. There was no suicide note to be found.

Doc reached out for the invoice. And began reading. "This might explain it. The older scars and the rehab experience would have me believe that she was trying to quit. She must have stopped using until she was tempted again, or was tempted *by* someone.

"Unfortunately, her tolerance level had dropped and she probably injected the same amount into her system that she ended up with before rehab. Too much. Much too much. That led to the overdose."

"The question you need to answer, Joe, is who gave her the drugs? She just shot up and there is no needle, tubing, or other drug paraphernalia. Who took them? My bet is on the boyfriend."

Meadows came back into the room. "Nothing significant in the refrigerator except for three bottles of beer. Guinness Stout. Pretty strong stuff. Not many young girls care for the taste. It's definitely not my favorite. There's three empties in the trash."

The ambulance came to take the body down to the morgue. We called California's Department of Family and Child Services to take the little girl. They would try to find a relative if they could. Otherwise they would have to begin the process of finding a suitable couple, if possible, to adopt her.

We went back to the station. Meadows was clearly shaken. "All I can think about is that little girl tugging at her mom to wake up. She may have psychological issues with that her whole life. How can a mother do such a thing?"

"The thing you have to remember, Linda, is that drug addiction doesn't always happen to people who lack moral principles. Good people are influenced by a lot of bad people and alcohol and peer pressure makes younger people more likely to try it . . . just once . . . to see how it feels. Heroin makes you feel euphoric . . . the first time you try it. That feeling affects the brain and you crave it again. Quitting is not as easy as turning off a light switch. Repeated usage changes the brain and interferes with the ability to resist urges to take more."

"When did you get so smart?"

"I've been around Doc a long time. He's seen a lot of drug abuse in his life, both as a coroner and as the legal officer in Nam. Did you know that the driver of the tractor trailer that killed his wife and daughter was found to have been using marijuana before he got in his rig? "

"Jill, the deceased mother, was actually trying to quit. She probably hated being addicted. You found the evidence of her going to that drug abuse center. But relapse is common. Especially if you are continually exposed as I imagine she was with her boyfriend. We don't even know if he injected her against her will."

"We need to find the boyfriend. I'd like to fry his ass!" Meadows sounded pissed.

Doc finished with the fingerprinting and called it in. We searched our database and found the boyfriend quickly. All three of the empty beer bottles in the trash had his fingerprints on them. He was already in our system: Possession of drugs, larceny, auto theft. He was sentenced at age 19 to jail for a year. I guess the judge felt sorry for him. He came from a good family; he was young, white, good looking and an athlete. He also was very remorseful at sentencing . . .

We put out a BOLO alert, 'be on the lookout', to all the police, bus stations, airport, border entry points, and hotels in San Diego. He was found at a ticketing booth at Lindbergh Field. As soon as he showed his ID, security was alerted and he was in custody before he reached the departure gate. Security searched his carry-on bag and found, among other things, a bag of white substance and jewelry. We were notified.

It didn't take long to get to the airport. Security police and our suspect were in a little office behind ticketing. We exchanged handcuffs and escorted him to our car. Meadows opened the door and put him in the back seat. She said "Watch your head!" as she jammed it up against the door frame. "I said, watch it, stupid."

He didn't say a word. Obviously, he already knew the drill and I figured he would lawyer up as soon as we read him his rights and asked him a question. We got in the car; Meadows drove. I turned to face the guy and I decided to ask him anyway . . .

"Is Bill Henderson your real name? Nice earring, by the way."

"Are you kidding me, you're holding my driver's license in your hand, asshole."

"I know, I just wanted to know if your name matches the name on your driver's license. You're not wearing your earring in the picture. Does it come off?"

"Fuck you. No, it does not come off. And yes, it's my real name, idiot."

"Good to know. You, William Charles Henderson, are under arrest for possession of an illegal substance, possession of stolen goods, selling drugs, and murder. I read him his rights and asked him if he understood."

"Yes, I understand . . . and I want a lawyer. I'm not the idiot here. But just for the record, I didn't kill anybody!"

"Did you know that's what every murderer I ever arrested said? And they were all liars, just like you." I wasn't asking questions now. "I'll bet she begged you to shoot her up with heroin; or maybe she didn't. Maybe you injected her by force. Maybe you didn't sell it to her, but you made sure she'd buy more later. They always want more. She OD'd before you left, that's why you removed the syringe from her arm and cleaned up the mess. I'll bet you didn't even try to help her . . . and you left her three-year-old daughter all alone with her dead mother. But you didn't forget one thing: you took the silver necklace from around her neck; the one with her initials on it. Yeah, that's right, we found that in your carry-on. To top it off, your fingerprints are all over her condo unit. Recent ones, in fact. You don't have to say a word, big man. You're going away for a long, long time . . . unless you get the chair."

We booked him and put him the city jail. He was on the phone with his daddy quickly. It wasn't too much longer before his lawyer showed up. He reviewed the charges . . . and the evidence. He asked us if there might be a plea deal. I told him that wasn't up to me. You'll have to ask the DA. She's a good friend of mine. I'll be sure to put in a good word for him. I smiled, and left him standing.

Meadows got a call from headquarters. She was needed at a crime scene over by Point Loma. I told her to go ahead, I'd meet her later if she needed help.

Family and Child Services notified us that they had located the deceased's mother. She was in traditional housing north of the city in Escondido. It's designed for low income or homeless people. They usually charge around 30% of the occupant's wages for rent. I think they are subsidized by one charity or another. She was working as a cleaning lady and indicated she had no money for a burial and wished her daughter to be cremated. She had had a falling out with her daughter over her use of drugs. She hadn't seen her since before the baby was born. It had gotten to the point where she had stolen everything of value of hers and racked up credit card debts that she couldn't possibly repay. She had to move out of her apartment. She was dead broke. Fortunately, there are places to go in the city if you need help and are willing to work. She also volunteered that as far as she knew, the father of the child was no longer in the picture and she did not know his name. She didn't know anything about anyone named Henderson.

Child Services indicated that unless this grandmother was willing to raise the child, she would be placed up for adoption.

I am still hoping the SOB got life!

The arraignment for William Charles Henderson commenced a day later. I decided to attend. His lawyer entered a plea of not guilty. Wonders never cease to amaze me. Based upon the charges, he was scheduled to go before a grand jury in two weeks. I almost laughed when his lawyer asked for bail. Let's see: the charges against him were murder, possession of illegal drugs, distribution of illegal drugs, and possession of stolen property. The prosecuting attorney would probably add others before the day of the grand jury. According to California law, there is a schedule assigning the amount of bail that can be awarded for each charge. The total for Henderson's charges amounted to over a million dollars. If you add in prior convictions of a felony *and* his attempt to flee the country . . . the judge quickly awarded no bail.

I called Doc to fill him in.

"Henderson is in jail and probably won't see daylight for a long time. He's scheduled for a grand jury in a couple of weeks and then will go to trial in the next three months . . . unless his lawyer waves his right to a speedy trial. In this case it's fifty-fifty. With no bail, he's sitting in jail. And it's crowded. I'm sure he doesn't like it. But waving the speedy trial gives the lawyer more time to prepare his case. Not sure what his defense is. I don't know if he knows that in our investigation we talked to all the neighbors and workers around that condo. We found a witness that places Henderson coming out of the deceased's unit at 10:30 the night before she was found. The man had been walking his dog and was returning to his unit three doors down the hall when this guy walked out of the door. As he passed he kicked at the dog and told him to get the fuck out of his way. He told the police officer if he had been thirty years younger he would have beaten the shit out of him."

I wished he had.

"Anyway, we called his lawyer to be present and put Henderson in a line-up with four other people similar to his height and appearance. We had our own lawyer there as well, Richard Schmidt. Just so everything was done legally and the identification could not be overturned. We also made sure they were each wearing an earring in their right ears. The witness picked him out immediately. The single earring in *his* right ear in the shape of a *syringe* seemed to help . . . and Henderson called *me* an idiot?"

I was still on the phone with Bob.

"Well, I can tell you more about the body. She was still in rigor when we found her the other morning. My guess, based on that and her internal body temperature, is that she died between nine and eleven the night before she was found. She definitely died of an overdose of heroin. There is also evidence of rough sexual intercourse prior to her death. It doesn't appear to me to have been consensual based upon the bruising around her left cheek and eye that would occur if she had been beaten. She was also nursing a loose left central and lateral incisor and busted lip. You might check to see if Henderson is right handed."

"Another nail in that bastard's coffin," I thought . . . out loud. "What do we do with the body now? We still have a problem; Grandma can't afford a burial and wants her daughter to be cremated. There are no other known relatives. She had no siblings."

"Well, there is a protocol for burying homeless people, people with no known relatives or people who just refuse to claim the body. If we can't find someone within ten days, we generally pay a funeral home to cremate the body and then we sprinkle the ashes out at sea. In this case you tell me that the only relative cannot afford a funeral or burial and will not claim the body. In that case, the city will cough up the money to pay for the bill. We don't use the same crematory every time. Politics. We can't be seen as favoring anyone in particular."

"Do you think you could arrange for the crematory at Heavenly Gardens to cremate her? Something is going on there, and I want to be in a position to find out what it is."

"Isn't that where James works?"

"Yeah. I'm sorry, Bob, but I have a job to do and sometimes it means stepping on people's toes. Your brother is clearly involved in something. He's hiding information that might solve our severed head case. I need to find that out."

"I understand. I'm afraid you're right too. James has had a dark side his whole life. I've tried to protect him, but it's gotten to the point that protecting him has just enabled him to become even more evil. I'll help you any way I can Joe."

Doc arranged for the body to be cremated as we discussed. He would personally drive it over to the crematory later that day.

I needed to find Meadows. I called her on her radio.

"Linda, what's up? Where are you?"

It wasn't like her not to answer her radio. I walked into headquarters and tried calling her at her home. Still no answer. "Has anybody seen Meadows? We were supposed to meet here this afternoon to discuss a case."

"She was headed out to investigate a possible homicide earlier." It was Lt. Hill. "Wait a minute. Peters called in a few hours ago to say it was a false alarm. I think it was out in Point Loma."

"See if you can reach patrolman Peters."

I radioed to Peters. No response. "Lieutenant, did Peters give you an address to the crime scene?"

"Yeah, it was out on Rosecrans." He handed me the address. "I gave it to Meadows."

I was getting worried; I needed to hear from Linda . . .

CHAPTER 49

MEADOWS

Meadows was not talking. She was on her back, lying unconscious, strapped to a metal table. Her left arm was bound to her side, but curiously, her right arm was free. Her feet were also secured to the rear corners of the table. She was naked.

Her eyes opened . . . to thousands of little lights dancing in her head. She blinked several times trying to clear them, and then the pain registered. The right side of her head at first, and then her right eye . . . which was actually swollen shut. Her mind was searching . . . what just happened? Where am I? How did I become tied to this table?

She turned her head . . . slowly. She was alone. The room was bare, completely empty except for a small table within arm's reach to her left . . . and there was a large knife on top of it. For some reason, her right arm was not secure. Either she had somehow broken loose earlier or . . . it was left free intentionally.

Could she reach the knife? What good would it do? At least it would be more than she had now. She would have to reach across her body to get to the smaller table. That was impossible from this position. She thought for a moment; then panic started to set in. She had to do something. Lying here waiting was not an option. The adrenalin started to kick in . . . maybe, she thought . . . maybe she could rock the table she was lying on enough that it would tip over and she could grab the knife as she was falling. "Are you kidding me," she screamed. Out loud. Then to herself: *You'll be lying on the floor on your side, or worse, still bound to the table. Will the knife cut your bonds?* She thought the odds were against it, but what did she have to lose? If she had the knife, she had more choices: free herself or fight whoever put her in this mess.

She started rocking. Slowly at first, then getting into a rhythm. The right legs of the table started to lift off the floor, then the left. Higher and higher. With one final heave, the table began to tip and she shifted her weight as much as possible to her left. As the table collapsed she grabbed for the knife with her right hand just as the smaller table flipped and she landed hard on the floor.

She was almost in tears as she held up the knife to her left eye . . .

"Congratulations! You constantly amaze me. I had a bet with my brother that you wouldn't be able to do that . . . and yet here I am ten bucks poorer." He laughed much too loudly.

"*You!* What are *you* doing here? What am *I* doing here?"

"Relax, Ms. Meadows . . . it is Meadows, isn't it? It wasn't always that, though, was it?

Interesting . . . you don't remember how you got into this predicament, do you? How about I refresh your memory. We've got lots of time."

"What are you talking about?"

"Surely you remember that, don't you? You cheated me out of over ten million dollars a few years ago. My brother and I lost our business. He had to find another job. That's how he became a cop . . . right here in San Diego. We couldn't let you win without a fight. I could never counsel that. It was only a matter of time before we got even. Now, here we are. You, flat on your ass, holding a knife. What good is that going to do for you?" He laughed again. "You really aren't as smart as you think you are." He walked over to her and stepped on her hand, releasing the knife. As he picked it up with a gloved hand and put it in a plastic bag, he teased. "Don't you feel foolish? You worked so hard to get this . . . you could have broken your arm . . . but you got it. How does it feel to only have it snatched away? From hope . . . to despair . . . how does it feel? How do you think I felt? I had to start over . . . you left me with nothing."

He started to turn away, then . . . "You know, I almost let it go . . . but then I saw you and your detective boyfriend fucking like dogs in heat in *my spa* . . . " His face was bright red. I could feel his rage.

"That's right. I had cameras installed outside when we built the house. You never knew that, did you? I saw the whole sordid spectacle. That's when I finally decided: I was going to get even. It won't be long now," he laughed. "Pretty soon you and your friends will be just like old Dean Meritt."

I glared at him. He really was sick. I decided to taunt him. Maybe he'd make a mistake. It couldn't be any worse than the mess I was already in. "Yeah, I feel like a fool . . . for ever having loved you. In fact, I don't think I ever did love you . . . it was only about the money. Without that, you were nothing. Look at you . . . five feet six inches on a good day. Mr. Big Shot developer. You never could handle been shown up beside a taller woman like me. No wonder you liked the shorter Latino girls. Your ego is way too big for the rest of you . . . and you know what I'm referring to . . . Mr. Wiggly." I managed a smile. "But it was the young ones that got you in trouble . . . not me. Fourteen and fifteen-year-old girls? Really? Small wonder you lost your business. It's a wonder they didn't put you in jail. They couldn't prove anything, but the inference was enough."

"Fuck you! Every one of those girls was a better lay than you." He was livid, but gathered himself. "Let's not argue. I think you already know where you're headed, pardon the pun. But I've got an even bigger surprise in store for you. Guess whose refrigerator is going to be found containing your pretty little head? That's right, I'm going to destroy one of your friends as well. Doc Hughs is already under suspicion. Your head, and this knife . . . the same one I used on all the other girls, will put the finishing touches to his guilt."

"Why would you think anyone would suspect Doc? He has no motive."

"I guess it won't hurt to tell you . . . who are you going to tell?" He was really in a laughing mood . . . "Did you forget I had a brother?"

It suddenly struck me . . . "Peters! The cop!"

"That's right. He's as pissed at you as I am. Not only has he been planting all those pretty little heads at accident scenes, but he's been keeping me appraised of your investigations. It appears that Doc is high on Kelly's list of suspects. You guys are really clueless. Let's begin with Doc's obsession with his daughter's death. Never mind his wife; this was always about his daughter. He talked about it after it happened . . . for years. He was despondent over the fact that she died so young without having a chance to accomplish anything. Remember? She was an unknown, no one knew her, no one missed her; only him.

"Those poor immigrant girls. Perfect for his plan. No one knew them, no one cared about them, no one missed them. He convinced himself that he was saving them from a life of misery while making them famous at the same time. He would give them some recognition. He cut their heads off . . . while they were still alive . . . while he told them how famous they would be. You call me sick? It won't be hard for us to convince everyone who is sick."

He was obviously psychotic; determined to compound my death by implicating others. "When I started this spree, it was all about getting revenge. I had to make sure you were at the scene of all the severed heads. Sooner or later, you would be implicated. Imagine a life in prison for something you didn't do?" He laughed again. "But this is even better. I'm going to plant that reporter's head in Doc's fridge along with yours. It'll be obvious who the killer is, won't it, Linda?"

"Wait. Why did you kill the reporter? How did she figure into your scheme?"

He looked at her. "That's the funny thing. We didn't kill her. I don't know who did. Her head was in a sack outside the police station . . . where my brother found it. He knew about the body belonging to Raines and figured it was her head. We decided to keep it and add it to your collection." He laughed again.

I closed my good eye. It was over . . . the fight was taken out of me.

"Enough chatter, Linda. Your days are numbered, but I'm not quite ready for the coup-de-grace. You're safe here for a while. I'm afraid I'm going to have to tie you up again, though . . . can't have you leaving so soon. You just got here!"

"Wait. Humor me. How did I get down here in the first place? I don't remember anything before I woke up on this damn table."

"Okay. Let me explain. "I've got to give my brother some credit."

"Do you remember the potential homicide call you got earlier? The one in Point Loma?"

"Yeah, but when I got to the address, there was no one outside; just a single police vehicle parked outside the residence."

"That was Alan's. You should have been more careful when you entered the house. That's how you got that nasty bump in the head. He wanted to shoot you, but that would have spoiled everything we have tried hard to produce: my revenge and hurting you. The eye thing, that was your own fault, which came when you landed headfirst onto the planter in the hallway."

He was laughing so hard he failed to hear the car pull up outside. It was Kelly. I heard him shout my name.

I tried to scream a warning, but my ex covered my mouth. "Not another sound, sweetheart. Let's see if we can surprise him like we did you." He smashed his fist sharply against my left eye. They were both closed now . . .

Kelly was still shouting my name, and I could hear him approaching the door leading to the basement, where I was being held.

Sean stood there by my side, covering my mouth. He only had his cutting knife.

I didn't know what was happening. I couldn't see anything . . . I couldn't scream.

Kelly kicked the door open. Seeing Sean, he yelled, "drop the knife . . . and get away from Linda."

Peters did as he was told, and as Kelly walked closer, Meadows screamed a warning, "Watch out for his brother! He's in the building somewhere." Too late, Kelly failed to notice Alan Peters come up behind him. It was a grievous error. Peters clubbed Kelly over the head with the butt of his gun and quickly bound his hands behind his back.

Now Shane Peters *really* started to laugh . . .

CHAPTER 50

Doc headed over to the crematory, Jill Baily's body inside the ME's hearse. He drove as if on a mission. He needed to confront his brother. To get everything out in the open. He was sure Jim was the killer . . . and he was determined to prove it.

Jim was inside. But he wasn't alone. As Doc entered pushing the casket, he was taken aback. Standing beside Jim was Manny . . . he was holding a gun, and there was a shotgun lying on the table.

"Please come in, Doctor. We've been waiting for you. There are some things we need to clear up. Besides the fact that you've been giving me a bad rap, you made a huge mistake. That unknown Hispanic girl whose head was plastered all over the San Diego paper? That was my older brother's sister. That's why I am here. Someone fucked up . . . and they are going to pay dearly. I know for a fact that your brother, Jim, had nothing to do with all those severed heads. Heads that you and your detective friends so conveniently have connected to him. Now, I'm no innocent bystander to a killing or two, but you should know that I had nothing to do with those heads either. That leaves either Detective Meadows . . . or you . . . as the killer. All I know is that I want these killings to stop. It's personal now . . . and the media exposure is putting way too much attention to this area . . . and that's also bad for business. I need for you to convince me why I should not hold you accountable for all those severed heads."

"Well, besides all the talk about me being depressed enough over my young daughter's death, I really had no motive. Killing innocent Hispanic girls wasn't going to bring my daughter back nor would it give recognition to a bunch of homeless women. It's important to note that in some cases, the heads were discovered before I even got to the scene. Plus, I had no way to get rid of the bodies. The morgue was always inventoried, and there is always someone there: we work in shifts. An unaccounted-for body would be identified immediately. Finally, you'll have to take my word that I didn't murder anyone . . . just as I have to take yours."

"Interesting. If you aren't the killer, and Jim is not the killer, and I am not the guilty party . . . who is left?"

"*Meadows!*" In unison . . .

"Where is Detective Meadows" It was Jim.

Doc went over to the phone on the table. "Let's find out." He dialed Lt. Hill.

"Meadows left hours ago to investigate a possible homicide in Point Loma. Detective Kelly went out that way to check on her about an hour ago. I haven't heard back from either of them."

"Send me the address. I'm going to head over there right now. Something strange is going on. You might want to send a back-up car over there."

"There's already a patrolman in the vicinity. His name is Peters."

Manny pointed with his revolver towards the door. "Let's go. You drive, Jim . . . and take my shotgun. I'll sit in the back."

CHAPTER 51

"**Could we have planned** it any better than this?" Sean Peters was standing beside Meadows. They had up-righted the table she was on and tied and gagged Kelly who was lying on his side against the wall. Kelly was awake, as was Meadows, although she still could barely see out of either eye.

"What are your plans?" Alan was getting nervous. "Someone is going to start looking for these two very shortly. I've already notified Lt. Hill that they were both here and left, probably heading to the ME's office.

Look, this place is not secure. Too many people have this address. I don't think we should dispose of the bodies here. Too messy and too many prints. You should not have used your cutting room to draw Meadows up here."

"You're right. I wasn't thinking it through. I had no idea Kelly would show up. No matter, it just makes it a little more difficult. Bottom line: we get to kill two birds at once! I'll gag Linda while you pull your car around into the garage so we can load them into the trunk. We'll dump their bodies up in the hills with the others, after we relieve them of their heads."

Alan Peters stepped outside and headed for his cruiser. He was about to open the door when Doc appeared in front of him.

" Officer, I'm looking for Detectives Kelly or Meadows. Have you seen either of them?"

"Uh . . . no." How long have you been here?"

"Not long. In fact, we just got here."

"We?"

"Don't turn around, officer . . . and put your hands on top of your head." It was Manny.

"Where is detective Meadows?"

Peters inadvertently stole a glance towards the house, "I don't have a clue. She left hours ago."

"Thank you, officer . . . but you're a liar. She's in the house." Manny cracked Peters over the side of his head with his gun. "Jim, grab his weapon and make sure he doesn't interfere with us. Doc and I will look for the detectives. I don't know what to expect once we're inside."

Sean Peters made it easy for them. When he heard the door open, he shouted, "Alan, come help me load Kelly in the trunk. But first, I think I'll make sure he never makes any more noise." He walked over to Kelly, holding a heavy cord.

Just then, Manny entered the room. "Excuse me, amigo, what have we here?"

Peters turned, confused at first, until he saw Doc Hughs enter the room. He dropped the cord.

"Thank God, you're just in time. I was just going to untie this detective when you came. There's a cop outside; he's dangerous. You've got to help us."

"That's why we're here, senor . . ." and he shot Peters in the left knee. Doc ran over to untie Meadows, who began to explain in detail what had just transpired. He quickly untied her and helped her dress. Jim soon entered, pushing Alan Peters ahead. He shoved him over alongside his brother and began to help untie Kelly and help him to his feet.

Manny listened carefully, then ordered everyone out of the room. "This is between the Peters' here, and me." He pointed for Alan Peters to get down on his knees.

"What about her?" Kelly asked, gesturing to Meadows.

"She can stay and watch if she chooses. She has earned the right."

"Detective Kelly . . . hopefully we will never meet again. Jim Hughs is not responsible for any of these murders; nor am I. And now we know neither is Doc Hughs or Detective Meadows. Do the right thing. Forget what happened here today. Do you agree? Your serial killer will not hunt again . . . "

"Agreed. But let me be clear: when we meet again, you're going to jail."

Meadows appeared deep in thought. "Linda, are you coming?"

She peeked out of her swollen eyes at Peters, shook her head, and smiled. "I'm coming."

Sean Peters was sobbing, "Linda, for God's sake, don't let this maniac kill me!"

"This is all your doing, Sean. I don't feel a bit sorry for you. But I do have one last question: who was Dean Meritt?"

Her Ex glared at her . . ." you call yourself a detective? Fuck you! The game is over . . . bitch"

As they walked to their cars, they heard two shots. The first bullet went through the forehead of Alan Peters. The second, through Sean Peters' right knee. Manny wouldn't shoot again . . . he had Peters' cutting knife . . .

As Kelly helped guide Meadows back to their car, he whispered, "We still have work to do . . . and we won't be done until Jim and Manny are behind bars. This case is far from over . . ."

END

EPILOGUE

KELLY

We had had all the pieces to the puzzle, but one . . . and that one was the key to all the serial killings: Sean Peters. Meadows and I went back to her home in La Jolla. Doc went back to work, and I lost all contact with Manny and Doc's brother. Mexico?

I wasn't naïve enough to think we wouldn't run into him later . . . in fact, I looked forward to it. But that could wait. Right now, I was sitting in my chair, looking at some files; Linda was doodling at hers. Her eyes were open, but still black and blue. She looked up at me and grinned: "I kept wondering who Dean Meritt was . . . and why Sean called into question my being a lousy detective. I think I've figured it out. The SOB teased us with an anagram. Dean Meritt unscrambled is . . . *Terminated*. Ironic, huh? His little joke backfired: He forecast his *own* ending."

I was about to comment, when Lt. Hill entered the office. "Do you know a Brian Chu?"

"Yeah, I do. But I haven't heard from him since around 1969 or 1970. We met in Viet Nam. He was a tunnel rat based near Na Trang. Why?"

"He called this morning. He said he thought you still might be in the Navy or the Reserves and had been calling various Navy facilities around the country looking for a Lieutenant, or probably more senior, Joe Kelly. No luck there, he eventually called the FBI; they gave him my number. I told him I would have you call him when you got in."

He handed me the number. I didn't recognize the area code. Just then, Meadows walked in.

"What's up?" She saw me staring in space . . .

"Do you remember about the circumstances surrounding my Silver Star?"

"Sure. I still can't believe you dropped into a dark hole filled with muddy water and who knows what else."

"Well, the guy that helped me into that hole was Brian Chu . . . you remember, the Chinese tunnel rat?"

"That's right, although I didn't know he was Chinese."

"It's funny, I didn't really think about it either. I guess when everyone is wearing the same uniform, we all look the same. Anyway, he called here looking for me. I have no idea what he wants, but it will be nice to talk with him again. I wonder what he is doing now?"

I needed to call Brian Chu . . .

ABOUT THE AUTHOR

Bits & Pieces is Robert Hutto's first attempt at formal writing. Now retired, he served in the Navy as a comprehensive dentist for over forty years. His experience in forensics and two deployments to Viet Nam in the late Sixties provide the background for his book. The characters are all fictional, as are their exploits, which take place in that time period. As a former commanding officer and a member of the Navy's Medical Inspector General team, he has traveled the world and now spends his time in Northern California.

DETECTIVES
KELLY AND MEADOWS
ARE BACK!

Drugs continue to be smuggled into the San Diego area
from many sources. All signs point back to Manny,
but there are connections to others as well.
Are they connected to each other? Find out in . . .

COLLUSION

Please turn the page for a preview

CHAPTER 1

18 December 1967: Cu Chi, Viet Nam

KELLY

The bell rang . . . again. Someone had just thrown in the towel. I hated that sound. It meant that someone had just given up. U.S. Navy SEALs are supposed to be tough. They have to be, just to get through BUDS, their Basic Underwater Demolition School. Out of my class of 112, only 23 passed. Many washed out because of injuries, many more just rang the bell . . . asking to quit. No one made you quit. It wasn't always the biggest or strongest who qualified. The mental part was almost as difficult as the physical. I think every one of us wanted to quit at one time or another. I know I did, but somehow, I found the energy to continue. That's the lesson they tried to instill. SEALs don't quit. Since I passed, I thought I was pretty tough . . . but at this moment, if there was a bell to ring, I would be ringing it.

There were five of us, I was the leader, a Lieutenant Junior Grade in the Navy. We had started with six, but almost immediately after we were dropped off the Army helo, one of our guys stepped on a booby trap. His foot fell into a hole with a large spike in the middle. It penetrated his boot and foot clean through. We had to cut the spike off and pull his foot out. The pain must have been excruciating. To make matters worse, the spike had been covered with human excrement. We had a corpsman, also a SEAL, who removed his boot and wrapped his foot in bandages. We radioed the helo to return to medivac him out. That left two enlisted Seals, and an Explosive Ordinance Demolition or EOD man, the corpsmen and me. We were tasked to ferret out one of the many tunnels the Viet Cong had dug throughout the region. One of our

SEALs spoke Vietnamese and the other one carried a camera. We wanted to document whatever we found.

This was normally an army mission. They had been discovering the tunnels here and around Cu Chi since 1966. There were miles and miles of them located mostly about 25 miles northwest of Saigon. The U.S. had actually built a large base of operation directly over the tunnels without knowing it. At night, the VC, or Viet Cong, would sneak out of the tunnels and attack various units. Soldiers would have their throats cut, supplies would be damaged. One night a bunch of helicopters were blown up. Ultimately, a few entrances were discovered. Carefully camouflaged, some of the openings were no more than one foot by one-foot square. Smaller in stature men, dubbed tunnel rats, were employed to search the tunnels. They had to be the bravest people on earth . . . or just plain crazy. We were told a tunnel rat would be guiding us.

Before we went, we were briefed by one of them. He was a Sergeant in the Army; short and skinny. He told us what we could expect in the tunnels.

"Always enter the tunnels head first . . . with your weapon leading the way. There will be little room to maneuver until you get further in. You will be crawling. Be aware of booby traps. The VC are really clever as well as devious. We have found hundreds of scorpions littered along the paths. They're not deadly unless you're allergic to their poison, but their sting hurts like hell. Once we ran into a poisonous snake tied to a rope hanging from the top of a tunnel that would strike at anyone who entered. Deadlier, are the explosives and weapons triggered to go off when you trip a wire. Remember, it's dark in there. No lights to let you know when the next turn is . . . and there will be several sharp left and right turns before you get to any area large enough to stand. Not that you'll be able to: the ceilings are normally no more than five feet high. There will also be several vertical tunnels leading down into more horizontal tunnels before you get to your objective."

He was pointing to an area of the map north of Saigon when he interjected, "Before you ask, yes, we did try to smoke them out. We even used tear gas. Didn't work. Because of the turns in the tunnels, both right and left as well as down, the gas never penetrated far enough to get results. Same with explosives. The only way to get them was personal: hand-to-hand combat. At first, we lost a lot of men, but soon you developed a kind of sixth sense. Your hearing became more acute, your vision sharper . . . even your sense of smell became more discerning. Even in the dark, you could almost *feel* the enemy just around the corner, waiting to shoot you.

The worst was entering the larger caves. There would be so much shooting, it was like a shooting gallery or the fireworks on the fourth of July."

He returned to the map. "Here is where you will enter. We're *pretty sure* the tunnel you will enter is clear of booby traps. It *should* also be clear of enemy personnel. I say, *pretty sure* because they have been known to come back. Based upon our experience with the North Vietnamese Army, or NVA, we have seen a pattern of their strategy: retreat, harass, attack, and follow. They retreat when we engage heavily . . . usually across the border into Cambodia, where we are forbidden to cross. As they retreat, they harass us along the way to slow our advance. That's where their tunnels come into play. When we fall back, they attack. As we retreat, they follow. Right now, we feel, and our intelligence seems to confirm, they are poised for a major offensive. That brings me to your mission, and Lieutenant Colonel Weaver has the floor."

LCol Weaver was a tall man, completely bald, and smartly dressed in his combat fatigues. He was holding one of those telescoping pointers. He wasted little time addressing us. "Gentlemen, your orders are twofold. First, you are to gather as much intelligence you can find in the VC operation centers located somewhere within these tunnels. This information could be vitally important to stemming what we believe is the start of a huge offensive. We've tried before, but have not been able to penetrate deep enough into this labyrinth. Second, and equally important, you need to rescue a group of Navy and Army medical personnel who were captured three days ago when a medical forward operating base was overrun."

It was all swirling in my mind, as we began to enter the tunnel. It also brought back memories of Officer Candidate School . . . "Mission first; people always." Maybe they were on to something . . .

The Army contributed to our mission further by having another tunnel rat lead us into the darkness. His name was Brian Chu. Yes, he was Chinese . . . American. His father was born in a village near Shanghai, China, but moved with his family to Taiwan, where he eventually became an officer in the Taiwanese Navy. They paid for him to get an engineering degree at the University of California at Berkley. When his obligation was up he immigrated to San Francisco and started a business near Walnut Creek, outside of the city. Brian was born two years later, on September 8, 1935, making him now forty-two years old. He didn't look it. He was five foot-five and built like a gymnast. We also didn't know he was a Lieutenant Colonel himself. Plus, he had been down this same tunnel before. It was located fairly near the Saigon River which ran roughly north and south through Viet Nam. A friendly Vietnamese farmer, loyal to the South, had told us this was the entrance that a large force of NVA had entered pushing many Americans, including women, with them two days ago.

We gathered around the entrance. Actually, we couldn't even see the entrance until Brian brushed away the leaves to reveal the cover. He lifted it to reveal the hole. It was about five feet deep and just wide enough that I could squeeze through if I took off my gear. Brian went first. "No talking," he warned. "I will shine the only light. Keep at least five feet between each of you. If there is an explosion we can keep casualties to a minimum. We will assemble at the first large cavern they have excavated." With that, he entered head first, his revolver leading. I think we must have crawled about thirty yards right and left before we went vertical again. Dropping down about five more feet we crawled about ten yards before we entered an opening. It appeared to be some kind of supply storage. There were bags and bags of rice piled neatly along the walls, along with uniforms and medical supplies.

"Those have been stored recently." It was Brian. "I was down here two months ago and this chamber was bare. The North is definitely planning a large-scale operation . . . soon."

We pressed on. The next tunnels were much larger . . . relatively. I still couldn't stand up, but at least I was not crawling on my belly. We made good time until Brian signaled us to halt. There was another much larger cavern just ahead. When I peered inside I could see it could probably accommodate at least sixty people. It was huge. In the center of it was a hole halfway filled with water. It must have been connected to the river and was their water source.

I started to say something, when Brian held up his right fist. He put his left finger to his lips. All eyes were on him and he shook his head side to side. He heard or felt something . . . I clearly did not. He motioned for us to go forward and hug the wall beside the next tunnel exit from that room. That way, no one would see us if they entered. As we did, Brian took out his knife and stood by the entrance. Soon . . . very soon, a lone VC entered. Brian swung his arm around him, smothering his mouth . . . and jammed the knife into his side; not once, but several times. When the VC slumped to the ground, Brian slit his throat . . . and spit on him.

He turned, looked into the opening, and gestured for us to follow him through. *Okay*, I thought. Brian obviously did not like these guys. I wondered what had made him so violent. What had he seen?

I soon found out. Another twenty yards. We went vertical again, down about five feet leading into another horizontal tunnel. I thought we must be at least twenty feet underground. Another large cavern. When we entered we could see bodies. Lots of them. They were scattered throughout in no particular order. Most were lying on cots, but there were too many bodies and not enough cots. As I looked around I could see bodies in NVA uniforms as well as naked ones. This must have been some kind of hospital, I thought. We started to check the bodies to see if any of them were still living. One of our guys noticed that a couple of the bodies were American. As we looked further, I could see that many of the bodies had been mutilated. In the far corner was what was left of a nude female. Her arms and feet had been cut off and a bayonet had been left sticking up in her . . . vagina. Her head was missing. I was clearly disgusted . . . and really angry. No wonder Brian was so brutal. He had probably seen scenes like this before. As we continued to search I noticed a uniform by the bed. It was of a Navy Officer . . . a Lieutenant J.G. As I picked up the shirt, I uncovered the head. It was . . . Mary! My Mary . . .

GLOSSARY

DEA – Drug Enforcement Agency. The lead federal agency in the country's war against drugs.

CIA – Central Intelligence Agency. A civilian foreign intelligence service of the federal government of the United States tasked with gathering, processing and analyzing national security information from around the world.

DNA – Deoxyribonucleic Acid. A molecule that encodes the genetic instructions used in the development and function of all known living organisms and many viruses. Unique to every individual. The first case using DNA in a U.S. Court case was 1987. It wasn't until 1994 that the Dental Identification Act was established, utilizing DNA as a definitive means of identification.

ME – Medical Examiner/Coroner

OCS – Officer Candidate School. Located in Newport, Rhode Island

SEAL – Navy SEa, Air, and Land unit. The United States' only all-terrain fighting crew.

ASAP – As Soon As Possible

NYCPD – New York City Police Department

CPSIA information can be obtained
at www.ICGtesting.com
Printed in the USA
LVHW082146050921
697037LV00017B/128